Praise for the Novels of Ralph Cotton

"The sort of story we all hope to find within us: the bloodstained, gun-smoked, grease-stained yarn that yanks a reader right out of today."
—Terry Johnston

"Cotton writes with the authentic ring of a silver dollar, a storyteller in the best tradition of the Old West." —Matt Braun

"Evokes a sense of outlawry . . . distinctive."
—*Lexington Herald-Leader*

"Disarming realism . . . solidly crafted."
—*Publishers Weekly*

AMBUSH AT SHADOW VALLEY

Ralph Cotton

A SIGNET BOOK

SIGNET
Published by New American Library, a division of
Penguin Group (USA) Inc., 375 Hudson Street,
New York, New York 10014, USA
Penguin Group (Canada), 90 Eglinton Avenue East, Suite 700, Toronto,
Ontario M4P 2Y3, Canada (a division of Pearson Penguin Canada Inc.)
Penguin Books Ltd., 80 Strand, London WC2R 0RL, England
Penguin Ireland, 25 St. Stephen's Green, Dublin 2,
Ireland (a division of Penguin Books Ltd.)
Penguin Group (Australia), 250 Camberwell Road, Camberwell, Victoria 3124,
Australia (a division of Pearson Australia Group Pty. Ltd.)
Penguin Books India Pvt. Ltd., 11 Community Centre, Panchsheel Park,
New Delhi - 110 017, India
Penguin Group (NZ), 67 Apollo Drive, Rosedale, North Shore 0632,
New Zealand (a division of Pearson New Zealand Ltd.)
Penguin Books (South Africa) (Pty.) Ltd., 24 Sturdee Avenue,
Rosebank, Johannesburg 2196, South Africa

Penguin Books Ltd., Registered Offices:
80 Strand, London WC2R 0RL, England

First published by Signet, an imprint of New American Library,
a division of Penguin Group (USA) Inc.

First Printing, May 2008
10 9 8 7 6 5 4 3 2 1

For Mary Lynn . . . of course

Prologue

Memphis Warren Beck stopped the buggy and looked back through the shadowy blue light of dawn toward the town of Little Aces. The glow of firelight in the distance had died, and by now he was certain Emma Vertrees, widow of Sheriff Dillard Vertrees, had made it back to town on Beck's big dun horse. Beck thought about it. Bringing Emma Vertrees with him had been a mistake, but luckily she had seen it before they had gotten too far for her to ever turn back.

Emma had once ridden the outlaw trail with Beck and the Hole-in-the-wall Gang, but that had been a long time ago, in the wild, restless days of her youth. Seeing him ride into Little Aces after all these years must have made her think she could relive the past. But something seemed to have dawned on her last night as the two of them fled the town beneath a hail of gunfire. She had suddenly stopped the buggy in the darkness in the middle of the trail and said to him, "I'm sorry, Memphis. I can't do this."

If she'd expected that Beck would try talking her into it, she'd been mistaken. He knew that the new sheriff of Little Aces, Vince Gale, lay bleeding in the dirt back in town, and he knew that there had been something at work between Emma and Sheriff Gale before Beck had arrived. Without a word on the matter, Beck had taken the buggy reins from her hands and said quietly, "Go back to him, Emma. I understand."

She'd attempted an explanation. "I—I don't know if I'm going back to Sheriff Gale, or if I've just been away from this too long and need the security of—"

"You never had to explain yourself to me, Emma," Beck had said, cutting her off gently. "I hope you and Sheriff Gale are as happy together as you and Dillard Vertrees were."

Those had been his last words to her before he sat listening to the dun's hooves turn and walk away in the darkness.

Beck smiled to himself in reflection, recalling a time gone by when Emma and he had lived wild and free, with the wide valley of Hole-in-the-wall, Wyoming, their sanctuary from the world, always there for them.

"But that was then. This is now," he'd murmured to himself in the darkness, realizing that just because he'd left Little Aces and a railroad detective posse behind didn't mean there wouldn't still be men on his trail.

The Railroad Alliance is still out here, he'd reminded himself, looking around warily in the grainy morning darkness as he shook the buggy reins enough to send the horse upward onto a higher trail. "So long, Little Aces," he'd said quietly, a free hand pressed to the bandaged wound in his side.

He traveled on throughout the day, stopping only long enough to water the horse at runoff streams along the trail. In the evening, stepping down beside such a stream, he let the horse lower its muzzle to the cool, clear water while he looked around at the rough, steep terrain and examined the healing gunshot wound in his side. He had another reason for stopping here besides watering the horse or checking his wound. Moments earlier he'd caught a glimpse of two riders moving quietly through the brush and bracken, off the trail to his left.

Without searching too closely, Beck had kept an eye on the hillside of rock and scrub cedar, hoping that whoever was out there might be innocent travelers who would come forward and show themselves. But that wasn't to be. When the two men did appear, they did so suddenly, out of the brush along the trail, on foot less than twenty feet away. *Detectives? Bounty hunters?* What was the difference?

"Raise them high, Warren Beck!" a voice shouted. "One move, you're dead!"

Hearing the nervousness in the man's voice and seeing the two had the drop on him anyway, Beck raised his hands chest high and relaxed, already watching for his chance to make a run for it. "Easy, fellows," he said, adding a weakened sound to his voice. "I'm wounded here. I couldn't put up a fight if I wanted to." As he spoke, he recognized one of the two men.

"Watch him close, Davis," Beck heard one man say to the other as they drew nearer.

"Neil Deavers, is that you?" Beck asked, cocking his head slightly as if it might aid his recollection.

"Yeah, Beck, it's me," said the serious voice, "but keep those hands up all the same."

Beck had deliberately lowered his hands an inch when he'd called the man by name. Quickly raising them again, he asked, "What are you doing packing a gun for the railroads? Last I heard you'd gained yourself a reputation wearing a badge somewhere. Kansas, Missouri—?"

"Things change, Beck," Deavers said, cutting his question short. As he spoke, he reached behind his back and pulled out a pair of handcuffs. "Here, cuff him, Davis," he ordered the other man, as Davis lifted Beck's gun from its holster and shoved it behind his belt. To Beck, he said in the same authoritarian tone, "Lower your wrists for him, Beck. The quicker you're cuffed, the quicker we can get you somewhere and get that wound looked at." He nodded at the bullet hole and the washed-out bloodstain on Beck's shirt.

"Obliged," said Beck, not about to tell him that the wound in his side had all but healed.

"Wait," said Davis Dinsmore as he took the handcuffs from Deavers. "You mean we're going to nursemaid him all the way across this high country, just so the railroads can kill him once they get their hands on him?"

"I'm no assassin," said Deavers. "We're taking him in alive, for the reward. What the railroad does with him is not my business."

"This thieving dog doesn't deserve any mercy," said Dinsmore with disgust. "If you don't have the stomach to put him down, I do." He leveled his Colt out at arm's length.

"Pull that trigger, Davis, you'll be dead before Beck hits the ground," Deavers said matter-of-factly, his own Colt cocking on the upswing and resting an inch from Dinsmore's ear. "I told you when you sided with me that I wouldn't stand for murder."

"But you'd kill me flat out if I put a bullet in this outlaw trash?" Dinsmore said in amazement. "That makes no sense at all!" He made no sign of lowering his gun.

" 'Making sense' won't be so important to you once you're feeding buzzards," Deavers said quietly. "Now, lower it or make it bark. I'm through talking."

Davis Dinsmore gritted his teeth, but he lowered his gun and let the hammer down. "All right, Beck, he saved your hide this time. Make one false move while we're on the trail, and I'll kill you, no matter what he says." He jerked a rough nod toward Deavers.

"Now holster it," Deavers said, seeing Dinsmore still hadn't settled the matter in his mind.

"Damn it." Dinsmore let out a tight breath, calmed himself and slipped the gun into its holster. "There, satisfied?" he asked Deavers.

Deavers lowered his Colt, uncocked it and said

without answering him, "Get the cuffs on him. Let's get back on the trail."

Beck cut in, asking them both affably, "Speaking of the trail, where are you taking me?"

Dinsmore growled, "That's none of your da—"

"We're taking you to Little Aces," said Deavers, not giving Dinsmore a chance to finish his words. "We'll turn you over to Colonel Dan Elgin's Railroad Security Alliance, the big posse that's been making a sweep to get rid of you and all your pals."

Beck shook his head slowly and said, "Good luck, Neil," as if he and the stern-faced lawman were on a first name basis. "I left Little Aces three nights ago. Colonel Elgin and his men were in the midst of shooting it out with the town sheriff and an Arizona Ranger named Burrack."

"You're out of your lying mind, Memphis Beck," Dinsmore said. To Deavers he said, "See how it's going to be with him? One lie after another, one trick after another. I say we kill him on the spot." As he spoke he'd snapped the cuffs around Beck's wrists and jerked them to make sure they were sound.

Beck only smiled, watching Dinsmore drop the key to the cuffs into his shirt pocket. "You overestimate me, my friend," he said. "I ran out of any tricks a long time ago."

"Don't call me friend, outlaw!" Dinsmore bristled, shoving Beck's cuffed hands away from himself.

"Tell me what was going on in Little Aces when you left, Beck," Deavers cut in, attending to what

Beck had said about Colonel Elgin and his railroad posse.

"Elgin and his men snatched two of Burrack's prisoners away from him and hanged them," said Beck, inspecting his cuffed hands as if to make certain Dinsmore had done a good job. "When I rode away they were having at it all over town."

"Snatched Burrack's prisoners? Dang," said Deavers. "So by now, the colonel and his men might be gone from Little Aces . . . from that whole hill area even," he mused, rubbing his chin as he wondered what would be their best move in order to turn Beck over to the railroad and collect their reward.

Beck shrugged. "I won't try to guess. The colonel might be nothing more than a name carved on a grave board by now." He studied Deavers' face closely to judge what effect his words were having on him.

"No lawman likes losing prisoners," Deavers said. But after a moment of further contemplation on the matter, he said to Dinsmore, "We might have to ride farther than we thought to claim the reward. Am I going to be able to trust you with him?"

Dinsmore took another deep, calming breath and said, "Aw hell, I just got my bark on for a minute there. I'm settled now."

"Good," said Deavers. "Then I can count on you to watch him, not kill him, while I go get our horses and bring them up?"

"Yeah, go ahead," Dinsmore said calmly. "You can count on me."

"Don't let him start moving around," Deavers said, recalling everything he knew about Memphis Beck and his slippery nature.

"I've got him covered, Neil," said Dinsmore, starting to sound a bit agitated.

"Don't let him get you into any conversations or answering questions for him," said Deavers as he stepped sidelong away toward the brush where they'd hidden their horses twenty yards off the trail. "He's quick with his hands."

"Damn, Neil, he's cuffed," said Dinsmore. "Do you think I'm a damned fool? Would you feel better if *I* went and got the horses?"

"Sorry," said Deavers. He stepped off the trail and walked away, deeper into the brush.

"Sounds like the man doesn't trust you much," Beck said, taking a slow step forward toward Dinsmore as he raised his cuffed hands, took off his hat and fooled with adjusting the crown.

Dinsmore stood staring coldly. "Beck, I don't care what I said. If you feel like stepping in close and making a play for this gun, just go right ahead and try it." He grinned. "I'm not backing off an inch."

"Even if I told you I have a derringer inside this hat aimed at your head?" said Beck.

"It's one more lie that I won't listen to," said Dinsmore. "Now, keep on coming real slow like. I'll burn you down and be done with you."

"No thanks," Beck said, stopping abruptly, looking concerned. "This is close enough for me. I believe you would shoot a man for blinking his eyes the wrong way."

"Now you're starting to understand me, Beck," Dinsmore said with contempt. He seemed to ease down a bit now that Beck stopped encroaching on him. "I have no use for your kind. As far as I'm concerned—"

His words stopped short as Beck's right boot swung up and around in a fast, powerful arc and connected with his jaw. Dinsmore's gun flew from his hand and he fell backward onto the ground, knocked cold. "Easy now," Beck whispered, settling the buggy horse who had become spooked by all the commotion. He stroked the horse's muzzle while he loosened its harness. "I'm going to turn you loose, let you go visit your kin. . . ."

Deep in the brush on the steep hillside, Neil Deavers hadn't heard a sound. He gathered his and Dinsmore's horses, led them all the way back and stepped onto the trail when he saw Memphis Beck standing with a gun aimed at his belly. Looking down, he shook his head slowly, seeing that the handcuffs formerly on Beck were now on Dinsmore's wrists.

"I didn't tell him to watch your feet," he said in a defeated tone.

"No, you didn't," Beck said flatly. "Now, lift the Colt easy-like and drop it."

"What are you going to do if I don't, Beck?" he asked warily. "I always heard you're not a killer."

The Colt cocked in Beck's hand. "You're picking a bad day to find out."

"All right! Take it easy." Deavers raised his hands chest-high, the two horse's reins in his gloved right fist. With his left hand he reached across his belly, lifted his gun from its holster and dropped it to the dirt. "You're not leaving us here afoot, are you?" He saw that the buggy horse was gone; the buggy sat useless on the trail.

"The horse is headed back along the high trail," said Beck. "If you catch him I expect he'll haul the two of you out of here."

"This won't help you, Beck," Deavers said. "The railroad is after you and they won't stop until you and your Hole-in-the-wall boys are all dead."

"Maybe," said Beck, "but that won't be today." He stepped forward and took the two horses' reins from Deavers' hand. "Start walking back the way you came until you know I'm gone."

Beck stood and watched until Deavers had walked ten yards back into the brush. Things were looking up, he told himself, swinging up into the saddle. Now that he'd gotten out of the buggy and was atop a horse he would make better time. One of his gang's hideouts lay just over the Arizona Territory line, some eighty miles southwest. There he would find English Collin Hedgepeth, Earl Caplan and the rest of the gang waiting for him.

"Let's get to it," he said to the horse, liking the idea of getting back among his own kind. With the tap of his heels he put Deavers' horse in a quick trot, leading Dinsmore's horse by its reins.

PART 1

Chapter 1

Valle Hermoso, Mexico

Arizona Ranger Sam Burrack stepped down from his horse in the middle of the empty dirt street in Valle Hermoso. He pulled his sawed-off shotgun from beneath the bedroll behind his saddle and let the reins fall to the ground. His Appaloosa stallion, Black Pot, stood firm as if he'd been hitched to a post. In the dirt lay two dead men: One, an elderly Mexican, wore a tin badge and a threadbare Confederate cavalry tunic; the other wore the range clothes of a vaquero. A few feet from the bodies a long smear of blood and drag marks led to the blanket-draped doorway of the Gato Negro Cantina a block away.

A voice called out in English from behind the cover of a mule cart a few yards away, "One of our vaqueros had the guts to nail one of them afore the other three gunned him down."

The ranger only nodded, walking on along the middle of the street as a shot rang out through the glassless window of the cantina. As he neared the town well, he saw a young Mexican crouched down with a Winchester repeating rifle in his hands. Sam raised a gloved hand in a show of peace when the young man swung the Winchester toward him.

With a look of relief, the young Mexican waved the ranger toward the cover of the low stone wall surrounding the well. "Are you hunting for these men?" the Mexican asked in stiff English, seeing the badge on the ranger's vest as Sam hurried in and crouched beside him.

"Yes," said Sam. He studied the blanketed door-way, then the small window where gun smoke wafted in. "They're all four murderers. They broke prison in Yuma. I've been on their trail over a week. At daylight this morning I found one of their horses limping alongside the trail. I figured they'd be coming here for fresh horses."

"*Sí*, it was for horses they came, and it was for horses that my brother, Ramon, and the village *guardia* died," the young man said with regret.

"I'm sorry," said Sam, realizing he had pushed these desperate killers in this direction. "I got here as fast as I could."

"*Sí*, but not fast enough," the young man said, nodding toward the bodies lying twenty yards up the street.

"No, not fast enough," Sam replied. He didn't flinch as another shot exploded from the window. "I'm figuring the others are gone. This one they left behind because he's badly wounded?" he asked, as if already knowing the answer.

The young Mexican only nodded. "My brother,

Ramon, was courageous. He fought back when they tried to ride away on his horse." He saw the questioning look in the ranger's eyes and added, "When I heard the gunshots, I came running. But like you, I was also too late to save my brother's life."

Sam detected bitterness in the young man's words, but he wasn't sure where it was directed. "All right," he said, getting down to the matter at hand. "I'm going to see who's in there and try to end this."

"So that you can go on in pursuit of the others?" the young man asked.

"Yes," Sam said, "so I can get them rounded up and keep them from killing anybody else."

The young man nodded and showed Sam the Winchester in his hands. "I will back your play," he said, as if using a term he had only heard that lawmen like the ranger might use. "I have the rifle this one dropped when my brother shot him. I fired upon them as they rode away. I think I hit one."

"Good for you," Sam said sincerely. Turning his attention back to the window he called out, "This is Arizona Ranger Sam Burrack. Who's in there?"

"It's Dick Hirsh, you damned lawdog!" a voice called out, followed by a pistol shot that thumped into the stone wall. "You want me, come in and get me!" Another shot exploded. "I'm all alone in here. It'll be just you and me!"

The ranger shook his head, then called out, "How bad are you bleeding, Hirsh? I see a lot of you smeared along the dirt out here."

"Not bad enough," Hirsh said with a dark laugh that lapsed into a deep, rattling cough. "I got . . . enough grit left . . . to kill half a dozen like you, *Ranger*!"

The young Mexican beside Sam said, "I will go in and get him for you, Ranger, to avenge my brother, Ramon." He started to move away in a crouch, but Sam stopped him by blocking his way around the well wall.

"Wait," Sam said, keeping his eyes on the blanketed cantina doorway. From the amount of blood along the ground he knew that the outlaw would soon bleed out. "Let's give him a couple minutes."

"I am not afraid of this murdering dog," the young Mexican said.

"I can see you're not," Sam said. He turned his face to the Mexican long enough to look the serious young man up and down. "What's your name?" he asked, hoping to stall him long enough to let his anger wane.

"I am Hector Sandoval," the young man said. He gestured a hand toward where his brother's body lay in the dirt. "Always Ramon and I are known as the Sandoval brothers. Now there is only me. Ramon's death leaves only me to carry on our father's name." He glared with hatred toward the cantina.

Seeing that he still teetered on the edge of making a run toward the cantina, Sam said, "I understand how you feel, but before you go charging in, let me see if I can get him to throw out his gun and come out on his own."

"You have no right to stop me, Ranger," Hector said firmly.

"That's true. I have no jurisdiction here," Sam replied. Thinking quickly he added, "But if I can talk to him, he might give me an idea where the others are headed. If I don't catch them, they will have gotten away with killing your brother. You'll never see them again."

"Will I ever see them again anyway?" Hector asked pointedly. "If you catch them and bring them through here on your way back to the border, will you allow me to do to them what I must to avenge my brother?"

"No," Sam said, "I can't promise I'll bring them through here. But you have my word that I won't stop until they're all either dead or headed back to prison. That's all I've got for you."

Considering the ranger's words, Hector let out a tense breath. "At least you did not lie to me the way I have come to expect you gring—" He caught and corrected himself quickly. "I mean, the way I have come to expect you *americanos* to do."

"I've got no reason to lie to you, Hector," Sam said quietly, watching the blanketed cantina door. "I'm here to do my job, nothing else."

"*Sí*, do your job," said Hector, nodding. "Talk to this killer and see what you can find out from him before he dies choking on his own blood." Hector spit on the ground in disgust.

Sam had no idea if the young Mexican's disgust was aimed at him, at the system of law he worked for or at the universe in general, but he had no time to think about it now. From up the street a small gathering of men had ventured out of hiding and began walking cautiously toward the well. They carried shotguns, pitchforks and ancient, wooden-stocked flintlock pistols. Leading them were the elderly American who'd called out to the ranger earlier, and an old mineral surveyor named Simon Gates. He carried a coiled rope at his side and slapped it angrily against his thigh as he walked.

The ranger used the townsmen as a reason to call out again to the trapped and wounded outlaw. "Hirsh, they're coming for you, rope coiled and ready. I can't stop them, unless I take you into custody."

No response came from inside the cantina. After waiting for a moment, Sam said, "Hirsh? Do you hear me in there?"

A single gunshot exploded, not from the window but from deeper inside the cantina. The sound stopped the advancing villagers and sent a few of them scrambling to the side. Hector asked the ranger, "Did he shoot himself?"

"Knowing Hirsh, I doubt it," said the ranger. "It could be a trick."

"A trick?" Hector asked curiously. "How can this be a trick?" He looked at the ranger in disbelief.

"With these men you always watch out for a trick."

"But what good would a trick do him when he is going to die?" Hector asked.

"Men like Hirsh don't stop until they're dead, Hector," Sam said, seeing that the young man had no lack of courage, but seemed to have no savvy about men like Dick Hirsh. "The prospect of taking a couple more lives might be all that's keeping him hanging on."

"Then he is not a man at all, but a devil," said Hector. He stopped himself from instinctively making a sign of the cross on his chest. "All of his kind must be stopped."

"Now you're talking," Sam said wryly. "Keep everybody back while I get inside." Without another word on the matter, Sam moved away in a crouch, following the circular stone wall around the well until he reached the point closest to the front of the cantina.

Hector watched him run to the cantina's front and press his back against the adobe wall beside the doorway. Using the shotgun barrel, Sam reached out, shoved the blanket to the side, peeped in, then slipped inside the cantina. As soon as he stepped inside, he stopped and looked over at Dick Hirsh lying sprawled on the dirt floor twenty feet away. On the side of Hirsh's head he saw fresh blood.

Dead . . . ? He didn't think so. He saw no spray of blood and brain matter along the floor or on the wall, but he did quickly take note that Hirsh still gripped a cocked Colt. Quietly, Sam said, "Hirsh, when you make your move with that pistol, I'm giving you both barrels."

In the dirt, Hirsh's gun hand opened slowly,

dropped the Colt and moved away from it. "Damn it, Ranger . . . all right," he growled, his voice sounding weak but still defiant.

His shotgun poised ready, Sam stepped closer, not convinced that was the only trick the wounded gunman had up his sleeve. "Which way are they headed, Hirsh?" he asked, looking all around the abandoned cantina, and seeing only a broken chair and an overturned table.

"I'll—I'll tell you, Ranger," the wounded outlaw said haltingly, his hand going to his *real* wound, the gaping bullet hole in his chest. "Come over here . . . so's I don't have to holler."

Here it comes, another trick, Sam told himself. But he stepped forward all the same. Behind him he heard Hector say from the doorway, "I'm coming in, Ranger. I told the men to stay back out of the—"

"No, wait, Hector," the ranger warned, seeing the overturned table roll sideways a foot as one of the escaped convicts sprang up from behind it.

On the floor Hirsh grabbed his Colt as the ranger's shotgun exploded at the rushing convict, picking the gunman up from behind the overturned table and flinging him backward. But he knew he didn't have time to swing the shotgun back around toward Hirsh before Hirsh pulled the trigger.

But it didn't matter. Hector reacted quickly, seeing Hirsh grab the pistol. Before the wounded outlaw could get a shot off, the Winchester bucked in Hector's hands and sent a round into Hirsh's shoulder, causing the Colt to fly from his grip.

"Damn it!" Hirsh moaned. "I'm shot again . . . shot twice by my own gun!" His voice, though still weak, sounded stronger than it had moments earlier.

"I will make it three times," Hector said, levering another round into the rifle chamber.

"No, hold your fire," Sam said, raising a gloved hand toward Hector to stop him from firing again. Stepping forward with his smoking shotgun aimed at Dick Hirsh, Sam said, "Hirsh, there're men waiting out there wanting to string you up. Either tell me where Suelo Soto and Nate Ransdale are headed, or I'll feed you to them. You can spend your last minutes swinging from a limb."

Hirsh let out a shallow breath and said, "All right, Ranger. That's Ted Shala . . . you killed over there." He gasped to catch his breath, then continued. "Soto, Ransdale and me were all . . . headed south, down through Sonora, going to lose ourselves."

Sam stared at him, wondering if he should believe a word of it. "Sonora, huh?"

Hearing the ranger's tone, Hirsh said, "It's the truth, Ranger. I don't owe . . . them two nothing." His voice grew weaker as he spoke. "It was Soto's idea . . . for me and Shala to gun you down. He could have . . . taken me with them, but *no* . . . he left us here."

"What's in Sonora?" Sam asked.

"I expect I'll . . . never know." Hirsh gave a weak grin; blood trickled from his lips. "Will you . . . ?"

Sam and Hector watched the outlaw's eyes

glaze over and turn blank. Sam let his shotgun slump in his hands as he stepped over and took a closer look at the other dead man lying sprawled on the dirt floor, riddled with buckshot. "Obliged for your help, Hector," he said over his shoulder as he opened the shotgun to replace the spent shell.

"You are welcome, Ranger," Hector replied. He turned the big Winchester back and forth as he looked at it. As far as he was concerned the repeating rifle now belonged to him. "Do you think he is telling the truth about Sonora?"

"He could be," Sam replied, "but I wouldn't count on it."

"When will you go after the other two?" Hector asked, cradling the rifle.

"As soon as I rest my stallion and find myself a good meal," Sam said, hearing the men venture toward the blanketed doorway.

"Careful, boys," Simon Gates said to the others in a gravelly voice. He held the front door blanket to the side and looked in, the coiled rope in his clenched fist. Inside the cantina, the men looked back and forth at the bodies on the dirt floor. "Hot damn, fellows," Gates chuckled. "It looks like our own Hector Sandavol is a bonafide gunfighting hero." He gestured his coiled rope toward the dead outlaws. "Let's get this trash cleared out of here. I think the town of Valle Hermoso owes us all a drink."

"I have no time for drinking," said Hector, turning toward the door. "My brother, Ramon, is lying dead in the street."

"I'll give you a hand," said Sam, following him out of the cantina.

Giving the rest of the men an annoyed look, Gates called out, "Well, what are you all waiting for? Let's give Hector a hand with his brother."

Chapter 2

The ranger helped the young Mexican carry his brother off the street while Gates and the rest of the men followed close behind, carrying Valle Hermoso's dead constable. The group stepped back and waited outside as Sam and Hector carried the body to a small plank-and-adobe shack where an elderly widow had quickly cleared a battered wooden table when she saw them coming. Two villagers laid the body of the elderly constable beside Ramon; then they backed out of the open doorway and joined Gates and the others.

The old woman patted Hector's shoulder in sympathy and left to fetch a gourd of water and a washcloth. Hector stared down at his brother's body for a moment, then crossed himself and looked at the body of the old constable.

"This one's name is Luis Gravis. He grew up here with our father." Gesturing at the dead lawman's worn-out Confederate tunic, he added, "President Davis promised him land in your country if he would fight for the Southern cause."

He gave a slight sigh and patted the constable's dusty, streaked forehead. "But we know how that turned out, eh, Luis?"

"I'll wait outside," Sam said quietly, backing away to give Hector time alone with the dead.

"I go too," Hector said stiffly, seeing the woman, ready to attend to the corpses, return. He turned and walked out the door behind the ranger. "I will visit my brother's body again before I leave Valle Hermoso, if there is time. If not, Ramon will understand," he added.

The ranger stopped out front of the old woman's shack and turned to Hector. "Before you leave? Where are you going?" he asked, realizing that he already knew the answer.

"I am going after those murderers as well, Ranger," he said.

As Gates and the rest of the villagers gathered closer around them, Sam said, "I have to tell you, Hector, I work alone."

"I said nothing about riding with you, Ranger," Hector replied. "I know this country as well as any man. I will have no trouble hunting these animals down." He jutted his chin with determination. "I do it for my brother. He would have done the same for me."

Sam wanted to say more on the matter, but he could tell that his words weren't going to make any difference to this strong-willed young man. He started to turn away and walk to where Black Pot still stood, diligently awaiting him in the dirt street. But before Sam walked away, Gates said to Hector, "We've all talked it over. We'd like you to take Luis Gravis' badge and be the town *guardia* of Valle Hermoso."

"I am honored," said Hector, "but I cannot be town *guardia*. Did you not hear me tell the ranger that I am going after the men who killed Ramon and Luis?"

"So?" said Simon Gates. "That's all right with us, right amigos?" He turned to the other men for support. "Ramon was one of us, don't forget. And Gravis was the law in Valle Hermoso." He pointed toward the door of the widow's adobe where the two bodies lay. "There're two good men lying dead. If you can bring the murderers in, we're behind you all the way. We'll make up a posse and ride with you until they're—"

"No," said Hector, stopping Gates short. "There will be no posse, not if I am *guardia*."

"Then you'll take on Luis' job and uphold the law here?" Gates asked.

Hector looked to the ranger, then back at Gates. With a slight sigh, he said, "*Sí*, I will be *guardia* for Valle Hermoso, at least for now. I will do it so I can hunt these men down." He pointed a finger at Gates as if for emphasis. "But I do not want a posse with me. It is better that I go alone." Even as he spoke, a young boy hurried into the widow's adobe and came running back with the bloodstained badge in his hand.

"Anything you say, Guardia Hector Sandoval," said Gates. He took the badge, wiped it off and pinned it on Hector's shirt. "On behalf of Valle Hermoso I welcome and congratulate you to office."

"*Gracias*," said Hector, appearing humble. "I will do the best I can." He looked around at the villagers and said, "Now I have to go. I must gather supplies and prepare my horse for the trail."

Gates looked disappointed, but he tried to cover it with a wide smile. "Shouldn't we celebrate first? Just a drink or two? It's not every day a man becomes a lawman."

"It is not every day a man loses a brother, or a town loses a good man like Luis Gravis," Hector replied. "I cannot celebrate a day such as this."

"You're absolutely right," said Gates. His smile vanished. "I meant no offense." He turned from Hector to the other men and said in a somber tone, "All right, men, let's go inside the cantina and raise our glasses in solemn remembrance of our dear friends. . . ."

Hector had already started walking away as Gates spoke. Watching the serious young man as he cradled the Winchester in his arm and headed purposefully toward the village stables, the ranger let out a breath, shook his head slightly and walked to where Black Pot stood waiting. He gathered the stallion's reins and caught up to Hector before he turned the corner toward the stables.

"Maybe it would be a good idea for us to ride together, after all, Hector," he said quietly, leading Black Pot behind him.

"Why now, Ranger?" Hector asked without slowing or facing him. "Is it because now that I am a lawman like you, we have become equal?"

"Wearing a badge does make a difference," Sam

said. But that wasn't the reason. The ranger saw that nothing he could say or do would keep Hector from going after the killers alone. It would be safer to ride with him than to have him out there searching for the same dangerous men on the same trail.

"But you are an *americano* lawman . . . a Territory Ranger," said Hector in a prickly tone. "I am only a village constable, *un guardia*," he said with emphasis. "To someone like you I would be only a lowly town sheriff."

"To *someone* like me, a lawman is a lawman," said the ranger. "It makes no difference whose badge is bigger or who can spit the farthest."

"Oh?" said Hector. "Then you are saying that all lawmen are treated with the same respect by everyone in your country?"

"No," the ranger said bluntly. "I don't speak for everyone in my country. I speak only for myself. Most people in my country have respect for the law, and for any lawman. But there are some who have no respect for anything or anybody . . . and no regard for life and death." He gestured a gloved hand toward the trail leading south out of Valle Hermoso. "You're getting ready to go after two such men. I'm offering to ride with you. . . . Take it or leave it."

Hector thought about it for a moment, then said, "*Sí*, I will ride with you, Ranger, because I want these men to pay for what they have done. We are both lawmen, you and I. We are both after the same thing."

"Then it's all settled," said the ranger. "We ride together."

Suela Soto and Nate Ransdale had wasted no time after leaving Valle Hermoso lying bloody in their wake. By the time they'd heard gunfire echo from along the street of the ordinarily peaceful village, they had reached a higher trail that wound its way upward through steep, rocky terrain. Leaving the two men behind had been no problem for them. Both men had been expendable.

"Sounds like somebody's dead back there," Nate Ransdale said. He slowed almost to a halt and looked back for a moment in the direction of the gunfire while Soto continued on without a backward glance.

"I'm hoping it's the ranger," Soto said, his horse's steady pace not missing a beat, "but I've got my doubts. I figured Shala was no match for the ranger." Suelo Soto had a small tattoo of two red teardrops dripping from the corner of his left eye. When his right hand was bare, Soto kept it closed enough to hide a large, circular tattoo on his palm.

Ransdale looked at him and grinned. "That ain't what you told him and Hirsh though." Ransdale had no idea where Suelo Soto came from. Spain, Portugal, Guatemala? He didn't know, but it was a fact that Soto had savagely cut more than one fellow inmate for speaking Spanish to him when it was assumed Spanish was Soto's native tongue.

"I told them both what I needed to tell them,"

Soto said with not even the slightest trace of an accent. He nudged his boot heels to the sides of a dark roan. He led the big brown and white paint stallion that had belonged to Ramon Sandoval on a lead rope behind him.

"Hirsh—that poor unlucky bummer," Ransdale commented, shaking his head in reflection. He nudged his horse roughly in order to get back beside Soto and keep up with him. "I never knew him to have anything go right in his life. Nothing but bad luck."

"Yeah, well . . ." Soto spit and said, "Even bad luck runs out. I saw that Hirsh was bound for buzzard bait as soon as we started planning this breakout." He nudged his roan a little harder as the trail steepened beneath its hooves. "I'm surprised one of the guards didn't kill him before he got out of range—the damned fool."

With a dark chuckle Ransdale said, "You don't even have a kind word for the dead, do you?"

"I've never had time for the dead or dying," Soto said bluntly, his roan's pace adjusting to the steeper climb without slowing a step. "Once a man is dead or shot up the way Hirsh was, he's no longer any use to me." Giving Ransdale a quick, sidelong glance he added, "That goes for anybody I'm riding with."

"I'll keep that in mind and try my best not to get shot," Ransdale said, his grin gone now as he got Soto's message.

"You do that, Nate," said Soto. "Here's something else you might want to keep in mind. Harvey Simms and the Hole-in-the-wall boys sent word to me in Yuma prison. They wanted *me* and nobody else. I brought you along for my backup, because I know you've got a reputation for being good with a gun. Your job is to cover my back. If you stop doing that, you're no more use to me than Hirsh or Shala. Think you can remember that and not let me down?"

"Yeah, I think so," Ransdale said stiffly, not liking Soto's attitude. "Think you can remember who helped you break out of that Yuma rat hole? Think you can remember it was me back there who killed the trigger-happy Mexican vaquero before he managed to get his sights on you?"

"Like I said," Soto replied matter-of-factly, "that's your job. Keep doing it, and you and I will get along real well." He cut Ransdale a sidelong glance, and with it a flat smile. "Before you hooked up with me, did you ever suppose you'd be riding with the Hole-in-the-wall Gang?"

"No, I never." Ransdale grinned. "But I knew when it came to robbing and raising hell, I always had what you'd call a 'natural gift' for it. I expect the Hole-in-the-wall Gang done themselves well attracting the likes of either one of us."

Staring off across a deep ravine at a winding trail circling below them, Soto spotted a single, two-wheel mule cart and said quietly, "Well, well, look what's going there."

"Hmm . . . ," said Ransdale, speculating as he stared. "Do you suppose there's anything of value in that cart?"

"I don't know," Soto replied. "Are you hungry?"

"I could eat, sure enough," said Ransdale. "All

that shooting and killing back there has got my guts growling for something."

"Then come on," said Soto, batting his heels to the horse's sides. "Let's get on down there and get ourselves some fine Mexican hospitality."

On the lower trail, the old man driving the mule cart had looked up and over and caught a glimpse of the two horsemen across the ravine before they'd ridden out of sight. Had he seen them in time, he would have raised his wide, straw sombrero to them in a courteous gesture. But since they had disappeared so quickly, he only shrugged a shoulder and turned back to the trail ahead.

In the cart bed behind the old man, his fifteen-year-old granddaughter looked up from the weaving work spread across her lap and stopped working long enough to ask him in their native tongue, "Grandfather, what is it like in Méjico City?"

The old man smiled to himself in reflection and replied, "Ahh, *mía pequeña*, it is difficult to describe a city of such magnificence. It is something one must see with his own eyes."

"But I know that I will never see it with my own eyes, *Abuelo*," she replied sadly with a soft sigh, returning her attention to the weaving work on her lap.

"How can you say such a thing? It is still the beginning for you. You have no idea what magnificent sights you will see in your life." Her grandfather smiled again, watching the slow sway of the mule trudging along in front of his reins.

"No," the young girl said in earnest, her voice

expressing some dark regret, "I have always known that I will never see Méjico City."

"Always you are the gloomy one," her grandfather said over his shoulder to her, his smile waning upon hearing the melancholy in her voice. "When I was your age, there were many things I thought I would never see. But I saw them." He considered his words for a moment. "Those things I have not seen. Who knows, perhaps I may still see them someday. If not, so be it," he added with resolve.

"It does not bother you," she asked, "knowing there are things you have always wanted to see or things you have always wanted to do, and yet you might never see or do them?"

The old man shrugged slightly. "If it is meant to be, it will be. . . . If it is not meant to be, then it will not be. Who am I to question what plans God has made for me?"

The girl declared quietly to herself, "I will never see Méjico City," and returned to her work.

The two rode quietly on for the next hour until the old man stepped down from the slow-moving cart and led the mule to a thin spring of water beside the winding trail. As the mule drew in the cool, mountain water, the old man listened intently to the sound of hooves coming along the back trail. Inside the cart the young girl rose up with her weaving in hand and asked, "Who is coming, Grandfather?"

Upon seeing the riders and the spare paint horse draw nearer around a turn in the trail, the old man said warily, "Sit down, *mía pequeña*. Stay out of sight until these two are gone."

But it was too late. As the men rode in closer and slowed their horses a few feet away, before acknowledging the old Mexican, Ransdale turned his horse toward the mule cart and called out, "Hello in there, young lady. You may just as well step on out here. We've already seen you."

"No! Stay down in there, *mía pequeña*!" the old man shouted to his granddaughter.

" 'Little one,' eh?" Ransdale grinned, recognizing the old man's words in Spanish. He raised himself in his stirrups for a better look down inside the tall mule cart. "Now, you stand up, *little one*. Let's just take a little look-see, make sure you're not holding a nasty ole scattergun or whatnot."

As the young girl stood up shyly in the cart, the old man said harshly, "What do you want from us? We have nothing of value for you."

Seeing the young girl clutch her thin shoulders and turn her eyes away from him, Ransdale said with a dark chuckle, "Oh my, but I dare to differ with you, old hombre!"

Staring at the girl for a moment as a warm breeze swept her dark hair across her face, Soto turned back to the old man, his pistol out of his holster, and said, "We come hoping you might share some food with us. My partner here is hungry from the long day's ride. Right, partner?" he called out to Ransdale.

"Not me. Not anymore," said Ransdale, without taking his eyes off the young girl. "There's some

things makes eating have to draw up and wait."
As he spoke he loosened his gun belt and stepped
his horse closer to the mule cart.

"No! No!" The old man cried out, seeing Ransdale's intent. "*Por favor*, senors! She is only a
child!"

"Shame on you, pard," said Soto, giving Ransdale a mock look of disgust. "Ain't this the very
thing that got you thrown into Yuma in the first
place?"

"It might have been a part of it. I can't remember everything," Ransdale said, reaching down
and lifting a knife from his boot well.

Chapter 3

Evening light had turned pale and grainy in the hill country by the time the ranger and Hector Sandoval came upon the mule cart sitting beside the trail. Seeing the mule lying stretched out dead in front of the cart, both men stepped down cautiously from their saddles and walked their horses closer, their guns drawn and ready for anything. Yet nothing could have prepared either of them for the grisly sight they found awaiting them at the edge of the stream.

"Oh no . . . ," Sam said under his breath. The body of the old Mexican was draped over a large rock, his lifeblood still flowing pink down the middle of the stream.

"*Santa Madre* . . . ," Hector whispered, his gloved fingertips instinctively making the sign of a cross on his chest. In the water the naked body of the girl bobbed facedown in the shallows. Her head was scalped to the skull bone so severely and completely that her gender could not be detected until the ranger stepped into the stream and turned her over.

Hector clasped a hand to his mouth and hurried a few feet downstream, as if to keep the ranger from seeing him lose control and heave violently. The ranger swallowed a black, bitter taste from his mouth and kept his eyes on the surrounding rocks and trees as he dragged the dead girl to the stream bank. He stepped over to Black Pot, took down his spare blanket and returned to the body. Hector came walking back, his gun slipping back down into his holster.

"Walk the horses down and water them," Sam said, his words still brittle and sharp with anger and outrage at what the escaped convicts had done.

"No, I am all right now," said Hector. "I can help do what we must."

"Good," Sam said stiffly. "Now walk the horses downstream and water them," he repeated. "That is what must be done." He gave Hector a grim look. "Nobody here is in a hurry. We got here too late to be of any help."

Forcing himself to look down at the dead girl, her face and chest slashed and mutilated beyond any possible recognition, Hector said, "What animal does something like this to one of its own?"

"Only man," Sam said flatly. His eyes still warily searched their surroundings. He flipped the blanket out and let it settle over the pale, tortured corpse.

Hector looked the ranger up and down. "Does

this not affect you? Do these people's lives mean
so little to you—"

"Stop where you are, *Guardia*," the ranger said,
cutting him off. "Don't start thinking you know
what I care about and what I don't." He nodded
toward the land surrounding them and at the
hoofprints leading away on the ground. "For all I
know these men could have staged this whole terrible scene, stunned us just enough to catch us
with our guard down. I have to try to protect the
living. I can't protect the living unless I'm one
of them."

Hector turned his eyes to the rugged terrain.
"But they know you are on their trail. Would they
dare stop long enough to set a trap for you?"

"They're *running*, Hector," said Sam, stepping
out into the water toward the old Mexican's body,
"but they're not running *scared*." As he spoke he
dragged the old man's body to the bank and laid
it beside the girl. "Yes, they will take time to set
a trap, or get drunk, or rob and kill." He nodded
at the girl's blanket-covered body. "Or, take time
to sate their own twisted pleasures."

"I must apologize to you, Ranger," Hector said.
"I had no right to say such a thing." He also nodded at the girl's body. "All of this has affected me
in a way I cannot explain."

"I understand," Sam replied. "I would be worried about you if it didn't affect you. Remember,
we're all after the same thing out here, we lawmen. We just go about it in our own ways."

"*Sí*, I will remember," said Hector. "Now that
I am a lawman, like you, I must learn not to let

such a sight bother me, no matter how terrible it is." Hector's eyes were fixed on the blanketed body. Shaking his head slowly, he added, "It might take me some time."

"Learn fast, *Guardia*," said Sam. "Time has a way of stopping short on a lawman." Turning to the horses, he took their reins and stepped away downstream, to let them drink in clearer water.

Catching up and taking the reins from Sam, Hector led the horses and said, nodding back toward the bodies, "Which of these animals do you think did this?"

"Both," Sam replied. While the horses dipped their muzzles into the flowing water, he stopped and scanned the winding trail as it reached upward around the hillside, then disappeared into the rock and trees. After a moment of consideration he said, "Nate Ransdale has been rumored with doing this sort of thing before. But he's never been charged with it. If I were to speculate, I'd say it was his doing, and Suelo Soto went along with it." He spit and ran a hand across his lips. "Far as I'm concerned, anybody stands by and allows something like this to happen is just as guilty as the one who did it."

"Yes," said Hector, "that is what I say too." He patted his horse's neck as it drew water. "We have been on their trail only one day and already their crimes have grown darker and uglier."

"They'll only get worse if we don't stop them, *Guardia*," said Sam. "If this is Soto's first time raping, killing and taking a scalp, it's only because nobody introduced him to it before now. We'll find out now what influence Ransdale has on him, even though Soto is the one in charge." He gave Hector a grim look. "If we don't stop them soon we'll find out if Soto has an appetite for torturing and killing innocent women."

"A woman?" Hector shook his head. "She was not a woman, this poor helpless girl," he said. "I saw her. She was *una niña joven*. A child so young and innocent she died not knowing such animals as this live in the world."

"Yeah," Sam said flatly, not wanting to talk about it any further, but seeing that Hector, like any man new to such situations, needed to get some things settled in his mind.

"I have seen it many times," Hector continued bitterly. "These men come into my country and think they can do whatever they please. It is as if my people do not count as human beings to these gringos."

"Ransdale is a Texan, but Suelo Soto is from far south of here, Venezuela I believe," Sam said quietly.

Hector stopped talking and took a deep breath. "Again I must apologize, Ranger," he said. "Not everyone from your world is bad, and not everyone from my world is good. It is a fact that wise men must come to realize."

"Apology accepted, and your reasoning understood," Sam said. "When a man hunts in the dark it's easy to want to shoot the first target he sees." Seeing that his stallion had finished drawing water, he reached down and took his reins from Hector. "We've got some daylight left. We best push on harder before these two get a chance to kill again."

"Wait," said Hector. "What about these two? We cannot leave them lying here this way!"

"I didn't intend to leave them lying, *Guardia*," Sam said. "I figure we can lay some rocks over them, keep the wolves and coyotes off them until somebody comes along and finds them."

"No," Hector said firmly. "We must bury them. There are things that must be done . . . words that must be said over them."

Sam stopped and looked at him. "Every minute we spend here makes the odds better that we'll find the same thing waiting for us along the trail. If you want to stay and bury them and say some prayers over them, do it. But I'm more concerned about the living right now. You've seen what these two will do next chance they get." He started to walk away.

"Go on then, Ranger," Hector said. "I will try to catch up to you when I am finished here. These are my people! I owe to them in death the same respect I owed to them in life."

Sam stopped in his tracks and took a deep breath. Maybe the sight of the dead young girl had hurt him more deeply than he cared to admit. Throughout gathering their bodies the question had nagged at him, how much of the mindless torture had happened while they were still alive? His hands clenched into fists as the question came and went again. "You're right, Hector." He let out his tight breath and with it released his fists. "These people have been through enough. I'll see if there's a shovel somewhere in the cart. We'll get them buried. You can say the words."

When Soto and Ransdale reached a stretch of flatlands between two towering hillsides, they stopped their horses long enough to sip tepid water from a canteen and look along the trail behind them. "We wasted too much time with the old man and the girl," Soto said, eyeing the fresh scalp hanging from Ransdale's saddle horn. The big paint horse stood beside him on its lead rope.

"Shhh," Ransdale said with a strange grin, running his hand down the long, glistening black hair. "You'll hurt her feelings talking like that."

Soto shook his head and squirted out a mouthful of water. "You really are as crazy as everybody in Yuma said you are."

"Crazy?" A flash of white-hot anger streaked across Ransdale's eyes, but he managed to mask it with his smile and said, "Nobody in Yuma ever said nothing like that to my face."

"Crazy doesn't bother me," said Soto. "I must be a little loco myself, going along with something like that back there."

Still stroking the long, black hair as if in fond memory, Ransdale said, "Yeah, I noticed I didn't have to talk you into it very hard, did I?"

"No, you didn't." Soto wiped his shirtsleeve across his mouth. "I expect a man is capable of just about anything once out of a hellhole like Yuma. It's been a long time since I had a woman."

"Me too," said Ransdale, "if you can call *la*

pequeña here a woman. Right, little one?" he said to the scalp at his fingertips.

"Young woman, old woman, what's the difference? It's done," Soto said, looking away from Ransdale and his morbid conversation with the dead girl's hair, and the way he caressed it as if it were alive. He spotted the thin cut of a narrow trail leading off across a rise covered with tall bracken and wild grass. In the distance he caught a pale spiral of gray smoke adrift on a breeze. "Are you still hungry?"

"I can eat, that's for sure," said Ransdale, still engrossed in fondling the silky, black hair. "What have you got in mind?"

"I think there's folks over there a few miles, if you can pull yourself loose long enough to go see."

"I believe I can," Ransdale said, bending slightly in his saddle, raising the long hair to his face and breathing in its fragrance. "Just so you don't think there's something wrong with me," he added, "I didn't take this hair just to be doing it. This thing is worth money in Durango you know."

"Apache hair used to be worth a few dollars but not anymore," said Soto, "especially not *Mexican* hair." He nudged his horse forward as he spoke. "You've been gone longer than I thought."

"I'm not talking about the government bounty on Apache scalps. I know that's over with. I'm talking about private collectors," said Ransdale. "I know a man who buys any kind of hair—Irish red, Swedish yellow. He don't care so long as it's woman."

"How much money are you talking about?" Soto asked skeptically."

"Not a lot of money, but some. Every little bit helps." He grinned again and nudged his horse along beside Soto, letting the long hair lie draped over his knee as if liking the feel of it. Shrugging he added, "So, if I can catch myself a woman alone and make a little something for my trouble, what's the harm in it?"

"It's none of my business." Soto stared ahead toward the faint waft of smoke in the distance, deciding not to take part in any more of Ransdale's bizarre indulgences.

"Wait a minute," said Ransdale. "Have you got a mad-on because those two are the same as you?"

Soto glared at him. "They weren't the same as me. They're Mexican. I'm not Mexican"

"I know where you come from," Ransdale said confidently. "It sure as hell ain't from this country. You might talk better English than the rest of us at Yuma did. Your ways might be a little more polished. But you're not American and I know it."

Soto ignored him as they rode on. When he did speak again, he asked, "Why did you cut up her face?"

As if resenting the question, Ransdale spit and said defiantly, "Why not?"

Ten minutes later, at a thin line of trees atop a low rise, the two stepped down from their saddles and walked forward until they looked down at a sun-bleached plank-and-adobe shack. "Goatherds,"

Ransdale said, eyeing a small corral where a few spindle-legged goats milled near a water trough. A few yards from the goats a large bitch dog with a thick, matted coat lay watching the animals as if they were her pups.

"Looks like dinner to me," Soto said flatly, glancing from the goats to the plank shack.

"I can get the rifle and pick the dog's head off from here," Ransdale said.

"I see no need to kill it just yet," said Soto. He watched a middle-aged woman step out of the shack, her graying hair gathered and tied up in a large bun atop her head. Behind her an elderly man, bowed deeply at the waist, ambled along, clutching a cane for support. "I bet these folks are accustomed to feeding every wayfaring pilgrim who comes along."

"Well, that includes us," said Ransdale. "We're pilgrims for sure."

"Tell me," Soto said, stepping back and turning toward the horses, "how much does your private collector pay for gray hair?"

"I don't know, but we'll damn sure find out." Ransdale grinned as they approached the horses. "I bet you start taking a liking to scalp collecting before it's over."

"Don't count on it," said Soto. "I'm in the business of opening railway safes without blowing them up. I'm not looking to change professions."

"I don't mean as a new profession," said Ransdale. "I'm talking about doing it for fun as much as anything else."

Soto only stared at him blankly as they gathered

their horses' reins, the lead rope to the big paint, and stepped up into their saddles.

In the littered front yard the woman stood watching as the two riders moved into sight from the shelter of the trees. She used her hand as a visor across her brow and offered a smile until she got a better look at the men. Then her smile turned troubled, and she said over her shoulder in a German accent, "Papa, get yourself back inside. Take Big Bess with you." She glanced around the yard and saw a smaller, younger dog staring toward the riders. "Take Little Bobby too," she added firmly. Under her breath she said in a worried tone, "This is trouble if I've ever seen it."

"What? What's that you say?" the old man asked in an ancient, crackling voice, his accent thicker than the woman's. He had to squint to see even a blurred image of his daughter. "Why must I get the dogs in?"

"Papa, don't question me," the woman said. "Get inside. Stay inside and keep your mouth shut no matter what happens out here."

"Oh . . . ," the old man said warily as understanding came to him. He turned his dim eyes toward the sound of hoofbeats, then shuffled back inside the run-down shack, calling both dogs to follow him.

Chapter 4

Having seen the old man and the two shepherd dogs disappear upon their approach, Suelo Soto stared at the shack as he and Ransdale reined their horses down and stepped them back and forth in the dirt. "I hope we're not interrupting anything, ma'am," he said politely, although his voice carried an unpleasant tone. "I've got a feeling there's things here we want."

"We don't want any trouble, Mister," the woman said. "Take anything you want and leave us in peace."

The two men stopped their horses and stared at her. Ransdale said as he eyed her up and down with a wicked grin, "Did you say *anything* we want?"

Her eyes moved across the long, freshly taken scalp hanging against his leg, but she pretended not to see it. The sight of the wet, gory artifact sent a chill of desperation up her spine, yet she managed to keep her voice steady. "Yes, you can have whatever you want without a fight—only please don't hurt my pa, or our animals."

"What makes you think putting up a fight would bother us any?" Ransdale said, his grin going away, replaced by a dark, malevolent stare.

Turning her eyes from Ransdale without answering him, she said to Soto, "Pick out a yearling. I'll clean it and spick it for you." She gestured a nod toward the small herd of goats milling nearby in a corral. "It's better that I cooperate, do what you want done, rather than fight you over every little thing, isn't it?"

"You're a whore, aren't you?" Soto said bluntly, causing Ransdale to snicker as if he'd meant it as a cruel joke or an insult.

"I used to be," the woman said, ignoring Ransdale for the moment and speaking only to Soto. "But I haven't forgotten how." She tilted her chin as she spoke and cocked a hand onto her hip as if compelled by instincts she thought she'd long abandoned. She felt herself steadily gaining a footing of control, and with it, courage. "In case you and your laughing friend want to know, my name is Clarimonde—"

"I don't want to know your name." Soto cut her off roughly. He gestured a finger up and down her. "Step out of that dress and let's see what you're carrying around underneath."

"Yeah and let your hair drop," Ransdale cut in.

Without taking her eyes off Soto, she untied the two strings holding her dress at her throat and let it fall to the dirt. Behind her she heard the bitch shepherd whine and scratch at the inside of the door. She heard her father call the restless animal down.

"I hate an unruly dog," said Ransdale, his hand going to his gun butt and wrapping around it. Yet his eyes stayed riveted on the woman's pale, naked breasts.

"The bitch dog is old. She doesn't mean anything by it," the woman said. "Neither of these dogs bites. You don't have to worry about them."

"These dogs look too damn much like wolves not to bite," Ransdale replied. "But you tell me if I look worried to you." He glared at her, his hand resting on his gun butt.

"No, you do not look like a man who worries about troublesome dogs when more pleasurable things are close at hand." Relieved that the scratching and whining had stopped, the woman eased a hand up her flat stomach and cupped a breast to keep Ransdale's attention drawn away from the door. She deliberately avoided looking at the fresh scalp at his knee as she reached up, pulled a long thin cactus needle from her hair, shook it out and let it fall.

Having noted her accent and the way she handled Ransdale, Soto chuckled and said, "Yeah, you've been a 'hurdy' girl all right. I can see your mind clicking right along. Don't try getting too bold on us," he warned. "You can see what my pard thinks of womenfolk."

"I will do only as you tell me to do," the woman said submissively.

"Whoo-ieee, I like the sound of that," said Ransdale. He looked her tall, naked body up and down and said with a tight, hushed voice, "Her hair's the color of wheat in the field."

"Keep hair out of your mind for right now, Nate," said Soto. "We're going to eat some hot goat meat and make ourselves at home here for a while." He glared at the woman and said, "Does that sound good to you, *Clarimonde*?" He deliberately used her name as if to let her know she had won something.

"Yes, that sounds good to me," she offered with a coy smile. Now that she felt she'd diverted their attention from the shack for the moment, she stooped straight down to pick up her dress. "I will kill our largest kid and prepare it for you."

"You don't need to dress on our account," Soto said, stopping her from pulling the weathered dress back up around her. "I might enjoy watching a woman go about her work without her clothes on."

"Might?" said Ransdale. "I know for damn sure that I would."

The woman straightened, picked up her dress and let it hang from her fingertips. Without letting her humiliation show, she nodded toward a smaller weathered shack thirty yards away. "I keep our butchering knives in there."

"After you then," said Soto, backing his horse up a step and allowing her to walk to the corral.

The two watched her select the largest yearling from among the goat herd and walk out, cradling it in her arms. They stepped down from their saddles and followed her to the shed. Ransdale took off his gun belt and draped it over his saddle horn as if preparing to force himself upon her as soon as they entered the shack. But a stern look from Soto kept him in check as they walked along, watching the woman stroke the kid's neck and speak soothingly to it in German.

Without looking around, the woman said matter-of-factly, "If I make you happy, I am hoping you will not kill my papa or the dogs before leaving."

Chuckling, Ransdale said, "It's not likely you'll get what you're hoping for—not with hair like this." He reached out with his gloved hand and ran it down her long hair hanging down her back.

Ignoring Ransdale's words, Soto said bluntly to the woman, "We're American convicts running from an Arizona lawman. I don't like leaving live witnesses behind us."

"But you have nothing to fear from us," said the woman. "No one here can say who you are. My papa does not see well."

Ransdale grinned cruelly and said as he watched the sway of her naked hips beneath her hair, "Then that leaves only you."

"You do not have to worry about me saying anything about you," she said. Still stroking the kid in her arms, Clarimonde reached out with a foot and shoved the weathered plank door open, then walked inside the shack.

"Oh?" Ransdale said. "And why is that?"

"Because I will ride along with you when you

leave," she said, pressing her cheek to that of the kid before setting it down atop a chopping block in the middle of the dirt floor.

"No fooling?" Soto gave Ransdale a look, then said to the woman, "And what makes you think you're going to be going with us?"

She leveled a gaze into his eyes as she picked up a long, sharp-pointed knife from a rack on the side of the butcher block. "Because I have lived here for a long time. I can show you ways out of this hill country that no American lawman knows about. I can take you deeper into the wilds of Mexico."

"Maybe we're not going much deeper into Mexico," he said, watching her play her hand at keeping herself and her father alive. "What if we're headed somewhere a little nearer to the border?"

"Nearer to the border? But if you are running from the law, shouldn't you try to get farther away from the border?" Clarimonde asked.

"Not just yet." Soto smiled. "What if I asked you to show us a fast way to Shadow Valley? Think you could do that without the law catching up to us?" His smile widened. "I mean, if it meant saving you and the old man's life?"

Without hesitation, she said, "I can take you to Shadow Valley on a gun runner trail that even the local villagers do not know about."

"Is that so?" Soto replied. "Then how is it that you know about it?"

With bold confidence she said, "Because I was once the concubine of the gun runner who forged the trail."

" 'Concubine' . . . ," said Ransdale. "That's just a fancier word for whore." He took a half step forward, but then stopped, noting the knife in the woman's hand.

"If you know a high trail to Shadow Valley, I'm interested," said Soto. "But if you're lying to me . . ." He let his words trail, leaving the consequence to her imagination.

"I am not lying," Clarimonde said, "and you will see that I am good at everything I do." As she spoke she pressed down gently on the kid's spiny back. The kid sank onto the block and lay staring blankly.

The two men watched her slide a low, wide, deep tin cup up against the thin animal's throat. With a deft stroke of the knife blade she opened a half-inch cut across a raised artery in the animal's frail neck and let the blood flow into the cup. The kid lay bleeding painlessly.

"Now that was slickly done," Ransdale chuckled. As the animal lay with its eyes closed beneath the woman's soothing hand, he dipped his fingers into the filling cup and flipped blood on Clarimonde's naked breasts.

Giving Ransdale a harsh stare, Soto cautioned him, saying, "Careful she doesn't do the same thing to you while you're not looking."

But Ransdale only laughed. He flipped more warm blood on the woman and smeared it down her breasts with his finger. Giving her a cold, menacing stare he said, "Not me, she won't. I'm always looking." He leaned in close to the woman and ran his bloody fingers down her hair. "One slipup, and you're going to look good swinging from my saddle horn."

Inside the shack the old man had paced back and forth for more than an hour, hushing the two shepherds when they piqued their ears and growled toward the sounds of harsh laughter and swearing from across the yard at the butcher shed. "Be still, Bess," he ordered the large bitch. "I know no more what is going on than you do. Now be silent."

But moments later when the aroma of roasting goat meat permeated the air, he stopped pacing and stood, anxiously wiping his palms on his trousers and squinting out a dust-streaked window toward the butcher shed. "Good, she is feeding them now. Soon they will go on their way and leave us in peace."

Yet, on the floor at his feet the distrustful old bitch rose slowly, this time growling louder as a peal of dark laughter resounded from the smaller shack. Close by the younger dog followed suit.

"*Halt die Schnauze, Bess! Sie störrisches altes Weibchen!*" the old man chastised the wary animal, resorting to his native tongue. Then, shaking his finger at the younger, thinner dog, he said, "You, lie down! What she does with those *schmutzige Schweine*, she does for all of us!"

But no sooner had he settled both animals than the pair sprang back up from the floor as a loud sound erupted from the butcher shed, as if someone had been slammed against the thin plank wall.

Cursing under his breath, the old man walked

to where a long, ornate shotgun hung on pegs above the mantel. "I won't sit here idly like a *dummer feigling*, no matter what my daughter demands of me."

At the sight of the old man taking down the shotgun, both shepherds began scurrying in circles around him. But he raised a hand toward them and said, "*Nein! Nein!* Both of you lie down and do as you were told!" Only when the two had settled grudgingly down onto the floor did the old man pick up his walking cane, step out onto the porch and slam the door behind himself.

From a place where they had built a fire out back of the butcher shed, Ransdale turned with a mouth full of hot goat meat and called out to the open doorway, "Suelo, here comes the old man. He's packing a scattergun." As he spoke he lifted his gun from his holster with greasy fingers and added with a glistening grin, "But don't get up. I've got him."

Inside, on a dirty blanket lying on the dirt floor of the butcher shed, the woman cried out, "No! Papa!" and shoved Soto from atop of her. Soto only rolled over and laughed as he watched her snatch her dress from the dirt, hold it to her bosom and run out the open door. "Crazy whore," he said to himself, pulling the cork from a dusty bottle of whiskey Ransdale had found when he'd rummaged the shack, "lives here with two wolves and a madman."

Standing, Soto lifted his gun from its holster on the butcher block and walked out naked, the bottle in one hand, his cocked revolver in the other.

"Please! It is not loaded!" the woman cried out, having run forward and grabbed the shotgun from her father's hands. She broke the empty shotgun down quickly and held it out for Soto to see, keeping herself between the old man and the two killers. "He is old and foolish in his head! Don't hurt him!"

Ransdale turned to Soto, his gun out at arm's length toward the old man. "You call it, Suelo. I can kill either one or both for you."

"Hold up," Soto said. He walked closer to the woman and took the shotgun she held out for him to examine. Behind her the old man struggled to shove her out of his way. Soto looked at the unloaded shotgun, shook his head and tossed it aside. "Foolish is right," he said, staring at the old man's confused and squinting eyes. "Old man, your daughter, Clarimonde, just kept you from making a bad mistake."

"Get out of here, all of you!" the old man shouted, uncertain of even how many men were standing before his blurred eyes. "You are not welcome here!" Struggling against his daughter's firm grip on his wrists, he raged at her, "I know what is going on out here! I won't stand for any more of it!"

"Get back inside the house, Papa!" the woman shouted, turning loose on his wrists and giving him a shove. Soto stepped in and shoved him at the same time, causing the old German to fall backward to the ground.

"You heard her, old man," Soto said. "Get inside before we nail your shirt to your chest." He slid an arm around the woman's naked, sweaty waist and drew her against his side. "Your daughter belongs to us now." He looked up and down Clarimonde's bruised and dirt-streaked body, her hair hanging matted, half covering her face. "Right, hurdy girl?"

"Yes, that is right, Papa," she said, feeling a surge of hope in spite of the pain, the shame and humiliation the two men had brought upon her. "Get back inside. I belong to these men. I am leaving here with them." She drew herself even closer to Suelo Soto's side as if they were lovers. "You stay here with the dogs."

"Yeah, old man," Ransdale called out, grinning, tearing off another mouthful of meat now that the shotgun had been tossed aside, "you can go to the dogs as far as she cares."

"I will get rid of him," Clarimonde said quietly to Soto. Slipping away from his side, holding her dress to herself, she stepped over and helped her father back to his feet. "Papa, listen to me," she whispered quickly, picking up his cane and placing it in his brittle hand. "I am taking them to Shadow Valley. Tell the lawman who comes looking for them. Now, stay inside and keep quiet until we are gone. Please help me keep us alive. These men will think nothing of killing you, the shepherds, every one of us."

The old man started to shout something, but uncertain of what he might say, Clarimonde clasped a hand over his mouth and raised her voice loud enough for both Soto and Ransdale to hear. "Shut up, you old fool, and stay away from me, or else I will take a stick to your back!"

"Whoo-ieee," Ransdale called out. "Old man, I'd say this gal has given you up for a better deal." He looked at Soto and gave a knowing wink, neither of them fooled into thinking the woman had anything more in mind than staying alive and finding her way out of their hands. "I believe she's fell in love with us."

Chapter 5

The old German sat in silence at a small table for a long time, his head bowed and his eyes closed until the old bitch pawed at his leg and whined so insistently that he could no longer ignore her. Rising from the table, his cane in hand, he walked out onto the porch and squinted toward the silence and the aroma of wood ash and roasted goat meat. No sooner had he opened the door than both of the shepherds shot past him toward the spot where the men and the woman had stepped into their saddles and ridden away more than an hour earlier.

Seeing no movement other than the blurred image of the dogs, the old man walked across the yard, picking up the shotgun from where Soto had thrown it to the dirt. "My daughter is gone," he murmured brokenly to himself. "Once again I find myself alone in this godforsaken *wilder platz.*"

In the nearby corral the herd of goats crowded the rail, bleating and craning their thin necks in hungry anticipation. Ordinarily the shepherds would have run around the fire, barking and begging for scraps of meat at the old man's feet. But today they only circled wide, sniffed the ground in the direction the horses had taken and raced away along a thin, up-reaching trail into the high, rocky hill country.

"Go on with you, then—you can leave me too. Who needs two unruly *hunde* always underfoot!" The old man cried out, waving an arm in despair as the dogs' blurred images disappeared into the brush. But no sooner had he made the remarks than his eyes filled with tears. "Both of you come home this minute! Do you hear me, Bess? Stay away from those men! Clarimonde went with them to protect you! Stay away from them!"

He stood silently until the last of his echo had sunk into the rocky hills. Then he sighed and walked dejectedly to a feed bin alongside the butcher shed. There he picked up a bucket of feed and an empty bucket for milking. With the empty shotgun clamped under his arm, he trudged out to the corral and went about his daily tasks.

An hour later, from the edge of the trail the two escaped convicts had ridden in on, the ranger and Hector Sandoval stopped their horses and warily searched the clearing before venturing in. "Do you know this man?" Sam asked, gazing ahead at the old German who had just stood up and walked out of the corral. He carried the shotgun in one hand along with the empty feed bucket. In his other hand he carried a full bucket of goat milk.

"He was not here the last time I came this way," said Hector. "I do not know him, but I know of him. He is an old German who tends goats with his daughter. These goatherds move about like sparrows."

"Goatherds don't usually arm themselves with shotguns to do their milking, do they?" Sam asked. Nudging his stallion forward, he warily searched the front yard of the shack and the area around the butcher shed.

"No, they do not," said Hector, looking all around the yard and the hillsides. "They have large German herd dogs protecting their goats. I have heard that they look more like wolves than dogs."

"Do you worry yourself about wolves, *Guardia*?" Sam asked, recognizing a sudden tenseness in Hector and hoping to settle him as they rode closer to the old man.

The two caught a wafting scent of roasted meat in the air. "Only when there are wolves around," Hector commented, realizing what the ranger was doing. Nudging his horse along a few feet behind the ranger, he added, "But I think the wolves I speak of have already been here and gone."

"I think you're right, *Guardia*," said Sam, knowing that whatever tension he'd sensed in the man had passed as suddenly as it had appeared.

Ahead of them the old man had stopped and squinted toward them. As soon as he made out their blurred images riding slowly into view, he quickly set the bucket of milk at his feet and raised the shotgun to his shoulder. Sam stepped his stallion away from Hector's horse, putting some distance between them. "This is your graze.

You had better talk to him," he said quietly to
Hector. Then he remained silent, watching the old
man intently, sensing from his behavior that
something bad had happened here.

"We come in peace, goatherd," Hector called
out, seeing the old man stop and set the bucket
of milk on the ground. "I am the *guardia* of Valle
Hermoso. We are hunting for two very bad men."
He paused just long enough to let the old German
think; then he added, "Have you seen them? If
not, we will ride clear of you and be on our way."

The shotgun was lowered from the old man's
shoulder. He sighed deeply and said, "Yes, they
were here. They took my daughter, Clarimonde,
and left with her. I am going out of my mind with
worry and fear for her."

Now Sam spoke. "Lay the shotgun down, Mister. We're riding in. I'm also a lawman—Arizona
Ranger Sam Burrack."

"Yes, please, ride in," the old man called out to
them. As he spoke he stooped and laid the shotgun down on the dirt. "I am Herr Siebelz—
Adolph Siebelz. I will do whatever you ask to help
you get my daughter safely away from them."

"It is said that his daughter was once a prosper-
ous *puta* on the Barbary Coast of California," Hector said almost in a whisper as they nudged their
animals forward at a quicker pace. "That is why
they took her, instead of killing her and taking
her hair. They take her for their pleasure."

"No," said Sam. "We've seen how these men
take their pleasure. If she's alive it's because she's

struck a deal for herself. These men are keeping her alive for their own reason."

They stepped down from their saddles. Sam stooped, picked up the shotgun, checked it and held it sideways, letting Hector see that it wasn't even loaded. Squinting, the old man said, "Holding an empty shotgun is better than holding no gun at all."

"Only if you hold it as a club," Sam said, handing him the shotgun butt first. "How long have they been gone?" he asked.

"More than an hour . . . two hours at the most." The old man squinted harder, trying to make out the blurred badge on the ranger's chest. "She's not with them because she wants to be. My Clarimonde rode with them to keep them from killing us . . . from killing us and our two dogs. Now the two dogs are gone off trying to find her. She is a good daughter, my Clarimonde." He grasped the ranger's sleeve. "Please get her away from those men. Please bring her home. Whatever she has done, she does it to save me and our dogs."

"I understand," said Sam. He gazed toward the higher land beyond the clearing, gauging how far the party could have traveled in under two hours on such rugged, upward terrain. "We'll do our best to bring her home," he said, gently pulling his sleeve free. To Hector he said, "They must be riding to the high country to find a back trail into Sonora. Maybe Hirsh was telling us the truth after all."

"Oh, no, Ranger," said Siebelz, "they do not go

to Sonora. My daughter risked her life to tell me. They are going to Shadow Valley. She is showing them a hidden trail that takes them there."

"Valle de la Sombra," Hector said with a tone of dread in his voice.

Sam looked at him. "I've heard of it, but I've never been there. Do you know your way there?"

"*Sí*, I know my way there, but not on some hidden trail," said Hector.

"We'll keep tracking them," Sam offered.

"No matter the trail, once inside Shadow Valley, we are in a good place for desperate men like these to catch us in a trap," said Hector. "That is why they go there. Why else would they venture back so close to the border to get to such a place?"

Sam ignored the warning in Hector's voice and looked up eastward into the tall, rocky hill country lying above them. "Maybe they only crossed the border because there's something Soto needs down here." He studied the eastward ridges against a blue and perfect sky. "Whatever it is, he gets it, then he's gone back across the border with it. If he can get rid of us on his way, so much the better. . . ." He let his words trail in contemplation.

After a moment, the old German said, "Whatever these men are doing, when you catch up to them you can count on my daughter to do whatever she can to help you. This I vow to you."

Hector and the ranger both turned quickly at the sound of brush breaking on the far side of the clearing. Their guns streaked out of their holsters. But they both eased their guns down as they saw the tired younger dog come walking into sight, his head down, his tongue hanging limply. Having turned with them toward the breaking brush, the old German squinted, saying, "Who is it? Who is coming?"

"It must be one of the dogs you talked about," Sam said, watching the dog speed up into a worn-out trot at the sight of them. "Easy, boy," he said, he and Hector both standing perfectly still, guns in hand as the thin-flanked shepherd hurried in close, lunging, barking and snarling toward them.

The old man raised a hand toward the growling dog and spoke to it in German, causing the animal to settle down instantly and drop to the ground at the old man's feet.

"You must excuse Little Bobby," the old man said. "He is not vicious. He is only trying to protect me."

"I understand," said Sam. He and Hector both looked toward the trail to see if the other shepherd might be coming.

The old German stooped down, embracing and patting the exhausted dog. "So, you have spent yourself out and now you come home to me, eh?" he said affectionately to the animal. To Sam and Hector he said, "See? He is no more than a big, foolish child, this one."

"He is a big child, but one who could take a man's hand off if he wanted to," Hector commented.

"Yes, but only if someone were harming the herd, or my daughter or me," the old man replied. "That is how these mountain dogs are. That is why Clarimonde made me keep them inside while the men were here. She was afraid they would get frightened and attack the men, and the men would shoot them."

"So, she protected the watchdogs," Sam commented, seeing the irony of it. He looked down at the tired dog lying at its master's feet.

"It sounds strange to one who has not given himself and his heart to the herder's life, but it is how we do things, my daughter and I," the old man said.

Sam only nodded. "Will this other dog cause us any problems if we come upon her out there?" he asked.

"You will do well to beware of her," said the old man. "Bess is twice this one's size. She is an old bitch who thinks Clarimonde and I belong to her. She is very protective of us, as if we are her pups.

"Obliged for telling us," said Sam. "We will beware of her."

"If she tries to harm you," the old man said, "I know you must do what it takes to stop her. But I hope you do not have to hurt her. She is such a good and faithful animal."

"You have my word we'll do the best we can," Sam said reassuringly.

The old man looked relieved, but only for a second. Then he said, "I fear she will try to follow Clarimonde too closely and those men will shoot her—if they have not already."

Sam and Hector looked at each other, both seeing the fear and anxiety in the old man's squinting face as he rubbed his hands nervously up and down on his trouser legs. To take his mind off things if only for a moment, Sam said quietly, "In my saddlebags I have a pair of spectacles that belonged to a prisoner who didn't make it back to the territory. This might be a good time for me to pass them along to somebody who could use them."

"Sí," said Hector. "Meanwhile, I will water our horses and get us prepared to ride on. We are too close to stop any longer than we have to, especially now that we know they have taken a woman hostage."

Hearing Hector, the old man stood up stiffly from patting the tired dog and said, "My Clarimonde prepared our finest kid for those men. I will not feel that it was such a waste if you two will take it with you to eat on the trail. It'll save you time having to fix a meal."

"Obliged," said Sam, turning and searching through his saddlebags. "It will save us time having to stop and gather a meal. Every minute is going to count, catching up to them on these high trails." He turned back to the old man with a duster pair of spectacles in his gloved hand. "I'd also be obliged if you'll take these wire-rims off my hands and give them a good home," he said. The thin dog growled under its breath as he held the glasses out to Siebelz.

Squinting to recognize the spectacles, the old man scowled at the dog, saying, "Hush yourself, Little Bobby. Where are your manners?" To the ranger he said, "I have always hoped to someday

look through a pair of these and see the world as
I remember it to be."

"Let's hope they do the job for you," Sam said.

Siebelz put the spectacles on with a shaky hand.
Sam and Hector watched his eyes grow large and
full of surprise as he looked back and forth between them. "Oh my," he murmured as if in awe.
"It has been a long time since I have seen so
clearly. Oh yes, yes! They work fine for me! Thank
you, Ranger!"

Sam only smiled and touched the brim of his
dusty sombrero.

Siebelz turned in a complete circle with his arms
spread. His gravelly voice trembled as he looked
down at the panting dog and said, "For the first
time I can see you clearly, Little Bobby! My, what
a handsome young fellow you are!" He took a
step away from the dog and said, "Now come
with me. Stay out from underfoot while I pack
some food for these lawmen."

As the old man and the dog walked away, Sam
and Hector led their horses to a nearby watering
trough. The two washed trail dust from their faces
in the same tepid water while the thirsty animals
drank their fill. Slinging his wet hair back and
forth, Hector blew water from his lips and gazed
upward along the high, distant outline of rugged
hilltops.

"Strange," he said. "I started hunting these men
because of what they did to my brother and
Guardia Luis Gravis." His eyes searched back and
forth as if something might appear to him from
such a great distance. "Now it is important that I

catch them for this woman's sake." He looked at Sam. "For this woman I do not even know."

"It's the badge," Sam said. "It has a way of leading you into tight spots, makes you lay your life down for a stranger."

Sam ran a hand down his wet face and placed his sombrero back atop his head. Looking at Hector, he could see the young man waiting for more, as if the ranger had not finished what he had to say on the matter. But Sam only tightened his sombrero and picked up his gloves from beside the water trough. "Let's get going," he said, "and see where their trail takes us."

Chapter 6

Soto and Ransdale sat on the bank of a wide stream and watched the naked woman wade out until she stood knee-deep in the cool, rushing water. "That's far enough, *Clarimonde*," Soto called out. As always he spoke her name with mock emphasis, as if it were a joke or a nickname, not a name for someone of any significance.

She stopped and glanced back at them, making note of how far she had been allowed to go on her own. The next time she would try to stop before he had a chance to say anything. The less attention they had to pay to her the better, she thought. The less she had to be told what to do, the farther she could test the limits they held on her.

Clarimonde had learned a lot about these two in the short time since they'd forced their way in and taken over her life. These were rough, dangerous, crude, abusive men, but not too greatly unlike many of the men she had known in her past. She had survived the streets and brothels of the Barbary Coast among such men, she told herself as she dipped water in her hands and washed trail grit from her arms, her breasts.

Her hand went to a jagged, three-inch scar in the tender flesh above her right breast, at the edge of her armpit. With a cool head, clear thought and deliberation, surely she could survive these two, she told herself.

From the edge of the stream, watching intently as she dipped water and let it run down her long hair, Ransdale felt his cheek twitch nervously. "Damn black-hearted whore," he said, to keep himself from being aroused by her action. "What goes on in their heads, you think?"

Soto gave him a flat, sidelong look, then cut his gaze back to Clarimonde. "Getting themselves ahead in the game," he said, "the same as the rest of us." A few feet away, the four horses stood with their muzzles down, drawing water.

"This one would cut our throats while we're sleeping, and never bat an eye over it," Ransdale observed.

Soto grinned, his eyes fixed on Clarimonde's pale, firm flesh. "Yes, I admire that in a woman," he said, seeing her stoop down onto her knees and bow forward.

Allowing her hair to flow on the clear braided stream, she drank like some exotic creature from the wilds. "Hot damn," said Ransdale. "Does she know what she's doing to us?"

"Oh yes, she knows," Soto replied. "You can count on it."

Ransdale considered it for a moment; his cheek

twitched again, this time more severly. He swallowed hard and said, "I'm going to wade out there and beat the living hell out of her." He started to rise. Soto stopped him with a hand on his forearm.

Looking at him again, Soto said, "Calm yourself down, Nate. Why would you want to do something like that?"

Ransdale shrugged, but it was a stiff, awkward gesture that required effort in order to make it look casual. "You know, just to be doing it. I'm restless."

"Restless, huh? You want to do something? Walk off into the brush, take a minute and check back along the trail, see how it looks." He nodded toward the thick brush at the trail's edge. "Hurry up though. We need to get above these hills."

His face reddening, Ransdale understood Soto's suggestion and what it really meant. "Hell, I don't need to do nothing like that. We're not in prison anymore. I was just thinking out loud about the whore . . . smacking her around. Some of them like that, you know."

"I've got a feeling this one doesn't," said Soto, his eyes going back to the woman. "Besides, she's banged up enough already." He smiled. "We are not gentlemen, after all that cell time."

They sat in silence for a moment. Then Ransdale said with a slight chuckle, "I have to say, it's been a good trail so far. How many men break out of prison, run the border and come upon a whore just hanging out up here with a herd of goats?"

"Not many, I'd have to surmise," said Soto.

"None that I ever heard of," Ransdale said, settling down a little and watching the woman without the tight twitch in his jaw. "If this is all a taste of riding with you, I have to say it's an honor, *mi amigo.*"

"Don't ever speak Spanish to me," Soto said, his attitude bristling suddenly. "You've seen me cut men for doing it."

"I—I forgot for a minute," said Ransdale. "I meant no offense by it."

Soto cooled as quickly as he'd heated. Changing the subject he said, "Riding with me is going to get better and better, Nate. Just keep watching. Once we hook up with the Hole-in-the-wall boys, we're going to be the top aces in the deck."

"I believe it," said Ransdale. He looked back at the naked woman and saw her turn and walk back toward them. "If I ever doubted it to begin with, I sure don't doubt it now."

Soto also watched the woman. "If I'm not mistaken, this hidden trail she's taking us on is going to cut two days off our getting around these hillsides to where we're heading."

"Can you tell me just where it is we're going, yet?" Ransdale asked carefully.

Soto turned his eyes from the naked woman and looked Ransdale up and down. Grinning firmly he said, "To an old mining project. The people there used to work for my family. Once we get there, we won't care if the ranger catches up to us. In fact we might welcome it as a source of amusement."

When Clarimonde stepped out of the braided

stream and stooped down to pick up her dress, Ransdale reached out his hand and firmly gripped her wet, glistening buttocks. "A few years ago I couldn't do that without burning my hand, eh, whore?" He squeezed harder, staring at her long, wet hair. "You've lost some of the fire and honey since then. Hair is about all you've got left."

Clarimonde stopped what she was doing and froze in place, making no effort to resist as he roughly joggled her by the flesh of her behind.

"Get over here, whore," Ransdale said suddenly, his free hand going to loosen his belt. "I've seen all I can stand."

Clarimonde gave Soto a look that said little, yet seemed to call upon him to intervene.

"Save it, Nate," said Soto. "We've got to get going. I've told you how important it is to get above these hills."

"I know," said Ransdale, letting out a breath and turning the woman loose with a slight shove. "I was just seeing how well we're training her to do what we want." He sat upright, then pushed up onto his feet.

Clarimonde said humbly, "I have told you I will do whatever either of you want me to—"

In spite of her passive tone, the back of Ransdale's gloved hand swung around sharply across her face and cut her off. "Keep your mouth shut, whore!" he said. "Unless one of us tells you to open it."

Landing on her side in the dirt, she looked up at Soto as blood began to trickle down the edge of her lips. But Soto showed no sign of sympathy for her as he stood up and dragged her to her feet. Looking at the dirt down her side, he gave Ransdale an icy stare.

"I guess I get a little carried away sometimes," Ransdale said with a sheepish grin, rubbing the back of his gloved gun hand. "The whore's jaw is hard as a rock. Lucky I didn't bust a knuckle on it."

"Gain control of yourself," Soto said solemnly. "What good are you to me with an injured gun hand?"

"Come on, Suelo," Ransdale said, hoping to lighten things up. "My hand's all right. That was just a manner of speaking. I'd never break my hand over a whore. I just snapped, let her get to me for a minute, is all."

Soto seemed not to hear him. Still holding Clarimonde by her forearm, Soto looked her up and down and helped her brush dirt from her side with his free hand. "Are you all right?" he asked quietly, holding her close to him, so close she could feel his breath on her cheek.

"Yes, I'm all right," she replied, staring down, keeping herself supplicant to him. Her dress hung in her hand. She noted his breath had a sensation of coldness to it that she had experienced from only a few other men in her years on the Barbary Coast. To the man, those few had been murderers, bloodletters of the lowest order.

She didn't dare pull her forearm free, yet she nudged against his grip just enough to get him to turn her loose. Then she slipped the ripped and battered dress over her head and smoothed it down her front. "What do we have waiting ahead of us?" he asked. His tone implied that he might already know and was only testing her to see if she told the truth.

"Before we reach the top, we will pass a thin trail that leads back to an abandoned Spanish settlement."

"Abandoned?" Soto stared at her.

"There is only an old padre there, and three nuns. Sometimes there's a Mayan Indian couple who looks after them. They are all old and harmless."

"Mayans, huh?" said Soto, as if in contemplation. "I suppose we'll see how harmless they are."

Clarimonde ventured warily, "We'll miss them by almost a mile unless we turn onto their trail."

"But it's a sure bet they'll have food there," Soto said, watching her eyes for a response, "maybe some wine. I have never seen a priest who doesn't keep himself well oiled and well supplied." He looked at Ransdale and said as he had before the two had ridden down onto the mule cart, "Are you hungry, Nate?"

Ransdale grinned and gave the same answer he'd given before. "I can eat, sure enough," he said.

Gathering and mounting their horses, the three rode on, Soto in front, followed by Clarimonde five yards behind him. Ransdale rode a few yards farther back, enjoying the swing of the woman's long, wet hair with each step of the big paint horse. "I hope you don't think you're going to get away with teasing me this whole trip," he whispered to himself.

As if on cue, Clarimonde looked back at him for just a moment. With a flat stare she veered the paint horse quarter-wide, raised her dress all the way up her pale, bare thigh and caressed herself ever so slightly with her fingertips. "Oh my goodness," he purred under his breath. Then the paint horse straightened and Clarimonde nudged it up closer to Soto before turning her flat stare away from Ransdale.

For more than a half hour, the three climbed an ever steeper and rockier trail until they reached a place where a narrow, grown-over path broke away and vanished into a deep forest. "Here's the path just where she told us it would be," Soto said back to Ransdale. As he spoke he sidled over to Clarimonde, reached out and adjusted the front of her torn and disheveled dress to better cover her breasts. "Fix yourself up," he said. "Get ready to do what I ask of you."

She started to plead, to protest, to say whatever she thought might prevent them from riding to the old Spanish mission. But upon looking into Soto's eyes, she realized that nothing she could say would change his mind. "Tell me what you want me to do," she said submissively.

"That's my *Clarimonde*," Soto said, nudging his horse forward, the two horses walking side by side, his boot touching her bare foot.

Ransdale watched the two in torment and disgust. He spit in the dirt and ran a dusty sleeve across his dry lips. "I'll get my part of her, and then some," he whispered to some unseen force. "Make no mistake about that."

The old Spanish mission stood against the rocky hillside at the end of a narrow, stone trail. The entire fortlike structure had long been grown over in a tangle of hanging vines and a carpet of wildflowers, junipers and ferns. Inside the large wooden gates, the old Mayan Indian heard the voice of the woman call out from the trail; he immediately climbed to the top of a rickety catwalk atop the stone wall and looked down at her.

"Will you let me in, please?" Clarimonde called up to him, her voice slightly atremble. "I am a herder from the lower hills. I need food and water. Please open the door and let me in."

Without a word of response, the Mayan disappeared down out of sight. "What kind of black heathen refuses food and water to a poor woman traveling alone?" said Ransdale, starting to reach for his holstered Colt. "I'll shoot a way in if this is how they're going to act."

"Easy, Nate," said Soto, staring up along the ancient stone wall. "He's gone to get someone. They'll open the door for her. It's their custom."

The two sat atop their horses, out of sight behind a veil of hanging vines and twisted cedar branches. A silent moment passed; then a small door built into the larger door began to creak open. "There, you see?" Soto said with a half smile. "I know how these people think. They can't turn away a stranger."

"It's about damn time," Ransdale grumbled

under his breath, sizing up the old woman who walked out on brittle ankles and motioned Clarimonde down from her saddle.

"What's going to keep our dear Clarimonde from ducking inside and locking us out?" Ransdale asked, getting anxious.

"She won't," Soto said confidently, "She's too afraid of what we'll go back and do to the old man."

"There's no way we'd ride back all that way just to kill that old turd," said Ransdale.

"But she doesn't know that," Soto grinned. The two nudged their horses forward as Clarimonde and the old woman started to lead the paint horse through the open door.

Hearing the hoofbeats across the stone path behind them, Clarimonde clutched the old woman's forearm and whispered tearfully as she held the small door open for the advancing killers, "God forgive me for what I have brought here."

Chapter 7

From his room high above the ancient stone courtyard, the old priest heard the sound of horses' hooves and angry voices. Hurrying to the balcony, he looked down in time to hear a short scream from the young French nun who had run from her garden at the sight of the old nun being knocked aside by the two galloping horses.

"Oh no, they are inside the wall!" the priest gasped, seeing one American down from his saddle in the middle of the courtyard while the other sat atop his horse, looking up toward his chambers as if he knew where to find him.

"Good day to you," Soto called out, his wrists crossed on his saddle horn. "I hope we didn't arrive at a bad time." He spread his hand toward Ransdale.

The old priest's eyes followed Soto's gesture to where Ransdale stood, knife in hand. Having knocked the young nun's straw sun hat from her head, Ransdale held her by her short-cropped hair. His horse, the paint horse and the other spare horse ran in wild circles about the courtyard. "Turn her loose this instant! She is an innocent, *a novice*! Who are you? What do you want here?" the priest demanded in a scorching tone.

Soto raised a gloved hand and motioned him down with his finger. "Get your pious ass down here before me, and we'll talk about it," he said in a grim tone.

"I am not coming down there so that you will have all of us under your power. These doors have withstood worse than you." The priest jutted his chin defiantly. "I have a gun up here!"

Soto said, "Then you had better get ready to use it. He's going to cleave her head to the bone."

"You would not dare!" the shaken priest gasped in disbelief. "She is not yet a *monja*, but she is still a *hermana de la fe*!" he said instinctively.

"Say another word to me in Spanish," Soto replied casually, "I'll have my pard climb up there and cut out your tongue."

The priest bit his lip to keep from shouting what went through his mind. Hastily composing himself he said, "Even though she has not taken her vows, she is still a sister of the faith—"

"I heard you the first time," said Soto, cutting him off. "I hate the Spanish language. It offends me." He gave a cruel grin. "Are you coming down, or do you want him to scalp her and slit her throat?"

The priest looked over at the cruel, eager expression on Ransdale's face for only a moment, then relented and said, "I'm—I'm coming down. Do not hurt her, *por fav*—" He caught himself and corrected his words quickly, "I mean, *please*, do not hurt her."

"You learn fast, *old man*," Soto said, deliberately refusing to acknowledge him by his title, Padre. "On your way, how about bringing that gun you talked about. Hold it out with two fingers and drop it on the ground. Call it sort of a goodwill offering." As the priest disappeared back into his room, Soto looked at Ransdale and winked. Grinning, Ransdale held the terrified woman at arm's length, bobbing her up and down helplessly by her short hair.

"Am I going to get to eat this little French *sweet cookie* when we're through?" he asked. "It's all right by her, ain't it, *cookie*?" He bobbed her head quickly, then said to Soto, "See? She wants me too."

Lying on the ground a few yards away where Ransdale's horse had knocked her, the old nun, struggling in Clarimonde's arms, called out, "Turn her loose, you *pagano*, you animal!"

"Uh-oh," said Ransdale. "Didn't you hear how bad my friend hates Spanish?"

"Please, please be quiet," Clarimonde whispered into the old nun's ear, holding her against her side, half in her lap, trying to comfort her.

But the old nun would have none of it. She struggled against Clarimonde. "No! Turn me loose! You are no better than they. You are all *paganos*!"

Soto's Colt roared in his hand. Blood stung the side of Clarimonde's face as the impact of the bullet punched the old nun's forehead and sent her head snapping back. The gunshot resounded out like ripples on a still lake. Surrounding the fortlike walls of the mission, startled birds, screeching loudly, rose up from the treetops. Batting wings filled the air as if in dark applause.

"Are we all clear how I hate Spanish?" Soto asked flatly, the barrel of his Colt smoking in his gloved hand.

The old priest stepped out the front door of the stone building. He stood aghast, seeing the old nun lying dead in Clarimonde's bloody arms, his hands spread wide in disbelief. Even Ransdale looked surprised for a moment. But he recovered quickly. "Hot dang, that's what I call 'sudden.'"

From her bowed position, the young nun, seeing what had happened, screamed and tried to jerk herself away from Ransdale's powerful grip. Shaking her roughly by the hair, he growled, "All right, don't make nothing of it, sweet cookie! The old crow's dead. Don't get yourself killed too." He looked over at Clarimonde as he shook the young woman again. "Right, whore?"

Clarimonde looked down in submission. Soto shook his head. "What a waste of time," he said. "All this just to get a meal and water our horses." He looked back at the priest. "Step away from the door, old man. Where's the gun? I told you to bring it."

"I—I was only bluffing about having a gun," the priest said, staring at the dead woman still cradled in Clarimonde's arms. "I have no weap-

ons here. This is a—" He caught himself in time
to keep from saying the words in Spanish, *un lugar
santo.* "It is a holy place," he said instead.

"Holy . . ." Soto seemed to consider it. "Why?
Because *you're* here?"

"No," said the priest, "it is not holy because of
me, but because of God, and because of the ancient ones who have come before—"

"Save it," said Soto, cutting him short. "You
lied about the gun. I'm disappointed."

"I only tried to distract—"

"You lied," Soto said in a stronger tone. "So
now, it turns out that I lied in return."

Understanding what Soto meant, the priest said
in a humble tone, "No, please, I beg you in the
name of—"

"You beg me in the name of *nothing*," Soto
snapped. His eyes darkened, as if the evil in his
spirit had swelled up and taken him over. "You
lied! Now I lied. This is why we all go to hell in
the end. Who can stop the sin once it's made its
start?" He turned a quick nod toward Ransdale.

"At your service," Ransdale said eagerly. He
made a quick slash with the knife and kicked the
young nun away from him. She flew to the dirt
with a scream as he stood holding a ragged circle
of short-cropped scalp dripping in his hand. Clarimonde dropped the dead woman and scrambled
through the dirt to grab the young novice and
hold her screaming against her bosom.

The priest stood helpless, Soto's Colt cocked
and aimed at his chest, and called out through the

young nun's screams, "Cecille, be strong. Pray to
God for strength! Pray to God for strength!"

"I pray, Father, I pray!" the young novice managed to sob through her screams, her face buried
against Clarimonde, her fingers clawlike and trem-
bling above her bloody, glistening head.

"She gets done *praying*, get her cleaned up some
to where she's not stinking," Ransdale said to
Clarimonde as he held the short-haired scalp for
a closer inspection, fingering the dark, two-inch-
long hair. "I want us to get acquainted before we
leave." He grinned and slung the gore from the
underside of the dripping scalp. "This is 'holy
hair,' the way I see it."

Soto watched Ransdale closely for a second, always judging just how much he could depend on
the man. Finally he said flatly, "Put the 'holy hair'
away. We came here for something to eat, for ourselves and the horses." He looked at Clarimonde
as she comforted the maimed woman. "Is she able
to rustle us up a meal?"

"I'll do it," Clarimonde said, standing and pulling the young nun up beside her. "Please let me
dress her wound. She's in terrible pain."

"Wound?" said Ransdale, inspecting the bloody
patch of scalp before hanging it to dry on his saddle horn. "This thing isn't three inches around."

Hearing the young woman whine shrilly and
pitifully under her breath, Soto said to Clarimonde, "Go ahead. Get her settled down." He
turned his eyes to the priest, who stood watching,
still stunned by all that had befallen the ancient

mission. "You, old man," Soto said to him, "call the Indian out here. I need to see him."

"The Indian?" the priest said, Soto's words having caught him by surprise.

"The old Mayan I saw standing atop the wall when we rode up," said Soto. "Don't play dumb with me. I know he and his woman both live here."

"Oh, the Mayans," said the priest. He looked all around as if the Indians might be among them. "If he saw you coming, he and his wife slipped away into the forest. Mayans are a shy, retiring people. They run away at the sound of gunfire."

"Right, shy, retiring," Soto said dubiously. "Now call him out here, old man. I know he's coming. Let's get it over with."

"What do you mean? Why do you want him? He is an old man. He's harmless. He is no threat to you," the priest pleaded.

But as he spoke, Soto shifted his gun to his other hand, took off his glove and held his right palm out for the priest to see. "Do you recognize this?" he asked, showing a tattoo that circled his palm.

The priest almost gasped aloud. He shook his head and quickly made the sign of the cross. "You—you are one of them?" the priest asked, nodding at the tattoo, his face growing even more troubled and ashen than before. "One of *el diablo's*—" He caught himself about to speak in Spanish and stopped short. "One of the devil's own!"

"I am one of the devil's own," said Soto flatly. "Now, call the Mayan out here. We both know what I have to do to him."

The priest's eyes seemed to go blank for a moment. He glanced quickly toward the young nun as Clarimonde led her away toward the living quarters. Then he shouted loudly, cupping his hands to his mouth, "Run, Fiji, run! Do not stop! Do not look back! He is one of the cursed! Do not stop running—"

A bullet from Soto's Colt punched the priest in his right shoulder, silencing him. He staggered back against the closed door. Another bullet punched his left shoulder. He slid to the ground.

Ransdale raised his gun and aimed it, but Soto stopped him. "Don't kill him. Not yet."

Ransdale stopped short of pulling the trigger. He grinned. "Whatever you say. What the hell is he jabbering about anyway, you being one of the cursed? 'The devil's own'?"

"It was nothing. Forget it," Soto said in a tight tone of voice.

"*Forget it?*" Ransdale chuckled and shrugged. "All right, if you say so. But I have to say it's piquing my curiosity something awful."

The priest lay struggling to rise to his feet in spite of having lost the use of both arms. "He does not want to tell you . . . that he and his kind are devils . . . *demonios de los intestinos del infierno!*"

"What did I tell you about Spanish?" Soto said with an angry, disgusted expression. He shoved his Colt back into its holster and said to Ransdale, "Keep watch for an ax to come flying through the air, or a dart to nail you in the neck."

"Yeah? An ax?" Ransdale spun back and forth with his gun pointed and cocked. "You mean that old Indian we saw is dangerous?"

"He's a Mayan," said Soto. "It's his religious duty to try and kill me and anybody with me." He swung down from his saddle, stepped back to his saddlebags and flipped them open.

"What the hell is this all about?" Ransdale asked, looking back and forth, suddenly very serious. "Am I standing in the middle of some kind of religious rigmarole?"

"Just stay on your toes, and watch my back," Soto said, taking a straight razor from his saddlebags and opening it.

"Whoa!" said Ransdale, eyeing the razor. "It looks like somebody is about to lose something awfully important to them?"

Ignoring Ransdale's words, Soto said, "The Indian will be back, in spite of what the old man says about Mayans being *timid*."

Ransdale swallowed a dry knot in his throat, looking all around the courtyard. "I was kind of wanting to spend some time with that French sweet cookie, soon as she gets her head fixed up some. Suppose that Indian might have turned tail and run off, like the priest said?"

"Don't call this old fool a priest," Soto said sternly. "And trust what I tell you—the Indian will show up any time. A Mayan must do what he is sworn to do." He held his bare hand toward the priest and made the sign of the devil with his fingers. "Then I'll do what I'm sworn to do."

The wounded priest, unable to raise either hand and make the sign of the cross, murmured under his breath, *"Dios me ayude."*

Giving him a look of raw hatred, Soto stepped

forward with the razor in hand and said, "It's good that you're praying for help, old man. You're going to need all the help you can get."

Ransdale watched and listened intently, noting that Soto's voice had begun to take on a trace of an accent since they'd arrived here. "Are you getting ready to cut him like a steer?" he asked, watching Soto walk toward the priest.

Soto didn't answer. Instead, he walked past the priest, toward a fountain where water rose from beneath the earth and ran in a thin stream from the mouth of a laughing stone cherub. "Find a hammer and some nails," he said to Ransdale as he kneeled down at the short fountain wall and laid the razor on it.

"Sure thing . . . ," said Ransdale, staring bemused, watching Soto take off his hat, raise a knife from his boot well and begin slicing handfuls of thick, dark hair from atop his head and let them fall to the ground.

Chapter 8

In the nuns' sparsely furnished living quarters, Clarimonde finished cleaning and bandaging the wound atop the young novice's head. While she'd attended to the wound she had told the woman everything, letting her know the kind of men they were both up against. The young Frenchwoman took her by the forearm and said, "I will choose to die before I will submit to them."

"I understand," said Clarimonde. "And if you choose to die, then I'm certain you will die." She pulled her forearm away from her gently but firmly. "They will think nothing of killing you," she added flatly.

The young novice asked, "Do you think staying alive has been worth it to you? Will you ever be the same after letting them take away your soul?"

"Worth it to me?" Clarimonde thought about her father and the dogs, and the good, clean, simple years she had spent there attending the goats. She started to tell the woman that it was not for herself that she had gone along with these men.

But she stopped herself and said, "It doesn't matter what we think. Right now it matters only what we do."

"I will do what God leads me to do," the novice said, trying to sound strong through the raw, burning pain atop her bandaged head.

"Listen to me, Cecille," Clarimonde said, using the name she'd heard the priest use. "If there is a secret way out of here, you had better take it. I'll tell them that you managed to slip away from me."

"If I know of such a secret way out, will you come with me?" Cecille asked pointedly.

Clarimonde avoided the young novice's eyes. "No, I will stay. I know what I am doing. I will keep them busy while you get away."

"What will they do to you?" the young nun asked. "Beat you, torture you, rape you? I cannot have you suffer that for my sake."

"I would not be suffering for your sake." Clarimonde continued to look away. "But let me worry about that when the time comes. If there is a way out of here, take it. Take it now."

"No." Cecille stood up, stepped over to a wooden trunk and lifted the lid. She took out a clay jar, set it on the table and took off the thick lid. She dipped her fingers into a thick, gray oil filled with flecks of herbs and, reaching up under her arms, rubbed it on herself. "You must use this," she said to Clarimonde, sliding the jar toward her. "It is something the old Indian's wife made for me when I traveled to the villages. It is made to repel men."

The rancid smell caused Clarimonde to turn away from her again. "No, I won't use it," she said.

"Oh?" The novice gave her an almost accusing stare and said, "Don't you *want* them to leave you alone?"

"No," Clarimonde said bluntly, "not if it means letting them see I have done something deliberately to turn them away. It will only make things worse for me . . . the same as it would only make it worse for me if they caught me trying to escape." She stared at the young novice. "You used this oil before we arrived. I'll tell them I couldn't get rid of the smell. Perhaps it will help you—"

Her words cut short beneath a long scream and the pounding of nails coming from the courtyard. "Father! Father!" Cecille screamed. She tried to run out of the room to the courtyard, but Clarimonde, catching her around her waist, wrestled her back inside and slammed the heavy door. "Please, let me go to him!" she sobbed.

"There is nothing you can do for him now," Clarimonde said, shoving her back into the room. "When the time comes, they will do even worse to you, if you don't get out of here."

The young novice only had to consider Clarimonde's advice for a moment, the pain atop her bandaged head throbbing, intensifying with each beat of her racing pulse. "All right, I'll go. But I will tell you the way to go, so that you can use it if you get a chance to get away from them."

"No, don't tell me." Clarimonde stopped her. "If they think you told me the way out of here, they will beat it out of me. I might not be strong enough to resist telling them."

"You would rather take a beating for something you do not know, than be able to stop it by telling them what you *do* know?" The young woman looked confused by Clarimonde's logic.

"Just go. Go now!" said Clarimonde, taking no time to explain herself to an innocent. She gave the woman a shove toward a rear door and watched her hurry away. "Do not come back until you are certain we are gone."

Cecille grabbed the jar of oil and its lid from the tabletop on her way, then ran out of the room, slamming the rear door behind herself. Clarimonde slumped down into a chair and held her head in her cupped hands for a moment, wondering when her nightmare would end. Then she stood up, walked out the door into a stone hallway and followed it to a room where she found stores of cornmeal, dried beans and other food supplies. Without hesitation she took down a stained apron from a peg, tied it around her waist and went to work.

Outside in the courtyard, Ransdale stared at Soto, still getting used to his freshly shaved head and the strange tattoos that covered the top of it like a decorative skull cap. "With every day that goes by, I learn something new about you," he said. As he spoke he pitched the bloody hammer to the ground and stuck his hands out under the water from the stone cherub's mouth, washing them.

"Are you complaining, *mi amigo*?" Soto asked in a firm tone.

"No! Not at all," said Ransdale, stunned at hearing the words in Spanish coming from Soto's lips. "Just commenting is all." He slung water from his hands and finished drying them on his trousers. "Uh-oh," he said, his hands slowed to a halt, his right hand poised near his gun as he spotted the old Indian step into sight as if from out of nowhere. "Look who's here."

A glistening machete hung from the Indian's right hand.

"I see him," Soto said calmly. "I figured the old man's scream would bring him out. These Mayan converts never fly far from the nest." He nodded toward the wounded priest. "They need someone like this one to lay the whip to their backs." Stepping toward the Mayan, he spoke to him in a language that Ransdale did not recognize. The Indian replied in the same language and went into a crouch as if to defend himself.

"Huh?" Ransdale looked puzzled. "What did you say to one another?"

"I asked him what kind of fool stands with a machete before a man with a loaded gun," said Soto. "He called me a dirty name." He gave a thin, cruel grin, lifting his Colt arm's length with his left hand, level to the Indian's naked chest. "Can you imagine that?" He cocked the Colt. "He called me a *dirty name*?"

"*Por favor*, let him go, *por favor*," the old priest moaned from against the thick wooden door where Ransdale had spread his arms and nailed him into place.

"There this one goes again. He's talking Spanish

to you again," Ransdale said quietly, to see what Soto's reaction would be toward the priest.

But Soto ignored him. Instead, he raised his right palm toward the Indian and took another step forward.

"Yep, every day it's something new . . . ," Ransdale repeated under his breath, slipping his gun from its holster and holding it ready, even though Soto had the Indian covered.

Clarimonde had stiffened instinctively at the sound of the single gunshot from the courtyard. But she did not go to the stone window ledge and look out on the courtyard to see what had happened. Instead she kept herself busy kindling a small fire in a corner hearth on which to boil a pot of beans hanging on an iron pothook.

Had she looked out upon the courtyard she would have seen the Indian fall to the ground, mortally wounded, and she would have seen Suelo Soto walk over and take the machete from his hand. She would have also seen Bess, the shepherd bitch, slink into the mission through the open front gate and work her way around the perimeter, going unnoticed while the two men stood over the dying Indian like vultures, Soto taking off his shirt and laying it aside to keep from covering it with blood.

Clarimonde had no idea Bess had followed them across the high trails, until she heard a soft whine and felt a cold nose against her forearm as she fanned the small fire. "Oh my God!" she gasped, turning and looking into the big shepherd's panting face. "Bess! Bess. How in the world have you found me?" As she spoke she hugged the animal's coarse, brush-flecked head to her bosom. The big shepherd licked her face as if asking for her approval. Oh, Bess, yes yes, you are a *Gutes Mädchen*. Such a *good girl* indeed."

But no sooner had she tearfully hugged and praised the big shepherd than she pulled back and looked toward the open, stone-framed window. "But you cannot stay here. We cannot let them see you," she said in a harsh frightened whisper. She hurried to the window and glanced out just for a second, just long enough to see Soto standing naked and bloody above the Indian, his freshly shaved head bowed, the machete rising and falling viciously.

Clarimonde quickly looked away from the grisly scene, not letting the horror of Soto's action keep her from looking for a way to protect Bess. "We must get you out of here. These men are monsters. They will kill you!"

She quickly grabbed a handful of dried meat scraps from the tabletop and fed the hungry animal. Stooping, she hugged the coarse neck again and said, "I know you only came to protect me. But you have to go. We have to get you past these men. You must go back and stay with Papa and Little Bob." Tears rolled freely down her cheeks as she spoke to the curious face, knowing her words were not understood.

Leading the dog gently but firmly by the nape of her neck, Clarimonde looked back out onto the courtyard and said, "You must *go* quickly, while these two are not watching." She turned the animal loose with a bit of a shove toward the doorway, gesturing with her arm in a sweeping motion to make her command understood. *"Gehen sie,* Bess!" she ordered in German, telling the animal to *go. "Gehen sie."*

The dog circled slowly and whined as if in protest. Then, obediently she ran out the door and hurried away along the perimeter of the courtyard. Clarimonde watched intently, silently praying under her breath until the shepherd had made it most of the way to where the smaller entrance gate stood ajar. "Please *hurry,* Bess! You must make it out of here! You must!" Clarimonde whispered, seeing Ransdale strike a match and hold it to a freshly rolled smoke dangling from his lips.

But the big shepherd didn't make it all the way to the front gate. Ransdale caught sight of her as she hurried along silently, running low to the ground, partly hidden by a wall of shrubs and brightly colored flowers. "What the hell—?" he said in surprise, his Colt coming up cocked and aimed. "It's one of her damned wolf dogs!"

"Then shoot it," Soto shouted, the Indian's blood running down his chest, his arms, his face.

From the open doorway where Clarimonde stood, she screamed, "No!" just as Ransdale's shot rang out.

The shepherd, hearing the woman's voice, turned in time to see the man's gun buck in his hand. She felt the bullet whistle through the air only an inch from her lowered head. But before Ransdale's second shot exploded, the big bitch, fearful for her master's safety, spun in the dirt and sprang across the ground like a streak of gray furry lightning.

"Yiiii!" Ransdale shouted in terror, standing with his feet spread, unable to get an aim on the attacking animal. His third bullet ricocheted harmlessly off the stone tiles as the bitch dived into him. Instead of going for his throat, Bess clamped her powerful jaws around his crotch and slung her head back and forth viciously as his screams filled the air.

"Stop playing with the dog!" Soto shouted, reaching for his Colt lying in its holster on the ground where he'd laid it. He raised the Colt with a bloody hand and took aim.

"No!" Clarimonde shouted again, running from the doorway toward the blurred tangle of man and animal on the courtyard floor. But she stopped abruptly, her hands going to her mouth to stifle her scream as Soto's bullet hit the shepherd squarely in the side and sent it tumbling away with a loud, pitiful yelp.

"Help—help me, Suelo," Ransdale pleaded in an injured tone, both hands cupping his bleeding crotch. His Colt lay in the dirt a few feet away. "I'm ruined. . . ."

As Soto stepped over to Ransdale, the wounded dog yelped pitifully, struggling to get back on all fours. Clarimonde hurried toward the animal, but before she could get to her, Bess had managed to rise and stumble out the open entrance gate. "Stay back from that gate, Clarimonde," Soto commanded. She froze as she heard him cock his gun hammer.

Tearfully, Clarimonde said, "But she is still alive. I must go to her."

"She's as good as dead, and you know it," Soto said callously. As he spoke he lowered his Colt; the two listened to the painful yelping of the wounded shepherd disappear deeper down the hillside. In a moment it stopped altogether. "There, what did I tell you?" Soto said.

"What—What about me?" Ransdale groaned on the stone tiles at Soto's feet. He reached up with a bloody hand and tried to grasp Soto's naked, blood-slick leg.

"What about you, *mi amigo*?" Soto said harshly. "Like you said, *you're ruined*. Now I must get three of Satan's demons to replace you."

"No, wait," Ransdale said quickly. "I'm good. I'll be all right. I can still handle my job. I'll just get cleaned up some—"

"Adios, Nate," said Soto, cutting him off. He effortlessly moved his lowered Colt sidelong just enough to put a bullet in Ransdale's right eye. Ransdale fell back limply, his hand still clutching his crotch.

Clarimonde flinched at the sound of the gunshot. She stood weeping for the shepherd, her hands covering her mouth. "She—she only wanted to save me," she said brokenly, staring out toward the vast, rugged hillside beyond the mission walls.

Soto walked up close behind her; she could feel heat from his naked, blood-gorged body. "Nothing can save you *from* me, *except* me, dear Clarimonde," he whispered into her ear. "Is that what you want? Do you want me to save you?"

After a moment of silence, without turning to face him, Clarimonde replied, also in a whisper, "Yes, save me. Save me from you."

"Good." Soto smiled with satisfaction and looked himself up and down. "I'll go finish with the Indian. You prepare us some food for the trail. Let's get moving. The lawmen are bound to be close enough to have heard all the shooting."

Chapter 9

The ranger and Hector had been following only glimpses of partial hoofprints now and then on the rocky ground, at times finding traces of the shepherd's paw print in pursuit. But when they'd heard the sound of gunfire on the distant trails above them, they struck out toward it without hesitation. After an hour of pushing their horses, they'd made it to the fork in the trail and found clearer prints on the narrow, softer dirt path leading back toward the old Spanish mission.

"We can't stop now—we're too close," Sam said, noting the slant of sunlight falling over the slopes on the western horizon. He nudged Black Pot forward and added to Hector, "Watch out for a trap."

"*Sí*, I am always watching," Hector replied, nudging his horse along beside him.

Moments later beneath the canopy of overhanging pine and spruce, in the grainy light, the ranger stopped at the sight of the big shepherd limping weakly alongside the trail toward them. "Hold it,

Hector," he said, although the young lawman had already spotted the wounded animal and had drawn up his reins. "Here comes the big female shepherd the old goatherd told us about."

Seeing the animal stop and wobble unsteadily in place, the two stepped down from their horses and led them slowly forward. "Easy, girl. We won't hurt you," Sam said quietly, seeing the dazed and wounded animal take a stand, her blood-matted hackles standing high on her neck and shoulders.

But the shepherd would not be consoled. As Sam and Hector took another step, she growled deeper and bared her fangs, in spite of blood and saliva swinging from her flews.

"It's not working," said Hector, stopping alongside the ranger. "This one is not going to let us get past her on the trail."

"We've gotten too close to let these birds slip away from us now," Sam said. Yet, even as he spoke, the two stepped back cautiously until the shepherd's growl lessened.

"But what do we do about this wounded animal?" Hector asked in a lowered voice, seeing the big shepherd had faced them down in her weakened state.

Sam didn't have to consider it. "We're going to help her if it's not too late," he said. Without turning toward Hector, he nodded toward a tangle of bracken and downfallen limbs along the trail and added quietly, "See if you can find me a good long branch."

As Hector stepped away to the side of the trail,

Sam walked around his stallion, took down a coiled rope from his saddle horn and took out a rolled up length of rawhide strap from his saddlebags. The shepherd settled down, but watched both men closely, her loss of blood causing her to have to straighten herself up every few seconds to keep from losing her balance.

With the ten-foot-long pine limb Hector brought him, the ranger fashioned a snare. With an open loop on one end of the limb, and the rope wrapped around the limb leading up to his hand, Sam stepped forward, Hector right beside him, his gun cocked in case the shepherd found the strength to attack. "Easy now, girl," Sam said again as they moved closer.

But this time the shepherd had grown too weak to put up a fight. She faltered and went down on her hind quarters. Taking advantage of the narrow opportunity, Sam slipped the loop over her head and drew it tight before she had time to collect herself.

Feeling the rope grow snug on her neck, the big animal lunged and growled and fought, even summoning the strength to rise up once on her hind paws and snarl, then try to force herself forward. Sam held on to the limb and the rope and braced himself until her strength waned and she fell onto her side, lying panting in the dirt.

Handing Hector the limb and the rope, Sam said, "Keep some pressure on, while I get in there. I don't want her in my face."

"I've got her," said Hector, holding the limb steadily, bracing himself, prepared for anything.

With the length of rawhide from his saddlebags, Sam hurried in close and kneeled down beside the shepherd. Knowing that at any moment she could decide to make another lunge at him, he quickly hitched a muzzle around the middle of the animal's strong flews, wrapped it back around her head and tied it securely behind her ears. He let out a tight breath, patted her head and examined the deep gunshot wound in her side.

"You can ease off on it now," he said to Hector. "I believe she's lost too much blood to put up any more of a fight."

"*Sí*," said Hector, "if we don't stop the bleeding, I think she will soon be dead." He laid the limb down and stepped back toward his horse. "I will tear up an old shirt for bandages."

In the distance a streak of lightning licked across the sky, followed by a low rumble of thunder. "Hurry," said Sam, "we've got a storm brewing." He glanced in the direction of the thunder as he rubbed a gloved hand back along the shepherd's fading eyes. "This brave gal has come too far and done too much to be left out here to die."

In the first purple shadows of darkness the young novice had ventured back into the mission. With her came the Mayan Indian woman who had fled earlier under her mate's insistence. Before slipping back inside the walls, the two had watched the mission from the shelter of pines for a long time after the men and the German woman rode out along the high trail. Yet they still approached the mission warily. Once inside the walls, they quickly locked the entrance gate behind themselves.

Upon their arrival in the darkened courtyard, the two women lit torches, found the bloody claw hammer lying in the dirt and immediately removed the slender iron spikes that held the unconscious priest's hands nailed to the thick oaken door of the rectory. Then they laid the wounded priest on an old canvas gurney that the Mexican army had left behind at the end of some long-forgotten campaign against the dreaded Apache.

As the women started to raise the gurney between them, the priest groaned, "Don't move me . . . I—I must pray for the dead."

"Padre, you are awake!" the novice said in surprise.

"There is . . . a lawman coming," the priest added in a rasping voice. "Do not lock the gates."

The women gave one another a dubious look. "He is out of his head," the novice whispered. In the distance, thunder rumbled across the high valley floors.

"Listen . . . to me," the priest insisted in a weakening voice. "Prop me up. . . . Unlock the gates."

Under the priest's instructions, the novice ran to the gates, unlocked the small entrance gate and ventured a look up along the dark trail before running back to the rectory door. Together, the women cleaned and dressed the priest's wounds in the torchlight. They leaned the gurney up on a straight-backed chair so the priest could oversee the courtyard while they went about the grim chore of gathering the dead. Unable to raise his bandaged hands or his arms, the priest managed to say a prayer over the elderly nun as the two women carried her body off the stone tiles.

When it came time to gather the pieces of her mate's decapitated body, the Indian woman stopped the novice from helping her and gestured for her to attend to the priest instead.

From a short distance down the trail, Sam and Hector began hearing the eerie sound of the Mayan's mourning chant coming from the dim circle of torchlights glowing above the mission walls. "It sounds like they've been here and gone," Sam said gravely.

"I swear by the saints, if they have harmed these people . . ." Hector left his vow unfinished, realizing there was nothing more he could do to these men than what he had vowed to do in the first place.

"If they haven't been hit too hard, I'm hoping we can leave the shepherd here to be looked after and stay tight on their trail," said Sam, noting a flash of lightning in the east. "If this storm gets between us and them, it'll be hard tracking."

"I know," Hector said, resolving himself to patience as the two drew closer to the open entrance gate. "Stopping them is all that matters, storm or no storm." He pointed a hand upward along a distant, dark line of ridges. "Beyond those hills we will be inside Shadow Valley."

They rode on to the vine-covered mission walls.

The Mayan woman had finished the mourning chant by the time the two rode in slowly, their eyes searching the darker shadows outside the glow of torches the women had lit around the edges of the courtyard. The women gathered near the priest and stood silently, watching the ranger and Hector bow low in their saddles to get through the entrance gate, the wounded shepherd lying limp across the ranger's lap.

"I knew the law would not . . . be far behind," the old priest said in a strained voice. "Welcome to God's mission." As he spoke he gestured a nod of his head toward the two lawmen, and the Mayan woman hurried forward and reached up for the wounded shepherd as Sam stopped his stallion.

"*Gracias*, Padre," Sam said, he and Hector touching the brims of their sombreros in unison. When the woman stepped back with the unconscious shepherd in her arms, Sam looked over at Ransdale's body, still lying in the dirt, and said quietly, "I see we don't have to ask if they've been here."

"These men are ruthless . . . bloodthirsty savages," the priest said brokenly. "I pray that you . . . will stop them before they hurt others. Stop them however you can. . . . Let God decide what to do with their immortal souls."

Noting the gaping bullet hole in Ransdale's eye, and the ripped and bloody trousers at his crotch, Sam said, "It looks like the big shepherd got to him first, then Soto decided to finish him off, since he was no more use to him. I expect that's what got the animal shot?" He asked as if he already knew the answer.

The priest gave a look that acknowledged the

ranger's perception, and said, "I think you know much about such men as these."

"More than I care to, sometimes," Sam replied, swinging down from his saddle. "I'm Arizona Ranger Sam Burrack. This is Guardia Hector Sandoval, from Valle Hermoso."

Hector stepped down from his saddle right beside him.

As their boots touched the ground, the lawmen's eyes went to the Indian's body lying on a clean blanket his mate had spread on the stone tiles. The Mayan woman had gathered the pieces of his body and laid them carefully back in place, as if they might be reassembled. Beside his sliced-open trunk lay his bloody heart, a jagged bite missing from it. A few feet away the bloodstained machete still lay on the tiles.

"I wish we had gotten here sooner, ma'am," Sam said quietly to the Mayan woman.

"Hermano de Satán?" Hector whispered, studying the dead Indian's decapitated body for a moment longer. He looked to the priest with his question.

"Yes, he is one of Satan's Brothers," the priest confirmed.

Hector whispered, *"Que la Santa Madre nos proteja,"* in a guarded tone as he looked up in the night toward the dark, distant trails and crossed his chest.

"Sí, may the Holy Mother protect you both," the priest said, closing his eyes for a second, unable to cross himself.

Hector looked at the ranger, then back at the

old priest, and said in a guarded tone, "I have heard of the cult of Satan's Brothers. But I thought they had been banished from this hill country years ago."

"How does one ever banish the devil and his many demons?" the priest said in his weak, gravelly voice. "The devil and his demons appear and disappear at their own pleasure. The world south of here is filled with Satan's Brothers. There are even those who live at the end of Shadow Valley."

"How is the German woman?" Sam asked, taking the subject away from the devil and his family members. "Is she holding up all right?"

With a shift of his eyes the priest deferred the matter of the German woman to the novice who stood at his side. "I—I do not judge her harshly because she saved me from those men," the young novice said. "But I am not sure she wants to be saved herself."

"What makes you say that?" Sam asked, wanting to know all he could find out about the German girl before catching up to Soto. He knew what being held captive could do to a person's will—what tricks it could play on the minds.

The novice raised her dark eyes and gave the ranger a look. "I asked her to run away with me, but she said no, although I could not understand what difference her staying here would have made."

"Her father said they forced her to go with them against her will," Sam said. "She came along peaceably to keep them from hurting him and their shepherds."

"I understand," the novice nodded, "but she submits herself to those men. If I had to make the decision, I would die before I would allow them to use me in such a manner."

"Lucky for you, this woman took that decision out of your hands," Sam said.

The priest cut in, saying, "Please excuse Cecille. She is a novice who knows nothing of these sorts of devils and the misery and hurt they bring with them."

The novice's eyes lowered toward the ground at her feet in second thought. "Yes, it is true I know nothing. If ever I see her again I will beg her forgiveness for saying what I just said."

"I meant you no accusation, ma'am," Sam said. "I know there was no malice in what you said."

"*Merci, gendarme,*" she said, thanking him in French. She looked at the wounded shepherd lying on a blanket on the tiles, the Mayan unwrapping, tightening and rewrapping the bandages around the animal's chest in order to keep the bleeding from starting anew. "Until I can beg her pardon, I pray you will find her and send her back here. Meanwhile I will help take care of her brave animal."

Beside the ranger, Hector cut in, saying to the priest, "If there is nothing we can do here, I will attend the horses so we can get back on the trail before the storm." He gestured a hand toward a deep rumble on the dark eastern horizon.

The priest nodded stiffly. "Go. We will all be right here. This man must be stopped."

Chapter 10

Looking back into the darkness, Soto and Clarimonde watched as a streak of lightning split the night, followed by a deep growl of rumbling thunder. "You did what you said you'd do. You've gotten us to Shadow Valley," Soto said. "If we're lucky we'll be up on the eastern slope before this storm hits."

Clarimonde did not want to mention that he'd told her once they'd ridden through Shadow Valley she would be free to go. With this man, bringing up the matter could bring about her death. She'd decided it would be better to keep her mouth shut and let him be the one to mention her freedom. "The valley is full of overhangs where we can take shelter until the storm has passed," Clarimonde said above a strong, whirring wind.

"No," said Soto. "If we wait out the storm down here, when it's over we'll leave prints up out of the valley." He sidled his horse up close to the big paint she rode. Behind him he led Ransdale's horse and the horse Ransdale had kept for a spare. "You don't want to do that, do you? Leave prints for the ranger to follow?"

"I had not thought about that," Clarimonde said honestly. She grew frightened having him this close to her. Now that he'd reached Shadow Valley, she wondered what use she was to him. She'd seen how quickly and callously he had killed Nate Ransdale, a man he'd broken out of prison with. She had no doubt he could kill her without batting an eye.

"I know you didn't," Soto said, "but I thought about it. If we stay ahead of the storm, maybe even ride through some of it, by morning when it's over, nobody can tell that we ever rode through here."

"Yes, I understand," Clarimonde said, feeling relieved that he seemed to believe her. She felt even more relieved when he reined his horse away from her and turned back to the trail leading down into the depth of the dark, narrow valley.

As Soto rode ahead of her a few feet, he said over his shoulder, "Are you ready to leave me now, go back to your father, your goats and your shepherd dogs?"

Something about the way he asked sent a new chill up her spine. She was afraid to respond. "I have only one shepherd now, remember," she said, keeping her voice even, trying to show no fear of him.

"Oh, yes, I forgot," he said. "Ransdale killed one of them, didn't he?"

Clarimonde wondered if his words were a trap

of some sort. He knew as well as she that Ransdale didn't kill Bess; *he did*. She rode on in silence.

After a moment, Soto drew his horse back beside her and said, "You never answered me. Are you ready to leave me now?"

Clarimonde weighed her answer carefully, then said in a quiet tone, "No, I'm not ready to leave you."

Soto reached a hand over and stroked it down her long hair. He said in a gentle but what she thought to be an insincere voice, "But you will let me know when you're ready to leave, won't you?"

She paused, then said, "Yes."

"Good." Soto grinned in the darkness. Taunting her further he asked again, "But you're sure you're not ready to leave right now?"

Yes, he was toying with her, she told herself, the way a cat played with a wounded mouse. "No," she repeated quietly.

Soto gave a dark chuckle. "That was a wise answer, *Clarimonde*," he said. Making it a point to let her hear him uncock his big Colt, he slipped the gun back into his holster, dropped his horse back and gave the big paint a sound slap on its rump, sending it forward at a brisk clip along the dark trail.

Moments later a hard, wind-driven rain roared in sideways across a rocky stretch of tall wild grass, broom sage and scrub oak. They continued to follow the snaking valley floor for more than an hour until the water rushing around their horses' legs became too swift and powerful and filled with bracken and downfallen branches for the animals to negotiate.

"Hold on. We're going up," Soto shouted against the raging storm. Knowing she hadn't heard him, he grabbed the paint horse by its bridle and pulled animal and rider along behind him, upward onto a steep, mud-slick path.

Clinging to the paint horse's wet mane, Clarimonde held on for her life as lightning struck along the hillside, casting the night a ghostly gray. In those sudden flashes she saw streams of runoff water crash against rock and spray wildly down over them. She caught glimpses of the animals struggling upward; she witnessed the spare horse lose its battle against the downpour and go toppling backward in a wild thrashing of limbs, loose rock and splashing mud.

"Suelo!" she cried out, feeling the paint start to falter and lose its balance beneath her.

"I've got you!" She heard Soto reply. From out of nowhere she felt him slip over onto the paint horse behind her and straighten the animal, leading his own mount behind him by its reins. "Lie forward!" he shouted at her ear above the roar of the storm.

She obeyed.

His arms went around her. Like it or not he brought with him a means of command, a way of taking the will of the animal and making it his own. With their weight forward on the paint, the strong animal seemed to balance more securely against the rush of water and the slick footing and dig and climb its way to the top of the steep hill.

As the animal stepped onto level ground through a coursing short waterfall at the lands edge, Soto said in a flash of lightning, "Are there times when the devil is a welcome hand?"

Clarimonde pretended not to hear him as he slid effortlessly from behind her and back onto his own mount and gigged it forward. Once again taking the paint by its bridle, Soto pulled the animal along across a flat, rocky mesa for the following hour until the storm began to lessen around them and roar and flash along their back trail.

Ten miles farther along a higher trail above Shadow Valley, the rain began to subside. The wind lessened and grew cooler, so much so that Clarimonde shivered in her wet clothes in spite of a blanket Soto unrolled from a dry, canvas-covered bedroll and spread over her shoulders.

"Come ride against my back," Soto half offered, half demanded of her.

Obediently, she crawled from her saddle over onto Soto's horse and wrapped the blanket around them both, too cold and too exhausted to even care. Behind them the storm spent itself out along the valley floor. Clarimonde knew that the law would have a hard time picking up their trail, but she was too tired to think about it right then. As the warmth of their bodies caught up to them beneath the blanket, she laid her cheek forward against Soto's back and drifted off to sleep.

They rode on through the night. While Clarimonde slept, Soto did a peculiar thing. Instead of staying on the high trail above Shadow Valley, now that the storm had passed, he rode gradually back down onto the valley floor.

At daylight Clarimonde awakened when the horse came to a halt beneath a large rock that stood like a powerful sentinel above the narrow valley trail. "Where—where are we?" she asked sleepily. "Is this still Shadow Valley?"

"Yes," Soto replied, looking up at the large rock and the man standing beside it. "This is the end of Shadow Valley, a place you know nothing about. My family had mine holdings here for many years, under an agreement with the Mexican government."

She looked all around, long enough to realize that Soto was right; she'd never ridden this far along into the valley. The valley had narrowed into more of a crevice sliced deep into the earth. Looking at the paint horse standing beside her, its reins in his hand, she asked Soto quietly, "Do you want me to get back on the other horse, now?"

"No," Soto said sharply, "stay where you are. I like feeling you against my back. You'll know when I've had enough," he added in a menacing tone.

She settled, but with a gnawing fear lying in the pit of her stomach.

From above them beside the rock a rifleman appeared and called down, "Who's there?"

Soto called out, his rifle lying across his lap, "It's me, Suelo Soto . . . one of the Cera Sotos who built the mine standing behind you."

"Suelo Soto?" the man called out in a gruff but stunned voice. His rifle lowered in his hands. "Forgive me, Suelo! It is I, Juan Mandega. Ride in, *por favor*, by all means, ride in!"

"That's what I thought," Soto said under his breath, punching his boot heels to his horse's side, sending it forward. Over his shoulder, he said to Clarimonde, "We'll find you some clean clothes and a trail jacket in here." He grinned without turning to her. "I can't have a woman travel with me in rags. What would the Hole-in-the-wall Gang think?"

The Hole-in-the-wall Gang? Clarimonde sat silently, wondering if he had any intention of ever turning her loose.

"We're going to rest here for a while before riding back across the border," Soto said. Then he asked mockingly, "Is that all right with you?"

"Yes," Clarimonde said, agreeing with him, knowing better than to question anything he said or did. "What about the law on our trail?"

"The law?" Soto said. "The law stops being a problem once I arrive at the old Soto Cera Mining Company."

Clarimonde asked nothing else. She sat quietly, not knowing what to expect as the horse carried them on along the rocky trail into the small, dusty mining community perched upon a bare hillside.

Once upon the main street of the large, abandoned mining operation, Soto wasted no time. No sooner had the few remaining inhabitants of Soto Cera gathered in the dusty street to meet him than he began issuing orders, sending three of the elderly miners to gather picks, shovels and ropes.

The old men hesitated only long enough to look to Juan Mandega for approval. As soon as Juan said to them, "Well, what are you waiting for?" the old men scurried away to do Soto's bidding.

As the old men left and a couple of others eased away before they were given orders to follow, Juan turned to Soto and said, "You must excuse them. It has been a long time since anyone from the Soto Cera family has been here to guide them." His voice turned humble. "I have tried my best to carry on in some small way—"

"You have done well, Juan Mandega," Soto said, cutting him short. "I'll see to it that my family hears of your loyalty."

"*Gracias,*" Juan said, his head bowed slightly.

"Now, let's get busy," said Soto. He took Clarimonde by the shoulder and guided her toward two women who stood watching nearby. "You two, take her and find her some clothes and a coat fit for the trail." He said quietly to Clarimonde, "Will this be your chance to escape? Think it over carefully before you attempt something foolish."

Turning to Juan Mandega, Soto said, "Is the iron door still in place? Are there still blasting supplies stored there where I left them?"

"*Sí,* everything is where you told me to keep it until you returned," said Juan. He managed a thin smile. "No one has been brave enough to move it."

"Then let's go get it." Soto grinned. He slapped Juan on the back and gave him a half shove toward a tall mountain of rock standing seventy yards away.

But Juan hesitated, and asked with a suspicious look in his eyes, "We heard that you were in prison in the Arizona Territory. But now you have escaped, is it so?"

"Yes, I escaped," said Soto, seeing he would have to offer some sort of explanation. "There is a lawman on my trail. I'm going to close the main trail through Shadow Valley and make him have to double back and take another trail through here."

"And by that time you and your woman will be gone," Juan said, getting it.

"That's right," said Soto, knowing he needed this man's help to get everything done in time. "I knew once I got here, I could count on you, the way my family has always counted on you. Was I right in thinking that, Juan?" he asked, staring closely at him.

"*Sí*, you were right," Juan nodded, giving in, knowing it would be fatal to deny this man.

"As soon as I am gone, ride down to the south end of Shadow Valley, to my brothers in Satan. Tell them to send my brother demons from hell to follow me. Tell them to see into my mind and they'll know what to do when the time comes."

Juan's expression turned grim at the prospect of riding to the darkest end of Shadow Valley. But he swallowed a knot in his throat, and said "*Sí*, when you are gone I will go and tell them." He couldn't bear thinking what would happen to his family and himself if he didn't do as he was told.

The two turned and walked toward a mule hitched at an iron ring along the edge of the dirt street. "Now, help me load my supplies," said Soto.

The storm had cost the two lawmen precious time. But there was nothing they could do about it now, Sam thought, leaning low on his saddle and searching the wet ground for any sign of the horse's tracks. Beside him a few yards away Hector said, "He could have ridden up at any point along this valley trail." As he spoke he looked upward, searching along the ridgeline above them.

"Keep in mind that the storm slowed them down just as much as it did us," Sam replied.

"Yes, the storm," Hector said with a touch of bitterness. "Just when we could have tightened the noose around his murdering neck, the weather turns against us." He spit in disgust. "The storm could not have come at a worse time."

"Storms come when they come," said Sam, straightening in his saddle and nudging Black Pot over to Hector. "We have to decide whether it just slows down awhile, or stops us altogether. Isn't that true, *Guardia*?" When he finished speaking he stared at Hector until the young lawman shook his head and gave a tired smile.

"It has slowed us down," he said, reining his horse back to the trail, "but it has not stopped us." He raised his face to the heavens and said loudly, as if speaking to all of nature itself, "Do you hear that? We are not stopping. We are continuing on."

Sam offered a trace of a wry smile and nudged his stallion forward. A half hour later the ranger stopped suddenly as the hoofprints of three horses appeared back on the trail. "Finally, we get a break," Hector said with a tight sigh.

But Sam found no relief in the prints coming down to the valley floor. He looked up along the ridges above and said, thinking out loud, "He rode all the way up there out of the storm. . . . Why did he ride back down afterward?"

"I don't know," said Hector, "but let's be glad he did. Now we found his trail. It is always good to find the trail you search for, eh?" He smiled, happy with their discovery.

"Yes, it is," said Sam, still searching the higher ridges, "unless for some reason he wanted us to find his tracks again."

Hector's smile went away as he let the ranger's words sink in. With a moment of consideration he said, "The farther we ride into Shadow Valley, the steeper and closer the walls will become on either side." He gave the ranger a knowing look. "He has something in mind for us there, where the valley grows too narrow to escape unless we ride a long way back."

"If we climbed up here, where he climbed down," Sam asked pointing first at the track on the ground, then up the steep hillside, "how much longer will it take us to catch up to him?"

Hector considered it. "I am not familiar with

that end of Shadow Valley, but always it takes longer to ride along those ridge trails. It will cost us much time. He can easily slip away from us."

"Then we'll take our chances on finding him again," Sam speculated. "I don't want to track a man who's leading me to where he wants me to be." As he spoke he'd already begun turning his stallion to the uphill climb toward the ridgeline.

"Neither do I," said Hector, turning his horse right behind him.

Three miles ahead of the lawmen, Soto paced back and forth restlessly, on a level landing in the hillside where he could see the large rock standing above the narrowed trail at the end of Shadow Valley. "What could be keeping him from getting here?" he asked himself aloud.

Hearing him, Juan offered an answer, having listened as Soto told him about the lawman on his trail: "Perhaps when he saw that the storm washed out your tracks, he decided to turn back and give up the chase."

"Naw," said Soto. "This ranger is not the type to give up."

Juan shrugged. "Then he is coming. There is no need to concern yourself. If he is the kind of man you say, it is not a question of *if* he'll be here, only a matter of *when*."

Soto took a breath and gave a thin smile. "You're right, Juan. What do I care when he gets here. The dynamite I made is in place and all set. I wanted to watch him die, but knowing I got him off my tail is enough for now. I've got bigger business awaiting me."

"Say the word, and I blow the rock and close the valley," Juan said, eager to get Soto out of the peaceful hill community.

"Yes," said Soto. "Blow it to hell. Then go send my brothers in Satan to find my trail." He smiled. "Tell them I give them the sign. I will make them rich." He turned and walked to where Clarimonde stood with the horses and a mule loaded with the supplies they'd taken from a storage cave in the hillside. "Get mounted," he said, running a hand down her long, freshly washed hair hanging from beneath a broad, straw sombrero. "We're leaving."

"What about the law," Clarimonde asked. She wore a pair of thin, white peasant trousers and a flimsy, collarless peasant shirt with a deep, open neckline. A faded striped serape lay draped over the paint's rump behind the saddle.

"I have taken care of the law one way or the other," Soto replied. "Either he'll soon be dead, or else he'll be backtracking the length of Shadow Valley, licking his wounds, wondering what to do next." His words made her heart sink.

"Oh, then we have nothing more to fear," she said, hoping he wouldn't catch the terrible look of disappointment she knew came over her face.

Soto smiled knowingly. "That's right, *Clarimonde*, we have nothing to fear." He cupped her breast with his gloved hand and said closer to her face, "From here on it's just you and me. We will have the devil's protection. We can do whatever pleases us." He liked the way she looked off into the distance, avoiding his eyes.

As the two mounted, Soto insisting she ride double, perched upon his lap, they watched Juan give a signal, and the earth rumbled underfoot as a blast of rock, dirt, smoke and hillside rose into the air above Shadow Valley and rained back down on itself. "I'd say my explosive-making skills have not suffered during my stay in Yuma," Soto chuckled, putting his heels to his horse's sides.

Three miles away at the upper edge of the steep hillside, the ranger and Hector both settled their animals beneath them and looked at the large rise of dust above the explosion. "There it is," Sam said, "the surprise that awaited us, had we fallen for it."

Hector crossed himself idly. "That is just about where we would have been if we had stayed on the valley floor and ridden on," he said.

Seeing the look on Hector's face, Sam said, "A miss is as good as a mile. Now that he thinks he's killed us or sent us backtracking, we'll get the upper hand while he slows down some and takes his time."

"The question now is which way will he go," Hector commented.

"Oh, there's not a doubt in my mind he's headed back across the border now," Sam said. "He's feeling too full of himself to quit just now. He thinks he's won the game."

"I will be crossing the border," Hector said, as if considering it.

Sam looked at him, and asked, "Will it be your first time?"

"No," Hector replied. "Always as vaqueros my brother and I went where the work took us. Many times we crossed the border. But this will be the first time I cross it as a lawman, hunting a man for murder."

"If you think you had better stop, I told you I'll see that Soto gets what's coming to him for killing your brother, Ramon, and Luis Gravis," Sam said, gauging Hector.

"*Gracias,*" said Hector. "I started out thirsting for revenge for my brother and Luis Gravis. But that is no longer the case."

"I understand," Sam said quietly, gazing ahead of them in the direction of the border.

PART 2

Chapter 11

———

Rusty Nail, Arizona Territory

Before Soto put his horse forward on the dusty trail into town, he said to Clarimonde, who rode the paint horse close beside him, "We'll be taking up with some business associates of mine near here. I'm going to trust you to keep your mouth shut about what brought you and me together."

"I'm not going to say anything," Clarimonde replied quietly, her eyes lowered.

"That's real good," said Soto, lifting his hat from his shaved, tattooed head long enough to wipe a bandanna across his brow. Adjusting the hat back down into place, he went on to say, "Because you can bet these people will tell me anything you have to say to them." He looked her up and down and smiled. "Before you say anything to anybody, remember the old Mayan, how he looked lying chopped up all over the yard."

"I—I won't say anything," she repeated. "I swear I will not." She paused tensely for a moment, then asked cautiously, "Why did you do that?"

"What?" Soto asked. "You mean kill him, or chop him up, or eat his heart?"

"Any of that," she replied. Her face lost all color, recalling what she'd witnessed that evening from the window of the nuns' living quarters.

"Killing is in my blood, especially killing Mayan Indians," Soto said matter-of-factly. "For generations, my family, the Soto Ceras, and the Mayans have been enemies. It's legendary. The old priest knew about it. It was my ancestors who showed the Spanish the land routes across South America. When my people killed an enemy in battle, they had a tradition of cutting out his heart and eating it." He looked at her intensely and bared his strong white teeth. "Does that sound uncivilized to you?"

She didn't answer, but a cold fear gripped her insides.

"In my family it is an act of religion. Don't let it shock you. If you think there are parts of Mexico that are uncivilized, you have no idea how much worse it gets where I am from."

As he spoke about his origins, Clarimonde noted how his voice took on a trace of accent. "And where is it you are from?" she asked, still cautious.

But he ignored her question. Instead, knowing the effect his words had on her, he continued, saying, "The Mayans once called us 'brothers of the dark monster,' because of how my people tortured and killed them, and ate their hearts. Over time, as my people spread out among the rest of the world, that name changed to 'brothers of Satan.' I do my part to keep the practice alive." He chuckled darkly under his breath. "For that reason I can summon demons at my command and they will travel the world to find me and protect me."

Were these the ravings of a depraved mind? She wasn't sure. But he was talking freely; she wanted it that way to find out all she could. "Your family once owned the mining interest in Shadow Valley. You come from wealthy people, yet you choose to live this way," she said.

"Yes, the Soto Ceras are wealthy indeed." He smiled at her again and said with a shrug, "I was educated in Amsterdam. I speak seven languages as well as the natives of those countries. I am schooled in the world of commerce and industry."

"Yet, you chose to be an outlaw," Clarimonde ventured, hoping to gain as much insight into the man as she could gather while he was in a talkative mood. Part of her survival in the rank brothels and on the throat-cutting streets of California's Barbary Coast had depended on her wits and wiles. She had hoped never to have to live that way again, but here it was thrust upon her. She listened, weighing his every word.

"Yes, I chose to become an outlaw instead." Again Soto's white smile sparkled. "But being an outlaw in America here is mild compared to being a Soto Cera in the jungles where I come from. Like all of my family before me, I can slice out a heart and eat it before it stops beating."

As he spoke he reached a hand over and squeezed

her thigh firmly, high up, near her open lap. "That's something for you to keep in mind," he added, half joking but half-serious. "You are a woman who has been around. You know how well a man will treat a woman who makes him happy. You've also seen with your own eyes how badly things will go for you if you anger or betray me." Kneading her thigh firmly, he said in a whisper, "So, make me happy, Clarimonde. Make me *very* happy."

"I—I will . . . I'll do whatever you want me to do for you," she said, shaken not only by his words, but even more so by the image of what she had seen happen to the old Indian. "Was Ransdale a part of this practice? Is that why he took scalps?" she asked.

"No," said Soto, letting his hand fall away from her thigh. "I didn't know Ransdale was a scalper until we got out here where he could indulge himself. It was his scalp collecting that brought the Soto Cera blood in me back to life," he said. "There's something about killing that never leaves a man once he's acquired a taste for it."

Clarimonde couldn't help but raise her eyes and stare at him, either in shock or disbelief.

"Nate was a low-minded animal," Soto continued. "He didn't even realize that when he asked me if he could eat the French nun, the 'sweet cookie,' he had the same deep craving for warm, raw flesh as the most raging savage in the jungle." A dark, piercing look came to his eyes.

"I . . . think I understand," Clarimonde offered. She said it only in hopes that it would gain her some better standing with him, something she would need if she was to ever free herself from him.

"Oh, do you now?" Soto said with a flat, cynical look in his dark eyes. Again his gloved hand went up onto her thigh, this time roughly, with urgency; he squeezed more firmly through the thin peasant trousers. Lowering his voice he said, "The only thing separating any of us from the beasts is our self-restraint." Clarimonde saw a pulse beating quickly in his throat. Again, he gave the smile. "My self-restraint knows better than to get in my way once I've tasted what I want."

Clarimonde stared straight ahead as the horses walked onto the dusty street. She had been given a better glimpse into the darkness of Soto's soul, and whether he had said things deliberately to frighten her and keep her in his power, or whether he was indeed the monster he had so casually defined himself to be, she didn't know. But she did realize that when it came time to make her break, she'd better know beforehand that her plan would work. From all she'd seen and all she'd heard from him, this man was more dangerous and more insane than anyone she'd ever met those years on the Barbary Coast.

They rode on in silence.

On the busy, dusty street, the two stepped down at a hitch rail out front of Modale's Big Diamond Saloon, a gambling and drinking establishment set up in a large, ragged army tent. No sooner had Soto's boots touched the ground than a young member of the Hole-in-the-wall Gang stepped up as if out of nowhere and asked in a whisper, "Are you Suelo Soto?"

Soto took his time before answering, looking the young man up and down as he hitched the supply mule and the spare horse between his horse and the big paint. "I might be. . . . Who's asking?" he said finally, sizing up the blue-eyed, youthful face as no threat to him.

"I'm Billy Todd Carver," the young man said, touching the brim of his flat-crowned hat. He breathed a short sigh of relief, eyeing the pack mule and its tied-down cargo covered with a dusty canvas. "Man oh man, am I glad to see you!" he said, still in a whisper, struggling to contain his excitement. "We've been looking for you the past two weeks." As he talked to Soto, his eyes went up and down Clarimonde, noting her clothes, her straw sombrero. "What happened to the convicts you brought to back you up getting away from the law?"

"They backed me up. I got away." Soto gave a thin, wry smile, taking off his gloves and stuffing them into his waist.

"Ha, I get it!" Carver chuckled, appearing a bit simple. "That's a dang good answer, sure enough." He gave an openmouthed grin. But as Soto started to take a step toward the ragged saloon tent, the slender young man suddenly stepped in front of him, blocking him. His hand flipped back his coat lapel and wrapped around the butt of a big Remington sticking up from his waist. His laugh, his foolishness and the openmouthed expression were gone, replaced by a dead-serious glare in his clear blue eyes.

"Did I do something to make you think you're talking to an idiot, Mister? If I did, maybe we best start all over, so you won't get yourself smeared all over the street—"

"Whoa, easy there, Billy Todd!" said Ben Kirkpatrick, another gang member. "There's no cause to be inhospitable here." The tall man spread the tent fly to one side and stepped out, facing Soto from fifteen feet away. He wore a shiny black, Montana-crowned hat and a pair of polished knee-high riding boots.

"I was hospitable enough, T." Carver kept his eyes on Soto as he answered. "I asked him a straight question. I expected a straight answer."

Eyeing the mule, with its load of canvas-covered cargo, the tall man said, "I'm Ben Kirkpatrick. You'll have to overlook 'Quickdraw' here. We've had lots of railroad detectives on our necks of late. It's got us all a little jumpy."

" 'Quickdraw,' huh?" Soto asked, returning Bill Carver's stare.

"Don't ever doubt it," Carver responded without backing away an inch.

Soto made no further comment as he looked around the busy street, taking note of three other men, stationed here and there, who were watching intently to see where this confrontation was headed. Those men were English Collin Hedgepeth, Hunt Broadwell and Max Short. Finally Soto turned to Kirkpatrick and gestured a hand toward Clarimonde.

"This is my woman, Clair," he said, shortening her name. To her he said, "Clair, meet Bill Carver and Ben Kirkpatrick, 'the Tall Texan.' "

Kirkpatrick stepped forward, took off his hat, bowed slightly at the waist and said, "My close friends call me 'T.' I hope you will do me that honor, ma'am."

Carver took a step back, took off his hat and bowed his head slightly toward Clarimonde, letting the confrontation drop. "A pleasure, ma'am," he said politely.

The Tall Texan offered a forearm to Clarimonde to steady herself with as she stepped onto the low boardwalk out front of the saloon tent. "Allow me, Miss Clair," he said.

Clarimonde's eyes went to Soto; then she declined the offer of Kirkpatrick's arm and stepped closer to Soto's side. "Well then," Kirkpatrick said cordially, "I have a buggy for the lady to ride in. I think it's time we rode out and introduced you both to Beck and the others. They've been waiting for you like a child waits for Christmas." He smiled.

"She'll ride her horse. I'm having a few drinks before I go anywhere," Soto said, stepping toward the tent fly, taking Clarimonde by her arm and leading her with him.

The Tall Texan and Bill Carver looked at one another curiously. "Beck doesn't like being kept waiting, Suelo," Kirkpatrick said.

Soto stopped and turned to the two men. "Let's get this straight right now. You boys hired me to do something for you . . . something none of you can do for yourself. As long as I'm the top ace in the deck, I'll say how I play my hand." He thumped himself on the chest, and added, "I'm having some whiskey. You can join me, drink with me or go on about your business, Quickdraw."

Carver and the Tall Texan watched Soto lead Clarimonde in through the tent fly. "Well well now, what have we here?" said Kirkpatrick, just between Carver and himself.

"Say the word," Carver replied, staring at the tent fly that had fallen back into place. "I'll go raise a goose egg on his head and throw him over a saddle."

"No, that won't help us any," said Kirkpatrick. "This job is too far along to have to go rounding ourselves up a new safecracker. We need him too bad to start right off having trouble. Let's get in there and drink some whiskey with him. I want to learn more about this woman. She doesn't look very happy to me."

"Damn it, T," Carver said, giving the Tall Texan a disgusted look. "Leave your hands off his woman. You just said yourself we can't afford trouble with him."

"I'm not after this man's woman, Billy Todd," said Kirkpatrick, leveling his hat brim and in doing so, giving the other three men a signal that everything was all right.

"As long as I've known you, you've always been after every man's woman," said Carver.

"Not this time, Billy Todd," said Kirkpatrick, ushering the young man toward the tent fly. "I want you to believe me. . . . This time I'm innocent. I only want to find out what the circumstances are with these two."

"Yeah, I bet," said Carver, walking in ahead of

him. "I'm not taking my eyes off you, T. Beck told us to wait here for Soto and bring him out to the cabin. Whatever is going on twixt these two is strictly none of my business. Whether she's happy or not makes me no difference. I want no part of some lovers' spat."

"Neither do I," said Kirkpatrick. "But 'lover of women' that I am, I hate to think she might be some poor gal who's being preyed upon and kept by some bully, against her will."

"Dang," said Carver, "that would make her no different than most every woman I know!"

"Don't be a knucklehead, Billy Todd," said the Tall Texan. "It always pays to know what's going on among those you work with."

Chapter 12

—

In a weathered cabin alongside a wide, shallow creek, Memphis Beck had just poured himself a tin cup full of strong coffee and started to sit down at the table when he saw the four riders come into sight through the open front window. Three of the riders were on horseback. The fourth, Ben Kirkpatrick, rode in the open-top buggy that sat low to the ground. The other three men had stayed in Rusty Nail to see if Soto had been followed and to keep watch on any other comings and goings.

"It's about time," Beck said to the men seated at the round wooden table playing poker. "It looks like our safecracker has arrived."

Looking up at Beck, Bowen Flannery worked a toothpick to the side of his mouth and tossed seven dollars to the center of the table. "Call," he said to Earl Caplan seated across from him. Then to Beck he said, "I was beginning to think this big-time, Portuguese, dynamite man had gotten a taste of free air and decided to duck back across the ocean."

Beck walked to the front door, saying over his shoulder with satisfaction, "Well, you can stop fretting over it, Bowen. He's here."

Bowen shrugged, saying to the others, "Who said I was fretting?"

Across from him, Caplan spread his cards on the rough tabletop. "Two pair," he said. "Nines over sevens." Then replying to Flannery he said, "You're always fretting over something or other, Bowen."

"Portuguese?" a young horse thief named Bill "Cruz" Cruzan asked as he tossed his cards to the table and stood up. "I thought he was supposed to be from Brazil, Peru, some place like that."

Beck said, "Wherever he's from, Cruz, he's here now. Let's go out and meet him."

"Two pair won't do it," Flannery said to Caplan, laying his cards down. "Three lovely ladies here." Raking in the pot with both hands he said to Memphis Beck, "For all the time and money we spent getting this man out of Yuma, we could have bred our own safecracker and raised him to suit ourselves."

"Next time we'll do that, Bowen," Beck said with a smile.

"I don't know what was wrong with the way I cracked a safe," Cruzan said.

"Nothing at all," said Caplan, "except you cracked it all over half of Wyoming."

They chuckled among themselves as they filed out onto the front porch and stood waiting, relaxed and confident as the four riders drew closer. Had these four not been recognized by rifleman

Dave Arken, who stood posted at a point above the main trail into the valley, three rifle shots would have warned the cabin long before the riders had made it into sight.

"Cruz, there's a difference between cracking a safe and blowing it all to hell," Beck said to Cruzan. "This man's family has mined, cut trails and excavated all over Europe and South America. He cut his teeth on explosives. Opening a safe is nothing to him."

Cruzan shrugged. "Strap a few sticks to something, step back and cover your ears. That's all there is to blowing something up."

"You're right, Cruz," said Beck, gazing out at the approaching riders. "That's why Suelo Soto doesn't use dynamite to get inside a safe."

Cruz responded, "But you said he cut his teeth on dynamite."

"No," said Beck, correcting him, "I said he cut his teeth on explosives—big difference."

"Not to me, there's not," Cruzan said sullenly.

"I think what Memphis is trying to tell you, Cruz, is that this man, Suelo Soto, whatever his name is, uses Swedish blasting oil," Flannery said. "Am I right, Memphis?"

"No, not even close," Beck said, watching the buggy and the riders grow nearer. "Swedish blasting oil is no better than dynamite. It's just nitroglycerin mixed with gunpowder. It still blows everything to hell—including whatever's inside the safe."

"All right, we give up, Memphis," said Flannery. "What is it this man does that's worth so much to us? Don't he put his trousers on one leg at a time?"

"Yes, but it's what he does after he pulls them up and buttons them," Beck said. "He's a wizard with explosives, knows how to boil nitroglycerin out of dynamite. Even knows how to make nitroglycerin from scratch, like whipping up a bowl of biscuit batter. That's the part we want to learn from him."

Bowen Flannery raised a brow and said, "Learn it from him?"

"Yep," said Beck, "I want some of us watching how he does it. We might need to do it ourselves some day."

"Like hell if I'll learn to mix explosives," Flannery laughed. "You're a smooth talker, Memphis Beck, but you can't sell me on that one."

"I'll learn it if he'll teach me," Earl Caplan volunteered.

"That's the spirit, Earl," said Beck. He stepped down off the porch, offering no more on the matter as the riders brought their horses to a halt.

"I mean it," said Caplan. "If that's what it takes to keep a man in this game, I'll learn it." He also stepped down to greet the arriving party.

"If you start mixing explosives, Earl, you had better not do it around me," Flannery said with a slight chuckle. "I want to leave this world in a long wooden box, not in a canvas bag."

Beck stood by and watched Soto step down from his horse, Clarimonde and Billy Todd Carver doing the same beside him. While Soto dusted himself with his hat, Beck took a step closer, looking at the strange tattoos on his shaved head. The other men stared curiously.

"Suelo Soto?" Beck asked, his hand resting comfortably on his gun butt. "I'm Memphis Beck." He continued in a businesslike voice. "When my men set up the prison break for you in Yuma, they told you three words to say, so I would know it's really you instead of some railroad detective." He paused, his hand tightened in anticipation on the Colt; then he said, "Tell us those three words."

Soto took his time, looking back and forth at the men's faces, watching their eyes turn stonier the longer he stalled. Finally, with a flat grin he said, "Filthy Rich."

Beck seemed to ease down; his hand relaxed on the big Colt. He smiled. "But that's only two words. I said give me three."

"No," Soto said confidently, "You had them tell me that you would ask for three, but that I should give you only two." He looked back and forth again, this time spreading his hands as he smiled and repeated, "Filthy rich!"

"Relax boys, it's him." Beck smiled and took a step closer.

Behind Soto and Clarimonde, Carver let his Remington drop back into his holster. In the buggy, Kirkpatrick let the sawed-off shotgun lie back down on the seat beside him. He stepped down while Beck introduced Soto to the other men. Clarimonde stood to the side quietly until Soto gestured toward her with his hand. "This is Clair. She is my woman," Soto said, as if in introducing her he was also issuing a hands-off warning to the men.

The men nodded respectfully toward her, tipping or removing their hats as they each looked her up and down with both caution and curiosity. Beck said, "Ma'am, welcome among us. We are in sore need of accommodations for womenfolk right now. But anything you need to make yourself comfortable, do not hesitate to let any of us know."

Beside Beck, Flannery cut in and said, "What about the fellows you brought along to help you get away?"

"Don't ask," the Tall Texan said, stepping over among the others.

"They're dead," Soto said flatly. He gave Kirkpatrick a look, then added, "I brought them as far as I needed them. Two of them stayed behind to take care of an Arizona Ranger who dogged us all the way across the border. My guess is that he killed them both."

"Too bad," said Beck. "One of those men was Dick Hirsh. He's the one who tipped us off about you in the first place. Hadn't been for Hirsh telling us, you'd still be swatting fleas in Yuma Penitentiary."

"Yes, too bad about him." Soto shrugged as if it meant nothing to him. "The third man I killed myself, before I got to Shadow Valley, the place where I picked up the supplies we'll need."

"You've been all the way to Valle de la Sombra?" Cruz asked using the Spanish name. "That's a *dang* long way south!"

"Yes, Shadow Valley is how far south I've been," said Soto, deliberately not saying the name in Spanish.

"Killed him, why?" Caplan asked bluntly.

"I killed him because he was too badly wounded to live," Soto lied straight-faced. "And I don't leave living witnesses behind to talk to the law." He looked back and forth among them and asked, "Is that going to cause me any problems riding with the Hole-in-the-wall Gang?"

"We don't kill our own," Flannery offered, giving Soto a condemning look. "Fact is, we try not to kill anybody. So far we've been lucky in that regard. It makes the difference between going away for a few years, or swinging from a rope."

"Never have killed one of our own. Never will," Cruzan added, with the same expression.

"We're all brothers here," said Caplan. "That's what makes us the best at what we do."

"I do things the way it suits me." Soto turned his eyes to Beck. "If that sticks in anybody's craw, I can turn and ride right now before my saddle cools. You can get yourself another man."

"Everybody take it easy," said Beck, looking at Soto, then at the others. "We all need a little time to get used to one another. Let's don't start arguing right off about how things ought to be done." He looked at Soto, interested in what he'd said about a ranger following them across the border. "Who was this Arizona Ranger who dogged you? Did you get a look at him?"

"It was Sam Burrack," Soto said, as if knowing that was the question on Beck's mind. "I know everybody here has heard of him. So, you all know why I'm saying those two men are most likely dead."

"Burrack . . . ," said Flannery, his eyes instinctively searching the distant horizon as if the ranger might appear at any second. "If he was on your trail south of the border, it's a fairly safe bet that he's on your trail right now."

"That's a bet you would lose," Soto said. "I made certain I shook him loose before I left Mexico with our load of supplies."

"Oh? How's that?" Beck asked, his eyes having also gone to the horizon at the sound of the ranger's name.

"I blasted Shadow Valley down on his head," Soto said matter-of-factly.

"Burrack is dead?" Beck asked pointedly.

"If he's not dead, he's busy tunneling himself up through two hundred feet of dirt and rock. Either way, he's not a threat to us." Soto offered a thin smile. "I thought hearing that would make you happy, one less lawdog to worry about."

"Yeah, sure, it does," Beck lied. Looking back on his encounter with Burrack near the town of Little Aces, New Mexico, Beck realized that while the ranger had been difficult, he had been fair. The ranger had not fallen under the influence of the railroad's reward money, or its political pull. Burrack had only done his job. Beck could not fault the man for that.

"What about the supplies?" Beck asked, changing the subject away from the ranger.

"Everything is there in the buggy," Soto said, thumbing over his shoulder.

Beck turned his gaze to the loaded buggy, seeing the pile of supplies they had transferred from the mule and covered with the canvas tarpaulin before leaving Rusty Nail. Stepping forward he said to Soto, "Let's take a look."

Clarimonde stood to the side and watched as the men walked over and gathered around the buggy load of dynamite. She had listened closely as they'd talked, trying to see whom she needed to get close to—who might help her when she needed someone on her side.

Even as she watched and listened, she knew that this was not the time for her to try making a move. These men were outlaws, notorious robbers who had drawn together in preparation of plying their trade. No matter whom she went to, no matter what she told them about her situation, they weren't going to turn her loose, not now.

Even though Beck and his men were known to be thieves, not killers, Clarimonde couldn't risk saying anything right now. This was a time to lie low, stay quiet. Soto had mentioned a big job awaiting him with Memphis Beck and the Hole-in-the-wall Gang. How big was the job? She had no idea. But it might be easier for them to leave her lying with a bullet in her than turn her loose and risk her ruining the plans.

She watched as Memphis Beck flipped back a corner of the canvas and ran his hand across the top of the bulging bags and small wooden crates.

"So this is what it all starts off as, all this to squeeze us out some pure nitroglycerin," Beck said. "Would it have been easier to mix it all down before you left Mexico, instead of hauling all this over the hills?"

Soto looked at him, wondering if it was a legitimate question or if Beck was only testing him. "Yes, it would have been easier carrying it," he said, keeping it straight and to the point. "But pure nitroglycerin is too unstable on its own. That's why it's mixed three to one with diatomaceous earth and sodium carbonate."

Cruzan stammered, "Diatom—Diatoma—What the hell?"

"Diatomaceous," Soto corrected him, looking at Beck as he spoke. "Without mixing nitro with something to absorb it, the least bump in the trail would blow nitroglycerin sky-high. If I had taken the time to turn it into dynamite, we would have had to separate it again once I got here. Boiling nitroglycerin out of dynamite can be risky without the proper setup and equipment. It's easier making it right here, from scratch."

Listening, Clarimonde noted that the slight trace of a Spanish accent that had crept into Soto's voice while they were below the border had now vanished. His English had become as clear as Beck's, or any man there.

"I see," Beck replied coolly, not giving Soto any clue as to whether his question had been honest, or just his way of finding out if Soto knew what he was talking about. "In that case, tell us what we need to do to help you get it done. We need to be out of here headed north in no more than a week."

Looking off toward a small weathered barn a hundred feet away, Soto said, "I'll need that building to do my work. It'll take the next couple of days. If we're through with introductions, I'll get started right away."

"Good enough," Beck said. He looked around at the faces of the men and said, "Caplan, Kirkpatrick, you two come with me. We're going to help him make—"

"No," Soto said quickly, cutting him off, not wanting to share what he knew with the rest of the gang. "I won't be needing your help." He nodded toward Clarimonde and said, "Clair will give me all the help I need." He looked at her and said, "Bring the horses. I'll bring the buggy." He looked at Beck and said coolly, "I'm going to have a deep hole dug in the barn floor . . . and I'll need ice, lots of ice.

"We can start diggin' the hole first thing in the morning," said Beck. "Ice might be a little hard to come by."

"As soon as I have a hole full of ice, I'll get started," Soto said firmly.

Beck looked around. "Where am I going to find any ice?"

"That's your problem," Soto replied in a dry, arrogant tone. "Just get it for me."

Watching the two gather the horses and loaded buggy and ride away toward the barn, Cruzan said to the others under his breath, "He's kind of an odd bird. I'm not so sure he's going to fit into this bunch."

"He's got a rude, belligerent turn to him," the Tall Texan commented. "He didn't mind keeping everbody waiting while he drank his fill before he'd ride out here."

Beck stared after the two riders and their buggy load of supplies. "Well, he's not going to share what he knows with us, that's for certain."

"I'd almost as soon put the job off than work with the arrogant turd," Carver said. He spit on the ground toward the barn.

"We're not putting it off," said Beck, watching Clarimonde look back at him from the open buggy. "He's our safecracker. Until one of us learns to make nitroglycerin and dynamite, we had better get used to him."

The woman's eyes had singled Beck out for a moment, as if asking both him and herself if she could confide in him. Confide what? Beck wondered. He considered it, watching the man and woman move closer to the old barn. He didn't know what it was, but there was something at play here, he was sure of it. Shaking the matter from his mind for the moment, he turned to the others and said, "All right, let's get the man some ice. Bowen, you're in charge of getting it."

"Get the man some ice, where?" Bowen Flannery said, spreading his hands. "Look around you, Memphis. We're in a desert."

"The rail station at Rock Crossing," Memphis said, the idea just coming to him. They're using insulated cars, shipping goods on ice from Missouri."

"Rock Crossing is more than a fifty mile ride from here," Flannery protested.

"Then you had better pick a couple of men and get started quick," Memphis shot back. "Take the train out of Rusty Nail as far as Dry Buttes. Steal a handcar to ride back. That'll cut your time in half both ways."

"What about our horses?" Flannery asked, spreading his hands.

Beck stared at him.

"Damn it." Flannery shook his head. Then he looked at Billy Todd Carver and said to Cruzan, "All right, let's go. We're bringing back ice."

Chapter 13

Clarimonde and Soto spent the night in the barn, the two of them sleeping on a pallet of hay-stuffed blankets in a warm, dry stall she had to prepare for them. The following morning in the first blue hour of light, she walked from the barn to the well out front of the house with a blanket wrapped around herself. No sooner had she walked out of the barn than Soto, naked, had stood up from the pallet and watched her through a crack in the wall planks. He carried his big Colt, his thumb poised over the hammer, ready to cock it if need be.

When Cruzan, who had spent the last third of the night on the porch keeping guard, stepped down to help her lift a bucket of water, Clarimonde turned him down. Soto smiled to himself, watching her draw the heavy oaken bucket of water from the well and carry it back toward the barn. At the well, Cruzan stood scratching his head. "I've never known a woman to turn down a friendly offer of assistance," he said to Memphis

Beck, who had stepped out onto the porch, a freshly rolled smoke in his fingertips.

"She's obeying her master, I'd say," Beck replied. Noting her bare feet and realizing that she wore nothing beneath the blanket, he watched her walk toward the barn. "Peculiar," he commented to himself, striking a match down a porch post and lighting his cigarette.

Looking toward the barn himself, Cruzan said, "Her master, huh? Well, as far as I'm concerned, this Soto fellow has no interest in ever being a part of our bunch. The sooner we can find somebody else who mixes explosives the better," Cruzan said, stepping back to the porch.

"Maybe we've already found that person," Memphis speculated quietly to himself, watching the woman until she disappeared inside the barn.

"Huh? What's that, Memphis?" Cruz asked, not hearing his lowered words.

"Oh, nothing," Beck said letting go of a stream of gray smoke on the crisp morning air. "Just thinking out loud."

Inside the barn, Soto had walked back to the pallet and lain down on his side, facing her in the dark as if he were still asleep. When Clarimonde stepped inside and closed the door, she set the bucket of water down and made her way to the kerosene lamp standing on a dusty shelf. She took a long match from a wooden box, lit the lamp and adjusted the light into a narrow, circling glow.

With better light to see by, she carried the bucket over, set it atop a wooden work shelf and poured water into a wash pan sitting beside it. She gathered her long hair, wrapping and twisting it atop her head to get it out of her way.

In the dim, golden circle of light twenty feet away, Soto watched her drop the blanket from around herself, pick up a small washcloth from the pan of water, wring it between her hands and begin washing herself. He watched her, enjoying every movement, every touch of the wet cloth to her skin. She was not a young woman, nor was she beautiful. Her face, her sinewy body, had long been seasoned, weathered and hardened by the harsh Mexican hill country.

But Soto didn't care. She was no limp or rigid piece of cold flesh. She knew how to apply herself to the act of pleasing men. She was his for the taking, and she had seemed to grasp instantly that what he wanted from her was her complete and total submission. He smiled to himself outside the glow of light, watching her hand touch the cloth to her most private areas.

She was something warm, something to do with at his pleasure after all the days and nights alone in his ten by ten prison cell. He liked the idea of her knowing how little it would mean to him when the time came for him to kill her. And they both knew that time would come, he reminded himself, liking that idea as well. After he'd finished with her, had his fun with her, had his fill of her, they both knew she was marked for death.

When she'd finished washing herself, she gathered the blanket and walked out of the light to the pallet. Soto opened his eyes. Reaching out and grasping her forearm, he said, "Leave it lie," as she stooped to pick up her dress and put it on.

She let the dress fall from her fingertips and watched him turn onto his back and throw off his blanket, exposing himself to her. "Do something about this," he commanded her. Then he smiled, seeing her stand up long enough to loosen her hair from atop her head and bow down over him with no hesitation, no sign of reluctance. To think Nate Ransdale would have scalped and killed this woman, he reminded himself. The man was a fool. No wonder he was dead. . . .

Moments later, as Clarimonde stood dressed, rewrapping and resetting her hair atop her head, Soto had stepped into his trousers, pulled them up, buttoned them and looked all around the barn. He walked to Clarimonde and gripped her hard by her buttocks. "We slept too late. Go over to the house, get us a pot of coffee and some grub. Don't let me find out you said a word to anybody about how we met. Do you understand?"

"I understand," Clarimonde said quietly, her eyes lowered.

"Don't be foolish enough to think these men are going to do anything to help you. They need me worse than anybody needs you." His grip tightened; Clarimonde struggled to keep from trying to pull away from him. He tapped the side of his head. "You're just a washed-out whore. You're not worth the cost of your feed." He smiled cruelly. "I have *knowledge.* They'll do whatever I want them to do. That includes skinning and salting you, if I tell them to do it." He took a deep breath of satisfaction. "I'm the only thing keeping you alive."

She winced under his increased grip on her behind. "I won't tell them anything, I swear it," she said. "I have given my word."

He turned her loose roughly, saying, "All right, then get going and hurry back here with some food and coffee. We've got a lot to do to get ready for when our ice arrives." He watched her try to hurry away, limping the first few steps from the pain his strong grip had caused her. "Who knows, maybe I'll have you help me mix up the first batch of nitro. You have a steady hand, don't you?" he said, teasing her.

"I—I don't know if you should trust me to do something that important," she said. "I have heard how dangerous it is."

"Dangerous?" Soto chuckled. "I'll tell you how dangerous. One false move and they would be picking pieces of you out of the trees."

Clarimonde shook her head. "Please don't make me do something like that," she said, for the first time begging him to not force her to do something against her will. "I wouldn't be steady enough to do it."

Soto's thin smile went away as he took a step toward her. "You'll do it if *I say* you'll do it," he said in a threatening manner.

Clarimonde shut up, her eyes still lowered. Knowing better than to say any more on the matter, she moved away toward the barn door. "Go on," Soto added, waving her away in dismissal as he reached for his shirt lying over a stall rail. "As

soon as we get this place set up to mix our explosives, I'm going to tell *Mr. Memphis Beck* to have
his men clear us out a room in the house all for
ourselves," he said, even though Clarimonde had
already left and shut the door behind herself. To
himself he added as he straightened his wrinkled
shirt, "He'll do it, too. That'll show how much he
needs me. . . ."

Outside, walking to the house, Clarimonde saw
Memphis Beck and another man watching her
from the front porch. As if acting upon a word
from Beck, the other man stood up and walked
inside as she drew nearer. "Morning, ma'am,"
Beck said, standing and touching his hat brim. "I
hope you were comfortable enough in the barn."

"Yes, thank you," Clarimonde said cordially yet
stiffly, Beck noted. She stepped onto the porch,
deliberately avoiding him with her eyes.

*All right, Memphis, you're the smooth talker. Here's
your chance. Get busy . . .* , he ordered himself.

"I want you to know that had we been ex-
pecting a lovely woman such as yourself, ma'am,
we would have strived to provide you with more
genteel accommodations," he said, hoping to
bring her eyes around to him.

But she replied without facing him, "We made
do with the accommodations on hand, Mr. Beck.
May I please have a pot of coffee and some food?"

"Yes, ma'am, you certainly may," Beck said. He
stepped over and knocked on the front door, even
through there were eyes watching them through
the windows. "Now that you and Suelo are up
and around, we'll get busy straightaway, digging

the hole in the barn. I sent three of my men to fetch some ice." He heard someone turn the door handle from inside. "Is there anything else you or Suelo might have thought of overnight? Anything else that me and my associates can do to help speed things along?"

The woman stood rigid without offering any sort of reply. Beck had to ask himself if she realized how much her silence and her lack of response told him.

All right then . . . Beck studied her expression.

The door opened, Beck's knock being answered by Dave Arken, who'd had been relieved from his job of standing guard along the trail. "Miss Clair," Beck said, "this is Dave Arken."

"Ma'am," Arken acknowledged with a curt nod.

To Arken, Beck said, "Dave, this is Miss Clair, Suelo Soto's 'companion.' She and Suelo have gotten a late start this morning. Fix them up a fresh pot of coffee and some breakfast."

"Sure thing," said Arken, taking a second to look Clarimonde up and down. "We just made a fresh pot of coffee. I'll pour it into a couple of canteens. There's plenty of beans, bacon and hot cakes."

"Good, Dave," said Beck. "Meanwhile, the lady and I will wait here and get better acquainted."

The woman appeared to grow tense upon hearing Beck's suggestion, so much so that when Dave Arken closed the door, Beck said to her, "Ma'am, I hope I didn't say something to offend—?"

"No, you didn't," Clarimonde said quickly, almost cutting him off. She made a quick, nervous glance toward the barn. Beck noted the gesture. "It's just that it's been a long trip, and I'm still worn-out from it," she said. As she spoke, a nervous hand went to a strand of hair blown loose by a passing breeze. She brushed the hair aside with her fingertips. "I'll—I'll be fine in a day or two."

"Of course you will. I understand." Beck smiled faintly, wondering if she realized just how much more her actions and expression had told him about herself and her situation. The thought crossed his mind that she might very well be doing this purposefully, her words and demeanor speaking to him too subtly to be questioned if she were ever confronted about it.

He looked her up and down and asked, "I expect you and Suelo have been together a good while?"

She gave no response. She only looked away as if any answer she gave might be the wrong thing to say.

I see . . . , Beck conjectured to himself, deciding that she'd been warned not to reveal anything about the two of them.

Beck quickly filled the silent pause by saying, "I thought you might have known one another a long time, the way he trusts you to help with the explosives."

Her eyes flashed onto his with a look of fear, then cut away. Still she gave no answer.

Beck picked up on her silence and pressed further, learning more as he went, in spite of her refusing to answer him. "That's quite a trade you have, mixing explosives. If you'll pardon my saying so, ma'am, I know of only a few men who can do it, let alone women." He studied her eyes from a side view as she looked off along the distant hill line, avoiding him. This woman knew nothing about explosives, and very little about Suelo Soto, Beck decided. *Shame on you, Soto, you tattoo-headed son of a bitch*, he thought. *You stole this woman somewhere along the way.*

"We had a devil of a time locating a man like Suelo Soto. Not to mention how much it cost us, breaking him out of prison to get him here." Now he paused, but only for a moment, weighing his next words. "Just think, had we known you were available, we could have gotten you instead, saved ourselves some time and trouble."

Clarimonde's eyes snapped back from the distant hill line and riveted on his, as if she'd just been stricken by a great revelation. Beck could see she almost said something; but then she had caught herself and he felt her pull back from him. Her eyes moved away again, going back to the distant hills with resolve.

Beck started to say more, but before he could, the door opened and Arken stepped out carrying two canteens full of hot coffee and a wooden tray with two tin plates of steaming food. "Here we are, ma'am," Arken said.

"Allow me, Miss Clair," Beck said, stepping in, looping the canteen straps over his forearm and taking the tray between his hands.

She walked along beside him, in tense silence until she stopped ten yards from the barn and said coolly, with what Beck could only consider a restrained double meaning, "Please, I'll handle things from here." For only a second her eyes met his squarely, then slipped away. There was nothing he could have said to Soto about her actions, her words or her meaning.

A clever gal . . . ? Beck asked himself, handing the tray and canteens over to her. *Oh yes . . .* She knew what she was doing, he decided. She had to know. Tugging the tray just a little before turning it loose, he forced her to look back into his eyes for just another second. "I hope you will rest up, do some thinking for yourself. I've always found the world to look much better after some rest and quiet thought."

Clarimonde ignored his words as if she hadn't heard them.

As she turned and walked on to the barn with the coffee and food, Beck touched his hat brim toward the barn door as if knowing that Soto stood there watching. It made no difference, he thought. There had been nothing said that either of them had to be concerned about. *I threw it out there, lady*, he told himself. *Let's see if you pick it up . . . see what you do with it.*

When he turned and walked back to the porch, Arken stood in the open doorway and asked, "Well, what do you say? Does this woman really know how to mix explosives or not?"

"She doesn't know anything about explosives," said Beck, looking back toward the barn. "But I've got a feeling she's about to learn."

Chapter 14

Taking the train from Rusty Nail to Rock Springs, Bowen Flannery, Bill Cruzan and Billy Todd Carver made it a point not to sit close together. When they arrived at Rock Springs, they left the train separately and walked away in three different directions. Flannery stopped at the station ticket counter long enough to read the train schedule. Then he walked on.

Ten minutes later the three met behind the rail express station and looked out upon a large rail yard filled with crates, stock pens and empty freight cars. At the far end of the yard stood a large building where insulated cars stood with their doors open, their cargos of fresh produce being unloaded onto four-wheel express wagons pulled by mules.

"I can't tell you how humiliating this is, stealing ice," said Flannery, bitterly, "after making a career of stealing cash and gold."

"Ice is almost the same as gold these days,"

Billy Todd said. "Leastwise, the railroads all treat it that way."

"Ice or gold, it makes no never-mind. If this is what it takes to get us to our big job, let's bite down and get it done," said Cruz, looking all around for a workman's handcar not in use along the rails. "Dang, this sure is a busy place. How does anybody find their way to jake and back?"

"I don't know," said Flannery, "but I'm counting on all this 'busy-ness' to get us out of here—riding in plain sight with a load of ice."

Spotting a handcar first, Billy Todd nudged Cruz and gestured toward a four-man work crew who had just stepped down from one and walked away, their picks and shovels over their broad, sweat-stained shoulders.

"Good show, Billy Todd," said Flannery, seeing the handcar, then looking back toward the insulated produce cars. Beside the produce cars stood a thick-looking stone building with no windows and only one large door. Above the door a sign read: WARNING—ICEHOUSE—KEEP DOOR LOCKED.

"All right, let's get started," Flannery said, putting a plan together on the spot. "Cruz, do you still have that rail detective badge?"

"Sure I do." Cruz grinned. "I wouldn't take nothing for it."

"Give it to me. We're going to put it to use," said Flannery. As he held out his hand for the badge, he looked from the icehouse to the workmen's handcar, searching out a track switch that would connect the two.

"What's the plan?" Cruz asked, rubbing his hands together in anticipation, seeing Flannery already had something worked out.

Badge in hand, Flannery said, "Short and simple. You two grab that handcar and meet me at the icehouse. I have some lock picks. I'll get us inside." With no more to say on the matter, he turned and walked away toward the icehouse.

"Short and simple suits me," Cruz said. He and Billy Todd shrugged at one another and walked away in the opposite direction toward the handcar. . . .

Moments later, at the produce dock, the foreman of the freight handlers looked down the track from the insulated car door and watched the handcar roll along the track beside him. "What's this . . . ?" He let his words trail, seeing a man in the dark suit standing at the front of the car, a rifle cradled in his arm, a shiny detective's badge on his lapel. "There's getting to be more detectives than there are freight hands these days," he growled under his breath. Seeing the man with the badge look up and stare him squarely in the face, the foreman gave a toss of his head and turned back to observing his crew. "Keep moving! There's nothing that concerns us out there."

Billy Todd and Cruz stood pumping the car handle up and down, keeping the handcar rolling at a quick yet safe pace through the busy rail yard. Without turning to face the other two, Flannery asked over his shoulder as they rolled on, "Billy Todd, did you relock that door the way I told you to?"

"I'm not going to dignify that with an answer," Billy Todd said, as if offended Flannery would even ask. Gazing at Cruz across the up-and-down pumping handle, he gave a wink. On both sides of the handcar sat large blocks of ice, wrapped in insulated covers. Even under the thick, quilted covers the ice dripped steadily.

As the handcar rolled on, out of the yard and along the rails out of Rock Springs, Flannery took a pocket watch from his vest and looked at it, calculating how long it would take them to get to Rusty Nail and how many times they would have to get off the tracks onto a siding to allow other trains to pass.

"All right, it looks like we'll be in Rusty Nail before nightfall with any luck," he said, taking off his suit coat and rolling up his shirtsleeves. "We'll take turns on the handle and keep up a fast pace."

"We had better travel fast," said Cruz, eyeing the large blocks of ice beneath the covers, "else, instead of ice, all we'll bring back is a bucket of cold water."

They rolled on.

Ten miles out of Rock Springs as the handcar sped down a long, steep decline, on a ledge above the rails, Neil Deavers gazed down and adjusted his binoculars until he could recognize Flannery's face among the three. Taken aback for a moment, he pulled the binoculars away from his face, batted his eyes and said, "I'll be damned." Then he raised the binoculars again and said to Davis Dinsmore, who sat atop his horse beside him, "All this time we've been looking everywhere for *Wal-*

lers, there goes Bowen Flannery, right under our noses!"

"Let me see!" said Dinsmore. Reaching for the binoculars he added, "Let's go get him! You know those others are Hole-in-the-wallers too!"

"Take it easy!" said Deavers, giving up the binoculars and watching Dinsmore stare down eagerly, gritting his teeth as he did so. "We've got Flannery. But he's small coins. Play our cards right, keep him at arm's length and he'll lead us right to Memphis Beck and the rest of the gang."

"Play our cards how?" Dinsmore asked, lowering the binoculars and handing them back to Deavers. "Every time we try keeping one of these slippery rats at arm's length, they slip through our fingers!"

"You do want Beck, don't you?" Deavers asked in a condescending tone. "After him kicking your nuts up into your belly?"

"You know damn well I want him," Dinsmore said, his face reddening a little in shame. "I haven't forgotten what he did to me. You don't have to remind me." He raised a wrist that still had one of the handcuffs around it that Beck had put there. "Every time I look at this I remember what he did to me."

"Then you need to settle down," said Deavers. "We'll keep back and stay on Flannery's trail. Like all these men, every trail leads to Memphis Beck." He pulled his horse back and turned it toward the path leading away from the ledge. Looking back he asked, "Are you coming?"

"Oh, yes," said Dinsmore, raising the single

handcuff and adjusting in on his wrist, "you can bet I'm coming. I can taste Beck's blood so bad I can hardly stand it."

On the handcar, Flannery said as they sped along downhill, "Don't look up, but I just caught a flash of something high up there on the hillside."

Cruz almost looked up, but then he stopped himself and asked with a concerned expression, "A rifle, do you suppose?"

"Awfully bright for gunmetal," Flannery said, his face slightly lowered, but his eyes tilted upward, searching the hillside from under his brow, scanning the small, rocky ledge protruding out of it. "Leastwise if it was a rifle, whoever was holding it sure missed their chance," he added as the handcar rolled around into a long curve and out of sight from the hillside. "We're safe for now."

The three let out a tense breath. "Dang, I'd hate to get killed stealing a handcar load of ice," Billy Todd said.

"I'd hate to get killed stealing anything," Cruzan added.

"I'd hate to get killed playing checkers, far as that goes," Flannery said. He studied the long, tall hillsides above them as the handcar sped on. "Maybe it was nothing back there. But we're going to treat it like somebody's tailing us, just in case."

"I always move like there's somebody tailing me," said Billy Todd.

"So you do, Billy Todd, and so do we all," said Flannery, still combing the hillside. "I say it only as a reminder. . . ."

*   *   *

In the darkest corner of the barn, Beck and the rest of the men had taken turns throughout the day digging a six-foot-deep hole and layering the bottom of it with clean straw. Suelo Soto had not helped with the digging. Instead he and Clarimonde had sorted through the supplies they'd brought in from the buggy the night before.

Opening the small wooden crates stuffed with packing straw, the two removed glass bottles of nitric acid, sulfuric acid and thick, pure glycerin, which Soto examined closely before closing them tightly. "Pure and perfect," he said with a smile, holding his thumb and finger out for Clarimonde to see as he rubbed them together. Clarimonde stared, expressionless, but at the same time she was paying close attention.

From another stuffed packing crate Soto lifted a bag of baking soda, a thermometer, a large glass separating funnel, a glass flask and glass measuring beakers. "When the ice arrives we will need water that has been boiled free of salts and minerals," he said to Clarimonde. Raising a finger for emphasis, he added, "It must be pure, cooled and sealed, for our purposes."

She said with slight reluctance, "Do you want me to boil it?"

Soto chuckled. "Of course I want you to boil it. Are you afraid of boiling water?"

"No, I just meant, what if I don't get it boiled pure, the way you said it has to be?"

"Let me worry about that," Soto said. "Do as I tell you, and stop being so afraid."

"I will," Clarimonde said, noting all the while that he seemed to enjoy knowing that she was frightened of this powerful and dangerous knowledge of his. "Should I go do it now?"

Soto looked at her in disgust. "Yes, do it now! Do it and keep your mouth shut to everyone. No one needs to know how to do this but me."

"I—I wouldn't know what to tell anybody if I tried to," Clarimonde said, standing and turning toward the barn door.

"Yes," Soto said to himself as she left, "stupidity is the thing I admire most about a whore."

On her way to the house in the moonlight, Clarimonde heard a team of horses pulling a buckboard wagon along the path toward the front yard. From the front porch she heard one of the men call out to the others inside, "Flannery's back with the ice! Everybody get out here. Let's lend them a hand."

"It's about time," another voice called out. "We expected you three hours ago."

Clarimonde hurried forward and stopped in time to see Flannery and the other two men jump down from the wagon. Behind the wagon stood their horses, which they had picked up in Rusty Nail on their return trip through town. "We thought we were being followed," said Flannery, "so we made some moves for caution's sake."

"How did it go?" a voice asked.

"Smooth as virgin's lace." Flannery grinned in the moonlit night.

"Smooth, ha," said Cruzan, he and Carver jumping down from the wagon. "We've traveled by horseback, train, handcar and buckboard! I'm dizzy from it."

"You were dizzy to start," Flannery called out, walking back, untying his horse.

"But did you get the ice?" Beck called out from the porch, stepping down, already noting the large blocks, the quilted insulated covers, as he stepped forward.

"We most certainly did," said Flannery, leading his horse forward, reaching over into the buckboard and throwing back the wet covers. "It's nearly half the size we started out with, but there it is." He slapped a hand on a dripping ice block, causing water to spray in every direction.

Seeing Clarimonde standing nearby looking on, Beck asked her, "Well, ma'am, will this be enough to do the job?" Having decided that she knew nothing about the process, he watched her expression to see how she would handle the answer.

Coolly, she managed to look him squarely in the eyes and say, "If it's not, I suppose we'll have to get some more, won't we?"

Beck liked the way she handled it. He smiled. "Yes, ma'am, I suppose we will, now that we know Flannery has such a knack for getting it."

Soto had heard the buckboard rolling toward the yard and walked over from the barn. Stepping in beside Clarimonde, he looked at her, then at Beck, then at the large blocks of ice.

"Is that going to be enough?" Beck asked, gesturing a hand toward the buckboard.

Before answering Beck, Soto looked at Clarimonde and said, "Get inside and get the water boiling." Then looking back at Beck, he said without answering him, "Get it to the barn and get it into the ground. As soon as I finish setting things up and the water cools, we'll start making the first batch."

"Tonight?" Beck asked, considering the darkness inside the barn. "By lamplight?"

"Yes, by lamplight," Soto said smugly. "I could do this with my eyes closed if I wanted to." He stared after Clarimonde as she hurried away up onto the porch and into the house. Then he turned without another word to Beck and walked away.

Stepping in beside Beck, Kirkpatrick said quietly, "He thinks a lot of himself, doesn't he?"

"Yeah," Beck replied, watching Soto walk toward the barn. "Much more than I'm starting to."

"What about this woman?" Kirkpatrick asked. "Is he holding her against her will?"

"I believe he is," said Beck. "But she'll never say so. He's got her too scared. She doesn't know whom to trust."

"What are we going to do about her then?" asked the Tall Texan. "We can't risk her running away while we're in the midst of this big job."

"She's not going to run away," Beck said. "She knows it's not in her best interest. I've felt her out. This woman knows how to take care of herself."

"I hope you know what you're talking about, Memphis," said Kirkpatrick.

"So do I, T," said Beck, watching Clarimonde fade from the moonlight into the purple darkness. A few seconds after the barn door closed, he raised a hand, rubbed the back of his neck and looked all around the hill-encircled land.

"What is it, Memphis?" the Tall Texan asked. "You look like something's got you spooked."

"I don't know what it is," Beck said. "All evening I've had a feeling we're being watched from somewhere far off. Didn't feel it before tonight. Then all of sudden there it was."

"We've got ourselves well guarded here," said Kirkpatrick. "There's nobody going to slip in here on us without our knowing it."

Beck shook off the feeling. "You're right. I must be more strung tight about this big job than I thought." They turned toward the house, yet his eyes still searched the dark purple horizon.

Chapter 15

Beck and the men looked down at the large blocks of ice in the hole in the barn floor. The blocks had been wrapped in their insulated quilt covers, and in turn covered with a thick layer of fresh straw. A few yards away the center of the barn floor had been raked and swept and covered with blankets to keep down dust. A five-foot-long wooden workbench had been set up, Soto's equipment and supplies sitting atop it.

"That's all we can do here," Beck said as he and the others rolled their wet shirtsleeves down and buttoned their cuffs. Gesturing toward Soto, who stood bowed over two buckets of chipped ice and a bucket of the boiled, cooled water atop the workbench, he said quietly, "We best get out of here, so our genius can work." A few feet from Soto, Clarimonde stood watching Soto intently, ready at any moment to turn her face away as if fearing he might look around at her.

"Now we're ready," Soto said, hearing the barn door close behind Beck and the men. Clarimonde

watched intently as he took two glass laboratory
measuring beakers from one of the buckets of
chipped ice and set them on the bench. One beaker contained what Clarimonde, not standing
close enough to read the measurement on the side
of the beaker, could only determine to be three
fingers of sulfuric acid. The other beaker contained
half as much nitric acid. Soto had set the beakers
in one bucket of ice to cool before mixing them
together.

"Come closer and watch how I stir this together,
very slowly, very carefully," Soto said to her.
"When I get everything mixed together, your job
will be to keep everything stirring for the next
two hours."

Clarimonde only nodded, stepping in closer.
She watched him slowly pour the two acids together into a glass flask sitting half-submerged in
the other bucket of ice. When the two were in the
flask he stuck the glass thermometer in it and said,
"This mix grows warm, but it will cool quickly.
When it reaches the right temperature, we mix in
the glycerin."

Clarimonde didn't dare ask what that temperature would be and alert him that she might be
trying to learn the process herself. Instead she
kept a secretive eye on the thermometer. Moments
later, when Soto raised it, read it and said, "There,
that is cool enough," Clarimonde could only note
that the temperature was somewhere under the
fifty degree mark. "Now," he said, "I add the
glycerin, slowly."

She watched as he added the heavy, syruplike

glycerin to the acid mixture, committing every detail she could to memory, knowing that anything she missed she could never ask about. She had to learn the process on her own or not at all.

"Now, we wait," he said, after several minutes of blending the glycerin into the acid mixture. Carefully, he pulled the flask up out of the ice and set it on the bench. Putting the thermometer down into the flask, he stepped back, rubbing his hands together, and said with what she read as a cruel smile, "The complicated part is done. You'll be doing most of the mixing now."

Clarimonde didn't respond. She was ready. She could do this, she told herself.

A half hour after he'd mixed in the glycerin, Soto stepped back to the bench and examined the milky mixture closely. "Pour the water into the funnel," he said over his shoulder to Clarimonde.

"Done," she said, when the last of the water had been poured.

"Now, carefully pour the mixture into it," Soto said, watching the milky substance of acids and glycerin without facing her. . . .

While the two worked deep into the night, on the front porch, Beck and the Tall Texan stared now and then at the light glowing through the cracks in the barn walls. The rest of the men had given up over the past two hours and gone inside to bed. After a while, Kirkpatrick sighed and took the last swig of rye from a whiskey bottle. "Does it always take this long to make nitro?"

"How would I know?" Beck replied, his eyes going back to the image of a silhouette passing back and forth through the light inside the barn. "How long has it been?"

Kirkpatrick checked his pocket watch, then shoved it back down inside his vest pocket. "More than four hours. I didn't know anything took this long to make."

Beck started to answer, but his attention went instead to the barn door opening and closing. The two stood up, watching the pale, grainy image of Clarimonde walk toward them in the moonlight.

"May I get some coffee?" she asked upon stopping at the edge of the porch.

"Of course you can," said Beck. Before he could turn to Kirkpatrick, the Tall Texan had already turned toward the door. "It's going to be stout."

"Stout will do," said Clarimonde.

Beck noted a difference in her voice. It sounded stronger, more confident—the voice of a woman taking the reins, he thought. As Kirkpatrick stepped inside the house, he asked her, "How is it going out there?"

"It's finished," she said, a certain amount of relief coming to her voice. "Suelo said to tell you we'll test some of it first thing in the morning."

"That's great news," said Beck. His tone lowered as he asked, "And how are you?"

"I'm fine, thanks," she answered cordially, in the same manner anyone would have replied.

"I see," Beck said, understanding that she was not going to take a chance at saying the wrong thing. Deciding not to push the matter, he said, "Then, I suppose we'll see just how good you and Suelo Soto both are at this come morning."

"Yes, we'll see," she said.

The front door opened and closed, and Kirkpatrick stepped out, carrying a hot coffeepot, a rag wrapped around the handle. "Watch it, ma'am. This is hot," he said, handing the pot to her carefully. "Take a good grip on the handle here." He held the pot around for her to take from him.

"I've got a good grip on it," Clarimonde said, her eyes moving across Beck's as she spoke.

Beck smiled, getting her message. He touched his fingers to his hat brim toward her and said, "Night, ma'am," and he and Kirkpatrick watched her turn and walk away in the moonlight.

"Well, that's good news," said Kirkpatrick.

"Yes, good news indeed," said Beck. "I think I'll turn in now, see what tomorrow brings us."

At dawn, Denver Modale, owner of the Big Diamond tent saloon, pulled his gallowses up over his thick shoulders and stepped out of the privy. He'd walked across the littered alleyway behind the big tent and started to step inside when a hand reached out of nowhere, grabbed his collar and slung him to the ground.

"Whoa! Don't shoot!" Modale cried out, looking up the open bore of Davis Dinsmore's cocked Colt, two inches from his nose. "I've got no money on me! I swear I don't!"

"Shut up, Denver, you pig! It's not a robbery," said Dinsmore, tipping his hat up enough for the saloon owner to get a better look at his beard-stubbled face.

"Damn it, Davis," Modale said, almost wishing

it were a robber instead of his former brother-in-law. "Why'd you knock me down like this? Are you crazy?" He started to get back on his feet, but Dinsmore's dirty boot pressed hard onto his chest, holding him down.

"Not so fast, Denver," said Dinsmore. "We want some information. I'm hoping you're not going to make us beat it out of you."

"Not if I can help it," said Modale. "I've got nothing to hide and nobody to hide it from. Ask what you will." Lying back beneath the Dinsmore boot, he saw Neil Deavers step into view. "Detective Deavers?" he asked, looking surprised and puzzled. "You're working with Davis Dinsmore?"

"Yeah, he is. What of it?" Dinsmore cut in. "You find something wrong with that?"

"No, it's just that—" Modale's words turned to a grunt as Dinsmore raised his boot and stomped it down hard on his chest.

"All right, Davis," said Deavers, "that's enough of that."

"Enough?" Dinsmore gave Modale an evil look and said to Deavers, "If you knew this sumbitch like I do, you'd want me to *kill him* and do it slow, the things he did to my sister, Belle."

"Back off, Davis. I'm warning you," said Deavers. He stepped in between the two and reached a hand down to Modale, helping him to his feet.

"That was all uncalled for, Davis," said Modale, brushing himself off. "We've seen one another other times. You never acted like this!"

"It just dawned on me this morning how bad I

hate your worthless guts, Denver Modale," Dinsmore growled.

"The fact of it is," he said to Deavers, "I didn't run out on his sister. She ran out on me. She comes from a long line of crazy—"

"That's it. You're dead!" said Dinsmore, cutting him off. He tried to shove his Colt around Deavers to pull the trigger.

"Damn it, put it away!" Deavers shouted, clamping his hand down over the Colt to keep the hammer from being able to fall.

"He's got no sense. You'll have to knock him in the head to stop him," said Modale.

But Dinsmore took a breath and stood back, letting Deavers take the Colt, uncock it and shove it back down into his holster. "There, now leave it holstered!" He turned back to Modale. "We're looking for Memphis Beck and some of his men. We tracked three of them near here on a handcar. We found the handcar on the siding near town. Have you seen any of them?"

"I hope you try lying," Dinsmore said under his breath, getting one more threat.

Modale ignored him and said to Deavers, "I have not seen Memphis Beck, and that's the gospel truth." He looked back and forth along the alleyway. Then he said in a lowered tone, "But I did see the Tall Texan and some others."

"Yeah? When?" Deavers asked, attentively. "Who were the others?"

"Two days ago, Kirkpatrick and Billy Todd Carver came to town, Billy Todd on a saddle, the

Tall Texan holding down a buggy seat." He
looked back and forth again. "They met a funny-
looking fellow with his head shaved and tattooed,
and a woman who acted like she didn't know last
night from next Sunday morning."

"This was two days ago, huh?" Deavers rubbed
his chin, trying to put things together.

"Yep, two days," said Modale. "They stood
right at the bar, the tattooed fellow drinking shots
of rye like the sky was falling. Kirkpatrick just
watched him like they halfway had a mad-on."

"Which way did they ride out?" Deavers asked,
starting to wonder if maybe the gang was holed
up nearby.

"Up toward the hill trails," said Modale, pointing toward a hill line in the distance. Looking past
Deavers at Dinsmore, he said, "Now, see, I said
all that without all the threatening and bullying,
didn't I?"

Dinsmore didn't answer. Instead, he looked
away as if boiling with anger.

"You've been most helpful, Modale," said
Deavers, "and I appreciate it." He turned to Dinsmore and said, "Come on, we'll ride up along the
high trails, see if we can get lucky and pick up
some tracks.

"Any time I can help, Detective Deavers, you
let me know," Modale said. "I see lots of strange
folks come and go. Lately they're hairless with
tattooed heads," he wheezed and laughed.

"He's not a detective, you dimwit!" Dinsmore
growled at him, ignoring his words. "He's a
bounty hunter! We both are. We make our living

facing bad men, not pouring whiskey and lighting cigars!''

"You go to hell, Davis!'' Modale said, hurrying toward the tent fly as he spoke over his shoulder.

Deavers gave Dinsmore a shove to keep him from going after the saloon owner. "Come on, I think we might be onto something. One of the men with Kirkpatrick yesterday was most likely Billy Todd Carver, since Modale said they were both here in town together. We need to tighten down on Kirkpatrick and Carver. I've got a feeling they'll lead us to the rest of the gang.''

Chapter 16

An hour later, at a seldom-used rail siding outside of Rusty Nail, the two bounty hunters came upon the handcar sitting out of sight between two steep hillsides where Flannery, Carver and Cruzan had left it. They approached it with caution. "How do we know this is the same one?" Dinsmore asked, his Colt in hand, his thumb over the hammer as they put their horses forward at a walk.

"Oh, this is the same one all right," said Deavers, both of them looking around as they rode in between the hillsides, each wary of a trap. "Look around you. It's the only thing sitting here not covered with a year's worth of dust." They looked around at the dust-covered remnants of a tin mine operation. A loose corner of corrugated metal roofing chattered on a morning breeze. At the corner of a weathered building, a scraggly jackrabbit peeped around a corner at them, then looped out of sight.

At the handcar, Deavers stepped down, his gun poised. He laid a gloved hand on a damp spot on the rough plank floor as if gauging what had been sitting there. "It's been wet," he said, speculating, remembering the two covered blocks of cargo. "What do you suppose they were hauling . . . ?" He let his words trail as he rubbed his damp gloved fingers together and stared at them as if searching for clues.

"It sure as hell wasn't water lilies," Dinsmore said almost in a whisper. He looked spooked at the idea of getting caught in an ambush in a narrow space between the two hills. "I say we had better back out of here while we can."

Deavers couldn't argue. But he took the time to look down at the wagon tracks leading in beside the handcar, and leading away to a narrow switchback trail up one of the hillsides. "One of them must've pulled a wagon in here, unloaded the handcar onto it, then ridden off up into the hills. There must've been something they needed awfully bad up in Rock Springs."

"Sounds right to me," said Dinsmore, not wanting to be there. "Why don't we do the same before we get our ears shot off? This is just exactly the kind of place where a man gets killed in an ambush."

"What were they hauling that would be so wet?" said Deavers, still pondering the matter as he stepped back into his saddle and nudged his horse forward between the buckboard tracks.

"I'm not going to guess," said Dinsmore, settling some now that they were headed up toward the switchback trail. "The tracks are fresh enough we'll able to ask them in person real soon," he said. Booting his horse a little, he added, "As soon as I get in kicking range of Memphis Beck, I'm going to nail his nuts behind his navel."

They kept on the wagon trail for over two miles until the tracks swung down a long hillside thick with pine and dotted with sharp drop-offs that fell straight down over a hundred feet. "I'll say one thing for Kirkpatrick and those boys," Deavers commented. "They will travel some dangerous ground."

"In the dark too, when they came down this way," said Dinsmore. "Do you suppose they knew we were following them?"

"I don't know how they could," said Deavers. "I think they just play things close to the vest all the time. That's why they get away with so much." He nudged his horse carefully down into the thick pines. "They sure don't make themselves easy to find or follow."

Twenty minutes later, just as they had lost the wagon tracks and stopped and looked all around in bewilderment, an explosion resounded beyond a long stretch of hills lying before them. "That's them!" said Dinsmore, having to rein his horse down to keep it from rearing beneath him.

A look of revelation came to Deaver's face as he collected his frightened horse and held it in check for just a moment. "It was ice! They were hauling ice!"

"Ice? What the hell for?" Dinsmore asked, his horse skittish, struggling against the reins.

"They're cooling dynamite," said Deavers. "I'd say we're catching them right before they make a run on a bank or express car somewhere." He gigged his horse. "Come on. We'll catch them unexpected while they're busy testing their equipment. . . ."

Two miles away, in a valley a hundred yards beyond the barn, Memphis Beck put his boot down on a twenty-foot uprooted cedar that lay on its side, its upper branches still shivering from its fall. "I call that some good hot nitro," he said with a smile of satisfaction.

"If it's all that good, we could soon be owning the railroads instead of robbing them," Kirkpatrick laughed. He tipped a mug of coffee toward Soto, who stood up from examining the cedar and dusted his hands together.

"It's good," said Soto. "But the next batch will be better, stronger." He looked at Beck with a trace of a smug grin and added, "I've been out of business for a while."

"Are you saying you need some practice?" Beck asked. He nodded down at the cedar. "It doesn't look like it to me."

"Explosives are my art," said Soto. "I know when it is good, but I also know when it is perfect."

Billy Todd stepped in, looking down at the tree, and asked, "What about opening a safe? I see it's strong enough. But what's going to keep it from blowing the money all to pieces?"

"What we just used is far too powerful to use on a safe, unless we are launching it into the sky," said Soto, taking to the attention. "I knead a measured portion of this into some good stiff clay. I stick a handful of the clay on the lock and on each spot where the safe has a hinge. The compressed impact of the explosion cracks the hinges and the lock, and the door drops off. It's all very smooth and easy."

"Will we try it out first on a safe, before we go on the job, Memphis?" Carver asked, his eyes carrying the question to Beck.

Beck looked at Soto, studied his searing expression for a moment, then said, "No, not unless Suelo feels like we should. I've seen enough. This man can deliver. We're ready to do this job." He asked Soto, "How soon can you have us the new batch you're talking about, all wrapped and ready to use?"

"As soon as you have found us some good creek bank clay," Soto said. "Meanwhile, we will use this other vial, just to make sure it is all of the same consistency." He gestured toward the glass vial of clear nitroglycerin in his shirt pocket. "This time we'll blast up a large boulder."

"Pick your target and let it blow." Beck looked all around the heavily treed, rock-strewn area, and said, "I'll get somebody out looking for the clay today. Anything else we can do for you?"

"Yes, one more thing." Soto looked at Clarimonde, who stood by, silently watching, listening. Then he said firmly to Beck, "I want the house for Clair and myself. We're not staying in the barn another night."

Beck kept cool. "Sure thing," he said. "You can have the big room. There's a bed there, no springs, but you can lay a pallet there and—"

"No, no." Soto cut him short, saying, "We don't

want just the bedroom. We want the house." He grinned. "You and the men can sleep out front."

Kirkpatrick started to take a step toward him, but Beck shifted around in a way to stop him without it looking too obvious. "The house it is, then," he said. He looked at Clarimonde and said, "Ma'am, I apologize for any inconvenience we've caused you."

Clarimonde only looked down. Beck knew she had nothing to do with Soto's demands. This was just Soto flexing his muscle, seeing how far he could push. Beck knew it.

Listening to the conversation, Carver asked Beck, "Do you want me to clear out the house, move all our gear out to the barn?"

Before Beck could reply, Soto said, "That won't do. I've got everything set up in the barn. You'll have to sleep out front, under the stars." He gave Beck a superior look. "That won't be any trouble, will it?"

Beck took a deep breath, his patience starting to wear thin. "No trouble at all, Suelo. Is there *any-thing else* we can do for you?"

Deavers and Dinsmore had heard the second explosion and followed the sound to the edge of a steep ridge. With his binoculars to his eyes, Deavers scanned back and forth, hardly believing his eyes. He saw the house, the barn and the gang members standing over a broken, upturned boulder lying in a bed of loose dirt. "My goodness, Davis," he said as he watched, "we have struck the mother lode!"

"Let me see! Let me see!" Dinsmore could not contain his excitement.

"In a minute. I'm counting," said Deavers, pulling away from him without taking the binoculars down from his eyes.

"Is Memphis Beck down there?" Dinsmore asked. "That's all I want to know." He raised his eyes and pleaded to heaven, "Please let him be there."

"Oh, he's down there all right," said Deavers, recognizing Beck who stood beside Kirkpatrick, even able to see the two outlaws' lips move silently as they spoke back and forth. "There's a woman with them," he said as he continued his recognizance. He looked at the large, broken boulder. "They're playing with dynamite, it appears. Here, you can take a look now."

Dinsmore snatched the binoculars and looked down eagerly, scanning quickly until his eyes found Memphis Beck. "There he is, that dirty sumbitch! You got away from me once, Beck, but you'll never do it again."

Deavers squinted and looked down with his naked eyes while Dinsmore used the binoculars. "We've got them where we want them," he said. "Now all we have to do is figure the best way in and catch them off guard."

He'd hardly gotten the words from his mouth when he heard the sound of a gun hammer cock near his ear. The three gang members from town had followed them and slipped up behind them as quietly as ghosts. Deavers froze as English Collin Hedgepeth said to him, "First things first, gentlemen. Get your hands up in the air, and get on your feet."

As the finely dressed outlaw stepped back, he slipped Deavers' Colt from his holster and slid it down behind his gun belt. Standing over Dinsmore, Max Short smiled menacingly and did the same, lifting Dinsmore's pistol from its holster. "Shame on you, talking bad about my good friend, Memphis Warren Beck," he said.

Rising to his feet slowly, his hands up, Deavers kept himself calm and said, "Who was it put you on us, Hedgepeth?"

"Who was it, indeed," English Collin grinned. "Ordinarily I would never tell. But in this case, the saloon owner, Denver Modale, insisted I tell you it was he who informed us." He looked at Dinsmore. "What have you done to the man? He really doesn't like you. He practically begged us to kill you real slow. He offered us money."

"That sumbitch," Dinsmore murmured. "He had better hope you kill me."

"Something else he asked us to do," said Short, still grinning menacingly.

"Yeah? What's that?" Dinsmore asked.

"This," said Short. He cracked Dinsmore hard across the side of his head with his pistol barrel and let him fall.

Deavers clenched his teeth and looked up from Dinsmore to Hedgepeth. "You boys are all spit and silver, smacking around an unarmed man while you hold a gun on him. I'd like to get any one of you on even ground and see who comes out the—"

Another hard swipe of Short's gun barrel cut him off.

Standing back holding their horses, Hunt Broadwell shook his head, chuckled and smiled as Deavers crumbled backward to the dirt. "What took you so long, Max?" he asked. "I thought he'd never shut up."

"All right, then, all done here," said Collin Hedgepeth. "Let's get them up and over their saddles." He stooped to help Short grab Dinsmore and lift him off the ground. "We'll have to see what Beck wants us to do with them."

"I hope this don't keep us from getting the big job done," said Short, struggling with the knocked out bounty hunter.

"Let's try to remain optimistic, Max," said Hedgepeth, the two raising Dinsmore and plopping him over his horse's back. "The main thing now is for the three of us to get back to town and keep an eye on things. You never know what might slip in while we're away."

Chapter 17

By the time Hedgepeth, Short and Broadwell arrived at the hideout, the two bounty hunters had awakened across their saddles to find out they had been tied down firmly, their hands tied in front of them. Broadwell had tied their horses' reins together to make them easier to lead. At the edge of the front porch, out of their hearing range, Hedgepeth, Kirkpatrick and Beck stood talking.

"It was Denver Modale who told us about them," said Hedgepeth. "He used to be that one's brother-in-law. Apparently there's bad blood between them." He raised his voice enough for the two bounty hunters to hear him say, "We were offered money to kill Dinsmore real slow."

Across his saddle, Deavers said to Dinsmore, "Don't worry. It's a bluff. These boys have a reputation for having never killed anybody."

"There's a first time for everything," Dinsmore said with a worried look.

"Settle down, Davis," said Deavers. "This isn't

the first time either one of us has been knocked in the head. We'll get through it."

Looking over at the two, Beck turned back to Hedgepeth and Kirkpatrick and shook his head. "This comes at a bad time. Soto was getting ready to mix a fresh batch of explosives for the job." He considered things, then added, "But we're lucky you three found them before they got in closer with rifles. They could have held us pinned here for a long time, maybe long enough for the railroad to send in its killers."

Beside him, Kirkpatrick said, "I know this means we've got to clear out of here quick-like. But what about our nitro?" Off to the side a few feet, Soto and Clarimonde stood watching, listening; Soto realized these two bounty hunters meant trouble. He needed the money he'd been promised for this job. No one was going to stand in his way.

"Soto will have to mix it when we get to a safer place," said Beck. "Right now we've got to figure out how to get rid of these two without them getting back onto our trail. There's too much at stake here."

Soto looked at Beck with a raised brow, as if he couldn't believe what he'd heard him say.

Beck ignored Soto's look and continued talking to Hedgepeth, saying in a lowered voice, "All right, you three take them up high somewhere and leave them."

"These men are resourceful," said Kirkpatrick, expressing some doubt.

"What else can we do?" Beck asked. "We're not

killers—'' As he spoke he cut himself short, seeing Soto walk toward the two bounty hunters. "Whoa, what's he doing?" Beck said.

"What the—?" said Kirkpatrick, watching Soto reach up above Dinsmore, who lay staring wide-eyed at him.

"Soto, stop!" Beck shouted, realizing what he was doing.

But Soto ignored him. Instead, he slid the vial of nitroglycerin down into the hapless bounty hunter's back trouser pocket.

"Please! No!" Dinsmore shouted, seeing what was happening to him.

Beck and the others started to run forward to stop Soto, but it was too late. Soto slapped Dinsmore's horse soundly on its rump and shouted, "Hyiieeee!" sending both horses bolting along the narrow path toward the trail. Then Soto flung himself to the ground.

"Get down!" Beck shouted to everyone, watching Soto cover his head with both forearms.

All across the yard everybody dropped as one, and just in time. The two doomed horses made it almost thirty yards before the jarring of their hooves caused the volatile liquid to ignite. Dinsmore's scream turned into a loud blast of fire, blood, horse meat and human flesh. Soto jumped quickly to his feet in the bloody aftermath, his arms spread like a stage actor accepting applause. The grisly rain splattered down on his raised face.

From the ground, the others stared at him, stunned as chunks of meat, saddle and bone thumped upon the roof and splattered all about the yard. Soto turned toward Clarimonde and the cowering men, undaunted by the gruesome carnage falling around him. "There," he said with a bloody-faced scowl of a grin, "we have seen how it works on trees, stone and bounty hunters. What else need we do?"

The Tall Texan was the first to his feet. "This crazy, no-good son of a—"

But Beck, Collin Hedgepeth and two others caught him before he could get to Soto. "Let him go," Soto shouted at them. "If he thinks he's got to settle, we get it settled now." He reached up and knocked his hat from his tattooed head. He stood with his feet spread shoulder-length apart, a knife from his boot gripped firmly in his right hand.

"Easy now, everybody!" Beck warned, turning slowly, looking all around. The men had risen to their feet, guns in hand, blood-splattered and shaking bits of flesh and bone from their clothing. "Bloodthirsty lunatic!" a voice growled. Only Memphis Beck's hand raised toward them stopped the men from advancing on Soto. "We're not killers, Suelo!" Beck shouted at him. "You had no right jumping out on your own doing this!"

"Not killers?" Soto laughed harshly, looking back and forth at the drawn guns and the angry, blood-splattered faces. "You could have fooled me."

"You know what I mean," said Beck. "This is not the way we do things."

"Then you are all fools," Soto shouted. He pointed a bloody finger. "You do not *kill*. Yet there you stand, ready to *kill* me, for *killing* two men who came here to *kill* us if they had gotten the chance." He shook his head and said, "I think it's time we made some changes in how we do things."

"Changes?" Kirkpatrick said under his breath. "Who does this arrogant bastard think he is?"

Clarimonde stood silent, watching, listening, noting that Soto's accent had begun to slip back into his words as he spoke. She caught Beck's eyes on her, but only for a second as if to see if she was all right. Then she watched his eyes go back to Soto.

"No changes needed in how we do things, Soto," said Beck. "We don't *murder* helpless, unarmed people."

"I do," Soto said shamelessly. He stepped forward as he spoke to Beck, as if stalking him with the knife.

The men started to move forward, but Beck held them back with a raised hand. "You don't want to come at me with that pig sticker, Suelo," he said in a grave tone, standing relaxed, but his right foot poised, ready to go into a roundhouse kick.

Soto shrugged. "Oh? Why not? What do I have to fear? As you say, you are no *murderer.*" He continued advancing.

Beck measured the distance, knowing when to make his move. "But you're not *helpless*, Suelo," he said, "and certainly not *unarmed.*"

Soto stopped, and not an inch too soon. One more step would have brought a boot to his face, *nitro or not*, Beck had already told himself. "Ah, you see," Soto said, grinning again, "I do this to make a point. To show you that we all reach a place inside us where we must kill sometimes in this life we have chosen for ourselves." He lowered the big knife and held it less firmly. "How close did you just come to that place as I walked toward you?"

This smug fool . . . Beck didn't need anything pointed out to him, like some newcomer being helped along by a more experienced hand. And what was this accent all of a sudden, Beck asked himself. But upon seeing the knife go behind Soto's back and down into its sheath, he eased down. For the sake of the job he decided to let the matter drop. "I get your point," he said. He stood in silence, leaving the next move up to Soto.

Clarimonde watched, weighing the force and presence of each man.

After a moment, Soto looked all around, raised a palm and said, "It looks like it has stopped raining."

Ignoring his remark, Beck walked away toward the house. Hedgepeth stepped in and said, "Want the three of us to go back to town, keep an eye on things?"

"No," said Beck. Then turning, he said to all the men, "Get yourselves cleaned up, packed and ready to ride. We're leaving here. This place is getting too popular. Those of you splitting up, riding alone, meet us at the Pierman spread, day after tomorrow. From there we'll ride out and do 'the job.'"

"Are you going to tell us what 'the job' is yet?"
Carver asked, flipping a bit of saddle leather off
his shirtsleeve.

"Not yet, Billy Todd," said Beck, "but you're
going to be pleased, I promise."

For more than a week the ranger and Hector
Sandoval had ridden from town to town, searching for tracks to follow, asking if anyone had seen
a man and a woman traveling the hill trails. Fortu-
nately, a few people had spotted them, enough to
keep the two lawmen pointed in the right direction. Their last lead had pointed them to Rusty
Nail. If nothing else, it would be a good place to
stop, rest and care for their tired animals, Sam
told himself, stepping down out front of Modale's
Big Diamond Saloon and reading the name to
himself.

"Hector," he said, "I want you to go around
and come in the rear fly just like we're here to
make an arrest."

"All right," Hector said. He wrapped his reins
and walked away around the side of the tent.

Sam waited a few seconds, then stepped in
through the front fly. As soon as he dropped the
fly behind himself, he saw Denver Modale duck
down, scurry along the bar and head out the back
way. But then he saw him stop suddenly and
throw his hands in the air when he saw Hector
hold the rear fly to one side and point his Colt at
his round belly.

"Jumping Jehosephat! More Mexicans!" Modale shouted.

The only two customers at the bar, two teamsters, threw their hands high. "Lower them," Sam said, stepping forward, seeing Modale turn toward him, his hands coming down some but not all the way.

"Is he with you, Ranger?" Modale asked, gesturing toward Hector Sandoval, seeing the *guardia* badge on his chest.

"Yep, he's with me," said Sam. "He's Hector Sandoval, *guardia* of Valle Hermoso."

"Never heard of it, or him either," said Modale, shaking his head. "Tell me what right he has holding a gun pointed at me that way." He stared at the ranger, seeing how far he could get pushing him. "I don't like anybody covering my exit." When Sam didn't answer, he went on to say, "Far as that goes, what right have you got coming in here bullying and demanding?"

"I haven't bullied or demanded anything from you, yet, Modale," Sam said, eyeing him closely. "The last couple of times I've walked into a place that has your name out front, all I've seen is the back of your shirt on your way out. I figure covering your *exit* would keep you around long enough to say howdy."

"Well, then . . ." Modale settled down and said, "Howdy, Ranger. I reckon that didn't hurt nothing."

"No, not a thing," said Sam. He nodded for Hector to holster his gun. Then he said to Modale, "I'm looking for a man named Suelo Soto. He has a woman traveling with him, a German woman."

"Whew," said Modale, "I was afraid you were

going to ask me about Memphis Beck and his Hole-in-the-wallers."

"Why's that?" Sam asked.

"That's who everybody else is wanting to know about these days," said Modale, "even former kin of mine."

"Are Beck and his gang around here nearby?" Sam asked, already wondering if there might be a connection between Suelo Soto and the Hole-in-the-wall Gang.

"I'll say they're nearby," said Modale. "Damn near the whole gang is squatting up there somewhere in the hills. I've heard three rounds of dynamite go off this morning. I expect they're getting set to blow an express car all to hell."

Sam's mind raced. *Explosions?* He thought about the blast that Soto set off in Shadow Valley. He thought about Memphis Beck and his gang always looking for good explosives. Two and two came together quickly. "What about the man and woman? Did you see them?" He felt that he knew the answer before he asked.

"Oh yeah, I saw them," he said. "The man stood right here, tossing back shots of rye like he'd hang come morning," said Modale. "The Tall Texan and Billy Todd Carver wanted him to leave. But this fellow was sort of lording over them, if you know what I mean."

"How long ago?" Sam asked, having heard enough to know that he and Hector were on the right trail.

Two, three days ago," said Modale, scratching his beard-stubbled chin. "At daylight this morning two bounty hunters came by looking for Beck and his men. Doing my civil duty I pointed them up there." His raised a finger toward the hills. "That's all I could do."

"Who are these bounty hunters?" Sam asked.

"Neil Deavers and Davis Dinsmore," Modale said without hesitation. "Neil is a good lawman, used to be anyway. Davis Dinsmore is a skunk of the worst order. I know—I used to be married to his sister. She was as bad as he is—once tried to stab me in the eye with a two-pronged meat fork."

Sam turned to Hector and said, "Let's go. I think we've just had some good luck fall our way."

"What about the Hole-in-the-wall Gang?" Hector asked as they turned and headed out the tent fly. "Won't they be on his side?"

"That's a good possibility," said Sam. "But if I know Beck and his men, they don't hold to murder and kidnapping. Knowing the woman is with Beck and his gang gives us better odds at getting her back alive when we take Soto down." They stepped up into their saddles and rode away. Looking out from the tent fly, Modale shook his head and said, "Damn it, I ought to start charging money for all this information."

Sam and Hector found the two bounty hunters' tracks and followed them all the way to the ridgeline overlooking the vacated hideout. From there they followed circling buzzards above the valley floor. In the afternoon sunlight the two rode out of the thick pines and into the front yard, having seen from the ridge that the place sat empty. "Looks like they left in a hurry," Sam commented, noting the front door of the house standing open.

Hector eyed the circling buzzards, then gestured ahead at more of the grisly, black scavengers strewn out about the yard. "Why are they scattered out this way? I have never seen them eat like this."

Seeing three buzzards busily feeding on dark carnage atop the roof of the house, Sam quickly understood what had happened and said, "It looks like man or animal was unfortunate enough to get caught in one of the blasts Modale told us about."

"I only hope this is Suelo Soto they are eating," said Hector.

Looking all around, the two began to recognize bits of cloth and leather, blackened with blood. A boot heel lay in the dirt. Off to the left Hector saw half a saddle lying on the ground, a confused buzzard pecking at it with determination. The trunk of one of the horses lay a few yards away, being feasted upon by the hungry birds. "I've a feeling this is the remains of the two bounty hunters," he said.

The two stepped down out front of the barn and walked inside. Standing over the hole in the barn floor, Sam looked down at the wet straw and said, "They've been mixing nitroglycerin, making dynamite. Soto was in prison for killing two men. But after what happened in Shadow Valley, I expect making explosives is his trade. I can't imagine Beck and his gang having any other use for him."

"Whatever the case," Hector said with a sigh, "once again we have arrived too late, and because of it, more people have died."

Walking out of the barn, Sam looked down at the fresh tracks on the ground, heading out of the yard toward the trail. "We might've showed up late, *Guardia*, but we're closer to the woman and Soto than we've been so far. If we press Beck and his men, he just might give him up."

"Give up one of their own?" Hector asked. "Why do you think they would do such a thing?"

"Just a hunch," said Sam, swinging up into his saddle, Hector doing the same. "We've got to get Beck and find a way to talk to him, let him know the kind of man he's riding with."

PART 3

Chapter 18

Jonas Pierman looked out into the morning sunlight and saw Memphis Beck and Bowen Flannery
ride in from the north, Flannery in a buggy, a man
and woman riding along behind him on horseback. Without hesitation, the cattleman walked to
a coatrack, took down his gun belt and strapped
it on. He took down a hat and placed it on his
head, then took down a riding duster and slipped
it on as he walked out front to the hitch rail.

"Bert," he said to the silver-gray gelding standing at the rail, "I think it's time we rode up on
the grasslands, check on the hands there."

Halfway down the long path leading to the trail,
Pierman rode over close enough to touch his hat
brim toward Beck and Flannery. Then he rode on
without a word. Beck didn't bother introducing
the wary-eyed rancher to Soto and Clarimonde.
Ever since his old friend Pierman had left the outlaw life behind him, he'd wisely avoided knowing
anything about what Beck and the rest of the gang
were up to.

Once inside the large, crumbling adobe hacienda, Beck turned with his arms spread. "Ole Jonas
has the best of it right here." He gestured toward
the north across the dusty front yard. "Right out
front he's got Arizona Territory on his left, New
Mexico Territory on his right." He turned facing a
back window and gestured out toward an endless
line of jagged hills. "Out his back door he's got Old
Mexico as far as the eye can see."

"Right now it all looks like more sand and cactus to me," Flannery said, slapping his dusty
gloved hand against his thigh. Then he eyed Beck
craftily. "But I take it the job is somewhere out
the front door, eh?"

Beck smiled and put him off, saying, "As soon
as the others all get here, I'll tell everybody at
once where we're headed and what we're going
to do there."

Flannery started to ask more, but Soto cut in.
"We have to get the explosives out of the buggy
and out of the heat, before the clay starts to
stiffen." He looked out the back window toward
an adobe spring house sitting at the edge of a thin
stream. "That should be a good place to store it
overnight." He motioned to Flannery. "Come help
me unload it."

Flannery only stared at him coldly.

"Let's give him a hand, Bowen," Beck said,
stepping in and keeping his words between Flannery and himself. "You've got to help me keep
things pulled together until we see this job
through."

As the three men unloaded the buggy and carried crates of the nitro-absorbed clay into the dark coolness of a weathered spring house, Beck managed to walk in close to Clarimonde and say almost in a whisper, "I hope you know everything you need to about making this stuff. I'm going to be needing somebody I can count on." He gave her a look that told her Suelo Soto wasn't going to be around much longer.

She felt a warm breath of relief move through her, yet she remained cautious about what she said. "I've learned everything he wanted me to learn," she said quietly.

Beck smiled faintly and kept walking.

Throughout the afternoon and into the night, the rest of the gang arrived, both singly and in pairs. The last to come riding along the path from the main trail at a fast gallop was Dave Arken. Sliding his horse to a halt at the hitch rail, he jumped down and said, "I could have sworn I was being tailed the last few miles coming in. It was plumb spooky. I thought it best if I swung wide a few miles from here and tried to shake whoever it was." He looked back again warily as he spoke. Then he turned back to Beck and said, "Anyway, here I am."

Beck also looked back toward the trail. Earlier he'd felt that same feeling of being watched that he'd had the night at the hideout. *Nerves . . . ?* he asked himself. He considered it for a moment, but then he dismissed the matter entirely and said, "Come on in, Dave. Get yourself a cup of coffee. I'll send out a couple of guards as soon as I tell everybody what we're going to do."

Inside the house, while the men gathered restlessly to hear what Beck had to say, Soto sent Clarimonde to wait out on the front porch. But seeing her turn to leave, Beck said, "She can stay."

"I say she cannot," said Soto, stepping up, facing Beck. "She is with me. She does as I tell her."

"You brought her in," said Beck. "You said she helps you mix the explosives. As far as I'm concerned she's done her share. That makes her a part of this operation."

"It's always been that way," Collin Hedgepeth said in support. "Everybody who puts in, *is* in."

Soto felt the others staring coldly at him, forcing him to back down. This was not the time to cause trouble, knowing they were all still angry at him for killing the unarmed bounty hunters. Spreading his hands, he said, "All right, she can stay." But as he sat down, Clarimonde felt his eyes upon her, and she knew that Soto would not forget this.

"Miss Clair, please have a seat, ma'am," said Beck, with authority. "We all appreciate the fine job you and Suelo have done for us." As he spoke, Beck flipped open a wooden crate full of long, empty rawhide pouches.

She knew what Beck had just done was to let Soto know that he had no voice or power in the gang. She also realized Beck was telling her that he'd had enough of Soto's belligerent manner, and now that he had the explosives he needed to do the job, Soto had better walk softly. This was Beck extending his hand to her. Was it time she took it? Yes, she believed it was, she told herself, relaxing down onto a comfortable leather ottoman among the men, avoiding Soto's searing stare.

When the meeting was over and the men had stood up and drifted away into ones and twos, Clarimonde made it a point to stay close to Beck. She did not want to be left alone with Soto after what had taken place. Even though she'd had nothing to do with any of it, she knew how ruthless and deadly he could get in the blink of an eye. She felt relieved to hear Beck tell everyone that tonight, for security's sake, they would all bed down in the large main room.

"Nobody but the trail guard leaves this group tonight. If this job gets discovered, we'll all know it didn't come from anybody here," he'd said in ending. His words had been a godsend to Clarimonde. She shuddered at the thought of what dark promise lay in Soto's eyes, were the two of them left by themselves.

"Whoo-ieee," said Dave Arken to Bowen Flannery and Earl Caplan, as Clarimonde walked past them to be closer to Beck's side. "I'm afraid this might be more unstamped Mexican gold coins than I can carry." He hefted a handful of the long, rawhide pouches that had been handed out from the wooden crate.

Earl Caplan smiled devilishly. "If it's too much for you, Dave, I'll be honored to help you carry it." He also held a handful of rawhide pouches to be loaded with gold coins from the train robbery.

"What always amazes me," said Flannery, "is

how does Memphis get this kind of information?"
He gave a bewildered shrug. "How does an American railroad sell minted gold to the Mexican government?"

Hearing part of the conversation, Beck stepped over, saying, "Who else has the means of brokering such a deal? The railroad has the means of transporting this sort of shipment. They can ship it right over onto the Mexican rails without being questioned."

"But how can the Mexican government pay for something like this?" Flannery asked. "They can't afford roads. They can't provide for their people."

"But even the poorest government always finds ways to deal in gold," said Beck. "It's a fact of life."

"Yeah," said Caplan, "besides, it ain't the Mexican government paying for it. The Germans are the ones holding the purse strings down here. You can bet they've figured themselves a cut off the top. That's why the coins haven't been stamped, right, Memphis?"

Beck only shrugged. "I'm not a politician. I'm a thief."

"What's the difference?" Billy Todd Carver asked with a laugh.

"I'm told there's a difference," said Beck, "but I've never seen it."

"Don't insult a thief like Memphis Beck by calling him a politician!" Kirkpatrick replied with a chuckle.

"Forget all that," Flannery chuckled. "I want

to know how you get this kind of information, Memphis Beck. I'm beginning to fear you are some sort of mystic."

"Don't lose sleep worrying about it," said Beck. "It might make you too tired to tote your gold when the time comes."

"Good point," said Flannery. He pulled a silver flask from inside his dark suit coat, twisted the top free and held it out toward Beck. "Indulge yourself, sir. This whiskey is distilled from a recipe handed down by my dear Irish forefathers."

"Obliged, but no thanks," said Beck. "I'm going to sit guard on the trail tonight. Your forefathers' recipe could knock out a field ox."

Dave Arken cut in, "Go ahead, Memphis. I'll guard the trail tonight."

"No, Dave, that wouldn't be fair to you," said Beck. "You're always sitting guard while the rest of us get our sleep."

Even as he protested, Beck had been hoping someone might volunteer for the job tonight. He'd wanted to stay close to the woman tonight in case Soto tried anything against her. He realized he'd put her on a bit of a spot, but there was no other way to ever let her know that he was on her side, except present it to her in Soto's face, the way he just did, and hope she believed him.

"It's fair to me," said Arken. "I like being up on the hills alone. It makes me feel peaceful."

"Are you sure?" Beck asked.

"Sure I'm sure." Arken grinned. "I wouldn't offer if I didn't mean it."

"Then here's to us, and to a railroad as crooked as we are!" Beck said, taking the flask and tossing back a sip.

"Here here," said the men in unison.

As soon as Beck had taken the sip of whiskey, Dave Arken stepped away to the door, and said over his shoulder as he shook the stack of rawhide pouches in his hand, "Sweet dreams everybody. See you all in the morning, when we head out to go fill these things."

Stepping over to the open doorway, Bowen Flannery watched the good-natured train robber ride away along the moonlit trail. "Dave never shut a door behind himself in his life," said Flannery, taking the doorknob and pushing the door shut.

A hundred yards into the purple darkness, Arken veered his horse off the trail. Taking a grown-over path leading up into a broken hillside, he followed it up through a maze of deeply sunken boulders and jagged cliff drop-offs. At a place a half mile below the crest, he stopped and looked down in the moonlight, seeing Pierman's hacienda in one direction and in the other direction the shadowy main trail snaking away toward the border.

He had traveled as silently as a ghost; when he stepped from his saddle to take a position overlooking the trail, he froze at the faintest sound of a hoof scraping a rock on a ledge below him.

Crouching, drawing his rifle, Arken eased over to the edge of a sharp drop-off, lay down on his belly and crawled forward enough to look below. Twenty feet straight down, in a thin slice of moonlight he saw the ears of a mule twitch. Beside it he could barely make out the dark silhouettes of three more mules huddled together beside a scrub cedar. He had no idea who was down there, or why, but he knew that Memphis Beck and the others had to be told, and told quickly.

Carefully he pushed himself back from the edge with his hands. But as he did so, the edge of the cliff broke beneath his hand. Dropping his rifle, he grabbed with his free hand to catch his weight and keep from falling forward. But more of the edge broke. "Oh no!" he managed to whisper. "Why me?" Then he felt himself tumble downward among loose dirt and rock, and land with a hard grunt on his back, only a few yards from the mules.

Struggling to catch his breath and rise onto his knees, he saw dark figures dressed in white step forward out of the greater darkness, some with their face hidden by wide-brimmed sombreros, one of them hatless, moonlight glistening on his shaved head. Arken saw machetes hanging from their hands as he tried to catch his breath.

"You fellows . . . are making a . . . big mistake," he gasped in a halting voice, seeing them close in around him, silently, deliberately—terrible apparitions unaffected by time. He fumbled with his holster, finding it had been emptied by his fall. He wanted to shout and warn Beck and the others, but there was not enough breath in him to make it happen.

"Well . . . damn you . . . make it fast," Arken managed to say, seeing the machetes rise above their heads in a flash of pale moonlight, knowing there was nothing he could do to stop them.

Chapter 19

In the night, Beck had awakened with a start, its cause he did not know. But upon opening his eyes, he looked across the sleeping forms strewn about on the floor. Everyone, including the woman, lay wrapped in blankets, sound asleep. The exception was Soto, who sat in the glow of the hearth, staring straight at him. He wore a cold, thin smile that hinted of his having something to do with Beck's sharp awakening.

Standing, Soto said, "Did someone just step over your grave?"

Beck only stared at him for a moment, then said, "If they did, they were wise enough to keep walking."

"Good one," said Soto, nodding. "I'll have to remember that answer." Standing he said, "I'll go get some wood for the fire?"

"Tell me something," Beck said, keeping his voice lowered as Soto weaved his steps through the sleepers lying about on the floor. "Why is it sometimes I hear an accent when you talk and other times I don't?"

"I have no idea why you hear whatever you hear," Soto said smugly, without stopping.

Beck stood also as if poised for anything as Soto walked past the woman who slept on a long, battered sofa in the middle of the room. "You and I are never going to be friends, are we, Suelo?"

Soto stopped at the door with his hand on the knob and said, "Is it that important to you that we are?" He smiled coldly again. "Or is it better that we remain business associates and become rich together?"

"I can live with that," said Beck, easing to a window and looking out as Soto stepped down off the porch, picked up two fire logs, turned and came back inside.

"See, I came back, all done," Soto said, stepping through the sleepers atop the hearth and laying the logs into the fire quietly.

"For us to become friends before riding out on this big job tomorrow, you'd have to give me that rifle in your arms, and let yourself go soundly to sleep," said Soto, "instead of catnapping with your hand wrapped around the gun stock. I would consider that a true act of trust, worthy of my friendship."

"Good night, Suelo," Beck said, as if not giving Soto's suggestion a second thought.

Three hours later as the first wreath of sunlight spread along the hill line, Beck stood up and walked out onto the front porch, hearing the sound of hoofbeats moving along the trail toward the house. "Wake up back there," he said over his shoulder. "We've got a rider coming! Dave gave us no signal."

Flannery hurried to his feet and to the door first, his Colt in hand. "Somebody slipped past Arken?"

"Unless it is Arken," said Carver, right behind Flannery, followed by Kirkpatrick.

"It's not Arken," said Beck. "Dave always rides straight in. Whoever this is keeps stopping."

"Wait," said Carver, straining his eyes into the grainy morning gloom. "That's Dave's roan horse, sure enough!"

They all watched the riderless horse move into sight, then stop and lower its muzzle to pick at a clump of trailside grass. "But no Dave," said Beck. He stared at the horse warily, then said over his shoulder, "Keep me covered."

Stepping down and hurrying forward, Beck retrieved the big roan and led it back to the hitch rail. Having looked out along the trail and seeing no one, he said, "All clear," and looked the animal over thoroughly for any sign of blood or foul play.

"The horse is fine," Kirkpatrick commented. He looked off toward the gray swirl adrift along the hilltops. "I never knew Dave to slip a saddle. Something's gone wrong up there."

"I'm going up," said Flannery. He stepped over and picked up his saddle he'd slung over the porch rail the night before.

As he stepped down to the horses that had been grained and watered and spent the night at the hitch rail, Beck called out, "We're all riding up there. If something's gone wrong up there, it'll be time we skin out of here anyway."

The whole group, ten men and the woman, rode up along the hill trail, following Arken's tracks in the first light of morning. At the spot where Dave had fallen, Carver eased down onto his belly, crawled forward and looked down. "Oh no," he said, staring down at the dismembered corpse lying in a bloody heap, the next level down, partly hidden amid a stand of low juniper.

"What is it, Billy Todd?" Flannery asked, seeing the look on Carver's face.

"It's Dave, the poor sumbitch," said Carver. "At least, the face looks like it might be his."

"I'm coming," said Beck. Having led Arken's horse back up into the hills with them, he passed the reins to Flannery, then stooped down and started to crawl out toward the broken edge. But Carver waved him back.

"This ledge ain't safe out here, Memphis," he said, his voice stricken with grief. "Ride down to the hillside and find a way to him. We can't leave one of our own lying here like this."

For the next half hour the riders searched until they found a thin path leading around the hillside to the ledge where Arken's chopped up body lay, piled out of sight in a juniper thicket. The men carried the body out one piece at a time and laid them loosely together on the dirt path. Standing over the gruesome remains, Beck said, "Whoever did this never meant for us to find his body. Luckily, you spotted it looking down from up there, Billy Todd," he said to Carver.

"He was a good-natured ole boy," Carver said, looking down, shaking his head. "Never harmed nobody."

"Yeah, I know," said Beck, "and to think I let him go and take my place."

"Don't blame yourself for this, Memphis," said Flannery. "Dave asked to take your place. Neither he nor you saw anything like this coming." He dropped the saddle and bridle from Arken's roan horse and slapped it on its rump, setting the animal free. As the horse trotted away and turned to the trail leading down to the hacienda, Flannery looked all around, seeing no sign of tracks, animal or man, in the dirt or along the rocky path. "What kind of craven devil does something like this and doesn't so much as leave its tracks in the earth?"

"Only something not *from this earth*," Cruzan said with a look of terror. He looked all around frantically. "I've heard of some awful things in these hills, things that ain't human."

"Stop it, Cruz," said Flannery. "Whoever did this to Arken is as human as you and me. Maybe they'd like for you to think they're not human." His eyes went to Soto accusingly. "That's the way they wield power over a bunch of scared, ignorant dirt farmers. But they're not devils. You'll see that if we can get our gun sights on them."

"You keep looking at me," Soto said coolly to Flannery. "Is there something you've got on your mind? Are you blaming me for this?" As he spoke, his hand brushed back across his gun butt and poised there.

There it was, Beck noted, listening closely to

Soto, hearing that slightest trace of an accent creeping into his voice.

"Yeah, I've got something to say," Flannery replied, his left hand answering Soto's challenge by sweeping back his lapel and revealing a big Colt in a shoulder harness up under his arm. His right hand lay poised and ready across his flat stomach.

"Get it said," Soto demanded.

"In all the years that there's been a Hole-in-the-wall Gang, there's never been an innocent person killed, and we've never lost one of our own," Flannery said. "Now that you're here, we've done both inside of two days. You're damn right I'm blaming you."

"Hold it, both of you. This is not the time or the place!" Beck said, not wanting anything to interfere with their plans. "We don't know who did this, and we don't know who could be on our back trail right now. One gunshot and this whole operation is off. Is that what you want, Flannery?" He looked all around at the grim faces. "Is that what any of you want? I know it's not what Dave would have wanted."

While the men spoke back and forth, Clarimonde spotted the butt of Arken's Colt lying half-hidden in the low-lying juniper thicket. She inched over to it, stooped and picked it up. Before anyone could notice her, she'd hidden the Colt beneath her serape, stepped back and breathed a sigh of relief. Whatever happened, she was no longer defenseless.

Settling the two men for the time being, Beck said to everyone, "Whatever differences any of us have right now, it's time to put them away. We've got to get Dave into the ground and get out of here. It's a long, hard ride to where we're headed."

As the men loaded the severed remains of Dave Arken into two blankets and hauled them around the hillside to a softer bed of ground, Clarimonde sidled her horse over to Memphis Beck and whispered between the two of them, "He did it. I know he did."

"Oh? What makes you say that?" Beck stared ahead, but listened.

Glancing back first and seeing Soto looking away across the rugged hills, she said, "He has talked about commanding demons from his cult following him ever since he killed Nate Ransdale, the fellow who helped him escape. I thought it was just his raving madness at first, but after seeing what happened to your man, I know it's true. His demons are tracking us. Suelo Soto is pure evil, no less so than the devil himself. You must get rid of him."

Still staring ahead, Beck said coolly, "I've got one little problem with getting rid of him." As he continued he turned a questioning gaze her way. "Once he's gone, who's going to handle explosives for us?"

She understood what he was asking. Having already given the matter much thought, she swallowed a dry knot in her throat and said, "I will."

Beck allowed himself a hint of a smile. "Have you studied everything? Do you know what he knows? Can you do what he does?"

Without mentioning that she'd only watched Soto go through the process twice, she said, "I know how to make the nitroglycerin, and I can combine it with the clay."

"Are you certain?" Beck asked.

"I am certain," said Clarimonde. "I am the one who mixed the batch we tested. I mixed the batch we're getting ready to use."

"Good enough," said Beck. "I'll get you a pencil and some paper. You can write it all down for me. I'll look it over."

"I'm sorry to have wasted your time, Mr. Beck," Clarimonde said coldly. "I didn't realize that you thought me a fool. With the process on paper, you would have no further need of me." She started to jerk the big paint horse away from his side.

"Whoa, ma'am," said Beck, grabbing the horse's bridle and pulling it back beside him. "I was only testing you. I apologize."

Clarimonde eased down and took a deep breath. Keeping the big paint horse beside him, she asked, "Well, did I pass your test?"

"Yep," said Beck, still looking straight ahead. "Help me get us through this big job. I realize that getting Soto out of prison was a mistake, no matter how badly I need an explosives man. Once this is over, he's gone. If you can do the job, it's yours."

Pushing on through the night, the ranger and Hector arrived at the Pierman spread so close behind Beck and his men that they poured themselves a cup of coffee that had been left on the cooling potbellied stove. "I say an hour at the most," Sam estimated, after picking up a thin, black cigar from an ashtray, and checking the burned tip for warmth and the rear for moisture.

Hector sipped his coffee with a tired smile of satisfaction. "Then why are we stopping? We haven't a minute to lose."

"We'll lose more than a *minute* if we don't feed and rest our horses," Sam pointed out.

"Yes, you are right," said Hector, rubbing his face as he began to feel the weight of the long hours in the saddle, and the effect it had started having on his judgment. "I will go attend the horses."

"No, I'll attend the horses," Sam replied. Noting the haggard look on Hector's face, he said, "It won't hurt for you to slow down long enough to get a meal in your belly and close your eyes for a while."

"*Sí*, perhaps I will, just for a minute," said Hector, slumping down onto a large, cushioned chair.

While the young *guardia* sat with his eyes closed, the ranger stepped over, took the coffee mug from his hand and set it on a nearby table. Then, he walked outside and led their horses to a water trough where he let the animals drink their fill as he searched and found grain for them inside a feed bin beside the barn.

Seeing the big, bareback roan milling shyly at the side of the hacienda, Sam walked over slowly with a handful of grain and held it out. "Come on, fellow, don't be bashful," he coaxed. "I can tell you're hungry."

The horse nosed forward. Sensing no danger, he nibbled hungrily at the grain as Sam looked him over thoroughly, trying to picture the animal's circumstances. "Why'd they leave you behind, fellow?" he asked. "Good horses being as scarce as they are out here." He looked out along the trail—the direction the horse had ridden in from—and up along the hill line. They had lost a man up there, he deduced. Somewhere beyond the hills Beck and his gang were riding toward a robbery of some sort. They had lost a man and turned his horse loose. *Why else was this animal not in a corral*, he asked himself. "No reason . . . ," he replied under his breath, rubbing the roan's neck as it munched the grain from his hand.

Suddenly the roan reared its head and nickered low, looking past the ranger's shoulder toward the hacienda. Sam spun around, his Colt coming up from its holster. But he saw nothing. Then, as he scanned both sides of the wide adobe house, through the open front door he caught sight of two ghostly white figures moving across the room and out of sight, toward the chair where Hector sat sleeping.

Running fast, the ranger sprang up onto the porch and through the open front door. With no regard for his own safety, he raced into the hacienda, his Colt up and cocked, in time to see two figures look toward him from where they stood over Hector, machetes raised high in the air. They stood hatless, their shaved heads covered with strangely colorful tattoos.

As soon as Sam's Colt exploded, one figure flew

backward onto the stone hearth. Hearing Hector's Colt explode from the chair where he sat, Sam saw the other figure spin upward and away, his machete flying from his hand.

"Hector, are you all right?" Sam called out as he spun in place, his smoking Colt scanning the room until he saw there were no more strange-looking figures in white ready to spring out on them.

"*Sí!* I'm all right." Hector jumped up from the chair, his Colt also smoking. Sam saw the worried look on his face as the young lawman sided over to him quickly, half-crouched. "We must get out of here, fast," Hector said, looking all around, then down at the two bodies. "There are more of them!" He crossed himself as he backed toward the open front door.

"Who are these people?" Sam asked, reaching down to grab one body by its shirt collar and drag it out onto the porch.

"They are demons, from the cult of Satan's Brothers," said Hector, calming down enough to drag the other body out, his Colt still cocked and smoking as he did so. "They are Suelo Soto's protectors—you can count on it."

The two stepped down from the porch and spread out, putting a few feet of space between them, covering each other as they made their way to the horses. At the hitch rail, out in the open, Hector calmed down, looking all around the wide-open front yard. "Come," he said. "We will get out onto the open trail. I do not like being at close quarters with these demons and the evil they embody."

Chapter 20

Fifteen miles south of the Mexican border, the seven-car train began a long climb up a steep hillside. The peak of the long hill had been blasted and parted into a deep V, allowing trains to taper down to level ground on their journey before traveling down the other side. Of the seven cars behind the smoke-bellowing engine, only three were legitimate.

The car following the engine carried the cargo of gold unstamped coins. The car behind it carried thirty well-armed Mexican soldiers. The car behind the troops carried a group of Mexican officers, and three German government officials. The other three cars and caboose were merely decoys to detract any public attention from the train's valuable cargo. But Memphis Beck and his gang were not detracted. They waited and watched the train intently.

Near the top of the steep uphill grade, Beck caught the first glimpse of the train rolling into sight beneath a bellowing wreath of gray smoke.

"Here it comes. Get ready, gentlemen," he said to Collin Hedgepeth and Earl Caplan, who set their horses beside him.

"Ready here," Caplan replied.

"And here," said Hedgepeth.

Looking up at the top of the hill, Beck murmured under his breath, "Soto, you had better be as good as you think you are."

The three pulled their bandannas up to cover their faces and nudged their horses forward onto the brush-covered side of the grade. Beck rode at the lead, judging how long before the train rolled along beside them, how much more the steep hillside would have slowed it down by then. Behind him Hedgepeth tugged his shiny derby hat down firmly and said, "I'm starting to get too old for this part of a job. I think next time some younger man should have a go at it."

"Next time, all right," said Beck, "but this time you're the one pulling the pin. We're all counting on you."

"Don't start with your worrying, English," said Caplan behind his bandanna mask. "I hate it when you start doubting yourself."

"I'm not doubting myself," said Hedgepeth. "I'm merely stating a point."

"Point taken," Beck said idly over his shoulder. "Now, spread out."

The three separated along the rails, Caplan riding higher up the grade away from the other two, Beck and Hedgepeth lingering near the cover of brush until the ever-slowing train began chugging along with much effort.

Inside the officers' car, one of the Germans raised a curtain just enough to glance out into the harsh sunlight. Then he dropped the curtain and said to the others, "We have nearly halted, Captain Guzman."

"It is a long, steep grade, this one," said a thin, young Mexican captain seated at a table set for breakfast. He sipped coffee from a floral, hand-painted mug. "But after this one we will be on much flatter land for most of the day."

"These excavations and new rail services are proof of Germany's commitment to a lasting friendship with your government," the other German dignitary took the opportunity to remind the Mexican officers.

"*Sí*," the young captain said in acknowledgment, "and as my uncle, Generalissimo Matissmo, has instructed me to say, sharing this gold with you is our way of saying *gracias*."

"I have a question of concern," said the other German, touching a white linen napkin to his wide, sweeping mustache. "With all of the armed guards we have aboard, why is it we have none posted atop the cars, or anywhere outside?"

"It is the generalissimo's idea, and a wise one to be sure," the captain said, tapping his forehead. "Why bring attention to what we are doing?" He grinned and added half jokingly, "The gold is *inside*! What better place to have my men guarding it?"

The German didn't see the humor in it. He frowned and gave the captain an icy stare.

But before he could comment, his fellow official,

Herr Steinven, said to the captain, "You must excuse Herr Frunhiem. It is a tendency of our government to be overprotective in matters of this nature. Perhaps we can learn something from your people in this regard." He gave the other German a searing look. "Eh, Herr Frunhiem?"

"I must admit it is true," Herr Frunhiem said, catching his comrade's subtle reprimand. "Forgive me my meticulous ways. I know that you and your generalissimo are far more familiar with your land and your people than I."

Sipping his coffee, the captain shrugged and said, "I commend you for your concern and close attention. But along this line there is never any trouble. The first thing the generalissimo did when he took power was start hanging banditos." He smiled. "Unlike our *americano* neighbors, our rails are safe." He raised his coffee cup as if in salute. "I say let them have their robbers and desperados. Here, we have no Jesse James, no Warren Beck. Here we know how to keep the gold in the proper hands."

Herr Frunhiem moved back and forth in his seat, his hands holding on to the table edge.

"Is there something wrong, Herr Frun—"

"Are we moving backward?" Frunhiem asked, cutting him off.

"Backward?" Captain Guzman sat with a baffled look on his face for a moment. But then reality snapped on in his head and he jumped to his feet and threw up a window curtain.

"Yes, *backward*, you fool!" shouted Stienven, both he and Frunhiem springing up from the table, jerking linen napkins from the front of their suits.

"Guards! See what is going on!" Guzman shouted over his shoulder, sticking his head out the window and seeing the engine and the gold car far ahead of them, chugging on, closing the gap to the top of the hill.

"What's going on?" Stenhiem raged out of control. "We are going *backward*, you uncivilized monkey! Do you have to ask?"

Without being ordered, two guards ran out onto the car's platform. One grabbed the iron brake wheel and, turning it frantically, tightened it down, hearing the metal on metal screeching sound beneath their feet. From the rear door of the troop car in front of them, young soldiers spilled out onto the platform and began turning the brake wheel on their car. The engineless train began to slow, but not much as the gravity of the steep grade pulled them downward.

In the engine, his Colt in hand, covering the engineer and fireman, Earl Caplan looked back at the severed train and chuckled beneath his bandanna. "If it gets easier than this, I'm giving it up." Then, turning back to the firemen who stood bent over a pile of firewood, he said, "Keep stoking! Keep her roaring!"

The sweaty face of the Mexican fireman turned up to him without stopping, his hand cramming chunk upon chunk of firewood into the open boiler door. "I'm afraid she will blow up if I keep stoking!" he said in Spanish.

Caplan looked ahead, seeing the gap closing

toward the deep cut in the top of the hill. "Keep stoking!" he repeated, waving the Colt. Alongside the engine, he saw Beck and Hedgepeth wave to him as their horses pulled away, running up the grade ahead of the engine and its single car. Once into the belly of the deep cut in the hilltop, the two nudged their horses up a thin path until they could look down on the train.

Beck's job had been to race alongside, leading Hedgepeth's horse until the pen had been pulled and the coupling opened between cars. Then he'd sidled in close enough for Hedgepeth to step down from the platform and back into his saddle.

"All right, English," said Beck, slowing to a halt atop the hill. He pulled his bandanna down from his face as he spoke. "Next time we'll get one of the younger men to do your part."

"Nonsense," Hedgepeth laughed, also pulling his bandanna down. "I have this part refined to an art form. Who else could do this as well as I?" He set his derby at a haughty angle atop his head and smoothed his hair back beneath the brim.

"That's what I thought," said Beck, gazing up toward the deep cut in the hilltop as the engine and the gold car approached it. "Get ready, Soto," he murmured to himself.

On the lower half of the grade, the severed cars had screeched and ground, and managed to all but come to a halt. Soldiers leaped to the ground and threw the iron wedging chocks under the wheels. The wedges scooted along loudly for a few yards, then brought the train to a jolting halt. Beck and Hedgepeth watched the doors to the stock car swing open and a loading platform drop to the ground.

"Come on. It's time we got farther back from here," Beck said, looking fifty yards to their left and across the deep cut to where Soto waved an arm back and forth, signaling that he lit a long length of dynamite cord that reached down into the rocky hillside above the tracks. "It's all up to our new explosives expert now."

A half mile inside the deeply cut hilltop, the rest of the gang waited restlessly on horseback. Seeing the two ride toward them, smoke from the engine's stack puffing and bellowing behind them, Kirkpatrick stood up in a buckboard, half-loaded with heavy rocks. Joyously, he said, "Here they come, and not a single shot fired!" Behind the buckboard, his big dun horse stood with its reins hitched to the tailgate.

No sooner had the Tall Texan said the words than a blast shook the ground beneath them, causing their horses to spook and have to be settled. Behind Beck and Flannery, the engine with its one car rolled along quickly, steam hissing from its overtaxed fittings. Behind the engine and the express car, a wide belch of rock, dust and smoke shot straight up toward heaven and folded back over itself into a mushroom head.

"Whoa!" said Cruzan, staring up as if in awe. "I don't think we'll have to worry about the *federales* getting through that for a while."

"Right you are, Cruz," said Kirkpatrick, standing, holding the reins taught on the two nervous

buckboard horses. "But let's not get full of ourselves. We need to work fast while we can."

Beck and Flannery had veered their horses off
the tracks, allowing the train to finish coming to
a halt. As soon as the rest of the gang had gathered around them beside the express car door,
Beck pulled his mask back into place and banged
on the door with his rifle butt. "Open up quickly.
There's been an explosion!" he called out in perfect Spanish.

The gang waited tensely, hearing bolts thrown
open on the inside of the door and a voice of a
soldier reply in the same language, "We felt it.
What was it . . . ?" His words trailed to a halt as
he slid the door open and he and three other
guards stared down at the guns pointed up at
them.

"Lay down the rifles!" Beck demanded, seeing
one soldier start to instinctively raise his rifle to
his shoulder. As the soldiers hurriedly followed
his order, Beck called out, "Step down! Hurry it
up!"

Jumping to the ground, Beck and the others
pushed them along. "Keep moving! Walk toward
the smoke. Don't look back," Carver said, watching them trudge along, still uncertain of what
had happened.

"So far so good," Beck said, stepping out of the
way as Kirkpatrick pulled the wagon load of rocks
in beside the open express car door. "Where's
Soto?" He looked around in time to see Soto ride
up, slide his horse to a halt, and step over onto
the buckboard and into the car, a coil of blasting

cord over one shoulder and a canvas backpack hanging from the other.

"How did the blast go?" Beck asked as Soto rolled the pack off his shoulder and set it on the floor.

"It went perfect. The mixture was hot, just as I meant for it to be," Soto said matter-of-factly. "They won't be riding up through the cut. It will take a crew of rail hands days to reopen this route."

Beck looked at Flannery with a slight smile. "Real good," he said. They watched as Soto opened the pack and took out six palm-sized balls of pliable clay, each wrapped in its individual piece of moist canvas. He picked up two of the balls.

"Bring two more," he said to Beck, gesturing toward the four bundles of canvas. Looking at Clarimonde, who stood among the men who had gathered in the open door, he said, "Light a cigar. Keep it glowing for me."

Clarimonde gave Beck a glance, then did as Soto had ordered her, seeing Beck pick up two of the balls and follow Soto to one end of the car.

Beck stood holding the two balls and watched as Soto examined the large, flat door of a safe built into the width and height of the express car. Shaking his head as he ran a hand over the smooth, thick metal, he stuck one of the balls of clay three feet up from the lower edge of the door, and pressed it as deeply as he could into the crack.

"What fools they are," he said. "They build it bigger and thicker, yet they still build it the same." He unwrapped the other ball, reached up, placed it the same distance down from the upper-right corner of the door and pressed it in the same manner.

Beck watched intently. This part he could do—this part he had done countless times. He looked around at Clarimonde as she moved forward, puffing on a thin, black cigar. She returned his knowing look and stood quietly as Soto turned to Beck and took the two balls he'd carried for him. "Want me to get the other two?" Beck asked as Soto turned back to the door.

"No," said Soto, "I won't need them. I brought them just in case these fools might have engineered something more difficult. I should have known better."

Beck nodded and looked at Kirkpatrick, who had stepped in beside him, waiting restlessly, a long iron pry bar in his hand.

When Soto had flattened the four balls of nitro-infused clay into place, he cut four short lengths of cord and stuck their ends deep inside, squeezing the clay carefully around them. He then tied the four ends to the end of the coil on his shoulder and began stringing it out toward the door as the others hurriedly stepped out onto the buckboard.

Soto didn't leave the car. Instead, he reached out the door to Clarimonde, took the cigar from her and stuck it in his mouth. He cut the end of the long cord from the coil on his shoulder, placed the other two balls into the pack and passed the pack out the door to Flannery.

"Aren't you getting out?" Beck asked, standing

beside Clarimonde as he watched Soto stick the glowing end of the cigar to the cord.

"No, I will stay here and watch. I want to see the instant of ignition." As the cord sizzled along the express car floor, Soto crouched low but kept his eyes on the thick metal door of the safe.

Kirkpatrick held the buckboard team steady. The men on the ground held their horses' reins in the same manner.

When the explosion went off, the entire car shuddered as the big metal door seemed to launch itself off the front of the huge built-in safe in a swirl of fire.

Soto saw the big door rock back and forth on the express car floor, the weight of it causing the car to sway from side to side until it settled. *"Perfecto,"* he whispered to himself.

Stepping in beside Soto, Beck fanned his hat back and forth. Seeing the safe door lying smoking on the floor, he called out, "All right, it's blown. Everybody get your pouches and saddlebags loaded and let's get out of here."

Chapter 21

As the rest of the gang hurried up across the buckboard and into the express car, saddlebags over their shoulders, Kirkpatrick climbed down to the ground and waited until everyone was inside. Then he led the wagon horses a few feet away, wrapped the traces loosely around an iron rail on the side of the seat and walked back to untie his big dun from the tailgate. Walking to the front again, he slapped the left horse soundly with a foot-long riding quirt.

"Hyiieeee!" he shouted, stepping back as the two horses bolted forward along the tracks. He watched them until they cleared the cut and veered off across the flatlands, toward a hill line three miles away. "There you go, Matissmo. You and your *federales* chase that," he said aloud to himself.

Looking along the tracks he saw the freed engineer and fireman walking back toward the cloud of smoke and Earl Caplan hurrying toward the express car. "You had better run, Earl. I'll bag it all up and not leave you squat." With a laugh he jerked his rawhide pouches from his saddlebags, hitched his horse quickly to the express car and climbed inside.

Gathered around the open front of the safe, the men filled their rawhide bags quickly. Beck had known from the start that no matter how many of the coins he and his gang bagged and packed away, there would still be a fortune in gold left behind. Seeing Carver stuff pouch after pouch inside his saddlebags laid out on the floor, Beck warned him, "Don't get too greedy, Billy Todd. If you can't carry it, what good will it do you?"

"Oh, I'm going to carry it, Memphis!" Carver said with a grin and a gleam in his eyes. "Don't you doubt that for a minute." He squatted down, hefted the saddlebags over his shoulder and struggled to his feet. His legs wobbled as he walked to the door and let the bags fall off to the ground. Then he hurried down, brought his horse over, and stooped down to do the same thing over again.

"Everybody get finished up," Beck warned, taking his watch from his vest and checking it.

"What about you, Memphis?" asked Hunt Broadwell, stooping the same way Carver had done.

"I'll get mine. You get out of here, Hunt," said Back, giving him a boost with his heavy saddlebags. "We'll see you at Pierman's in a few days."

Seeing that the men had begun walking out to their horses, their saddlebags filled, Memphis moved in and began filling pouches for himself.

Beside him, Flannery said as he fumbled with the
drawstring on a bulging rawhide pouch, "Memphis, do you realize we've made this job without
so much as a shot fired?"

"So far, so good," said Memphis. "Don't jinx it
talking about it." He busily dropped coins into
the rawhide pouches. A few feet away he noted
Soto doing the same, but seeming in no hurry,
with little concern toward gathering his share.

On the other side of Soto, Beck saw Clarimonde
standing back, as if afraid to have anything to do
with the gold. "Ma'am, a share of this is yours,
the same as everybody else," Beck reminded her.

Soto shot Beck a hard stare. But then he looked
away and went on filling his pouches.

Clarimonde gave Beck a concerned look, but she
made no effort to help herself to the gold.

"Hurry up, Memphis," said Caplan, one of the
last to fill his saddlebags with the bulging pouches
of gold.

Beck looked at him as he tied off his last pouch
of gold and stuffed it inside his saddlebags. "Go
on, Caplan," he said. "You don't have to wait for
me. Everybody takes off when he gets his share,
remember?"

"I remember," Caplan said, "but we all had a
private vote. We're none of us leaving until you
leave. So, hurry up."

"Are you out of your mind?" Beck stood, hefted
his saddlebags over his shoulder and walked to
the door. Outside, the rest of the men sat atop
their horses, waiting restlessly.

"No more than I ever was," Caplan replied. "Somebody has to keep you in line."

Beck shook his head and handed his saddlebags down as Broadwell nudged his horse forward and led Beck's horse up to the express car door. "What am I going to do with you men?" Beck said, swinging down into his saddle.

Behind Broadwell, Carver and Cruzan led Soto and Clarimonde's horses to the door.

In his saddle, Beck spun his horse in a tight circle with an arm spread and said, "All right, is everybody happy now?"

The men nodded and laughed and murmured among themselves. "I'm happy!" Carver cried out, waving his sweat-stained range hat above his head. "Let's go spend our money!"

"You heard him," Beck called out. "Everybody split up into ones and twos and disappear. Anybody needs me, I'll be at Pierman's for the next week. Then I'm going to disappear too." He looked at Suelo Soto and the woman and said, "Suelo, bad news, the woman is riding with me."

"Oh, is she?" Soto looked at him in surprise; so did Clarimonde.

"That's right, she is," said Beck. "I'm in charge. She's been a working member of this gang ever since the job started. That means she takes orders like everybody else. I'm ordering her to ride with me. I want information she's got."

"Huh-uh, any information you get will come from me, when *and if* I feel like giving it," Soto said. "I made it clear from the beginning, this woman is with me." His hand was poised near his gun butt.

"And I just made it clear she's not," Beck said with finality, leaving no pretense about what he expected this to turn into. He looked at Clarimonde, knowing that once he'd made this move, she would have no choice but to go along with it. She couldn't weaken and back down. "Move your horse away from him," he said to her, giving a jerk of his head. His hand lay also poised near the butt of his big holstered Colt. The men backed up their horses a step, watching intently. This was why Beck had wanted them to ride away without him. He'd intended to confront Soto one-on-one.

"Here's how it lays down, Soto," Beck said as Clarimonde sidestepped the big paint horse, putting space between herself and Soto. "You've brought nothing but trouble to us. You're a no-good, murdering son of a bitch. Now that the job is done, I've held up my end of the deal. Take your gold and ride away, or slip leather and throw down, here and now. However you feel like playing it is good with me."

Soto's face turned red with anger, then white with rage. He opened and closed his hand. But then, instead of making a grab for his gun, he managed to let go of a tense breath and ease down. A thin, tight smile came to his face as he relaxed his hand and pulled it away from his gun butt. "Over a whore?" he said. "I don't think so, Memphis Beck. These men might act like it's between you and me, but that's for show. I bury a slug in your chest, they'll be all over me."

"You're right for once," Kirkpatrick said, pulling his riding duster back, uncovering his big Remington.

"Stay out of it, all of you," Beck said evenly. "What happens here stays the way it is. Him or me." He looked at Soto. "That's as fair as I can make it."

"I gave you my answer," said Soto, backing his horse up a step. "You think this whore can mix you some nitro, make you some dynamite, or roll you some clay like I can? You're loco," he said. Slowly he turned his horse and rode away, without another word on the matter.

"Well," said Beck, "I didn't intend for any of you to be here when I did that. But it had to be done anyway."

The men sat in silence for a moment. Finally, Flannery said, "If you hadn't done it, one of us would have shot him sooner or later." He looked at Clarimonde and asked, "Ma'am, are you as good as he is, mixing explosives?"

Before she could answer, Beck cut in, "If she's not, do you want to call him back here and send her away?"

"Hell no!" Flannery grinned. "Begging your pardon, just curious, ma'am," he said, touching his hat brim toward Clarimonde.

The men laughed.

"All right, get out of here," Beck said. "Get out of here, unless you want to stick around and give all this back."

As the men disappeared, Beck looked at Clarimonde and said, "I'm sorry I had to do it that way. I know he's a killer, but it had to be done, else he'd own you the rest of your life."

"I understand," Clarimonde said.

"When we get to Pierman's, you'll be free to go," said Beck. "I have to keep you with me until then in case you run into *federales* between here and where you're going."

Clarimonde didn't answer; she couldn't right then. She gazed off in the direction Soto had taken, not trusting how easily he'd turned away.

"Ready?" Beck asked, riding over beside her. They booted their horses as one. In moments they were gone, the entire gang having vanished in every direction. The engine sat in silence on the rails, its engine metal cooling as the fire in its boiler burned out.

For an hour, Sam and Hector had followed the distant sound of the two explosions, the second explosion much less powerful than the first. From a hilltop overlooking the closed rail cut and the abandoned engine and rail car sitting above it, Sam scanned back and forth with his field lens and shook his head.

"We must've just missed them, *Guardia*," he said to Hector who set his horse beside him and scanned the area with a battered field lens of his own.

"But now we know for certain what the explosions were," Hector replied. He lowered his telescope, shrugged and added, "As if we didn't already know."

"Ever since Suelo Soto got his hand on some explosives, he's been a lot easier to follow," Sam said wryly.

Raising his field lens again, Sam saw the line of nine mounted men, seven of them *federales*, ride up into sight along a ridge running above the rail cut. "Here come two soldiers," he said, "a little late, but they didn't let the closed cut stop them."

Sam noted the two Germans in white linen suits flanking the lead rider. One of them was mopping his wet brow with a handkerchief as he struggled to stay in the saddle. Adjusting the lens closer, Sam noted the other German's angry expression, his lips moving rapidly toward the young Mexican captain.

"Somebody's catching it," Sam commented, watching the Mexican captain ride on, his face stoic, but his eyes ablaze.

"It is not a good idea to push this man too hard in front of his troops," Hector replied, also having adjusted his lens for a closer look. "A man in charge of others must maintain his self-respect, no matter what he must do to keep it."

"I agree," Sam said quietly.

They watched as the captain led the men down a winding path to the engine and express car, the German never ceasing his scorching reproach of the young captain. Both Germans followed the young captain, as if taking turns hounding him as he looked down at the wagon tracks, then gathered his troops and rode off following them.

"No, no," Sam said, as if they could hear him.

"That's a trick. Don't fall for it." But seeing the riders continue on, he shook his head, lowered the lens and said to Hector, "They fell for it."

"*Sí*, they fell for it," Hector nodded, also lowering his lens in exasperation. "But at least it will keep them out of our way."

The two turned their horses and rode back from the edge. "I hope so," said Sam. "We'll have enough to do figuring which tracks are Soto's and the woman's."

"Where do we start?" Hector said, looking down at several sets of hoofprints going in every direction.

"We look for two or more sets of prints that stay together," Sam said, looking back and forth, seeing where the gang had already broken apart, making any one of them hard to track. "This could cost us some time."

On the rolling land below, the Mexican captain and his men had ridden out of the rail cut, leaving a flurry of dust behind them. They followed the buckboard tracks over a low rise until they spotted the team of horses standing at the edge of a thin stream, nipping at clumps of wild grass.

Raising his hand, the captain brought his men to a halt. "What are we stopping for, you imbecile?" Herr Stienven demanded. "There sits the wagon with our gold in it! Go and fetch it back for us!"

"It could be a trap," said Captain Guzman, ignoring the insult and waving his sergeant forward with his binoculars for a closer look.

"It's not a trap!" Stienven bellowed. "There is

the gold and here are we! Let's get it before someone else steals it from under you!"

"Stop shouting at this poor ignorant buffoon,"
Herr Stienven," said Frunhiem in a calm, restrained tone. "We will leave the shouting to Generalissimo Matissmo, when he hears that his nephew
has lost the gold. Our friend the *capitán* here might
find himself raised in the air and impaled on a
sharp iron pole."

"Yes, indeed," said Stienven, "and if the generalissimo asks, I will personally suggest it to him."

Guzman swallowed a hard knot in his throat,
knowing the two Germans were right. "Sergeant
Valdez," he asked quietly, "how does it look
down there? Is this a trick, a trap of some sort?"

"*Capitán*," the sergeant said sympathetically just
between the two of them, "it is not a trap, but it
is a trick. There is no gold in the wagon, only a
load of large rocks."

"Large rocks?" The captain looked stunned,
then sick.

"Rocks?" shouted Steinven, hearing the young
sergeant's words. "There is no iron pole too tall,
or its point too sharp for you!" he screamed at
Guzman.

"We will see to it, you die slowly for this!" said
Frunhiem. "You and all of these baboons who
serve under you!"

The young sergeant started to turn toward the
two Germans in a rage. But Guzman stopped him.
"Sergeant," he said quietly and in an official tone,
"send down two men to retrieve the wagon. Have
them throw the rocks from it."

"An empty wagon?" Frunhiem raged at him. "Is that what we will deliver to those who are waiting for the gold? An empty wagon?"

"You saw inside the car," said Guzman. "There is much gold still there. We must protect it."

"Oh, now you must protect the gold," said Stienven, mockingly. "You ignorant fool! Now that two-thirds of it is stolen!"

"I cannot wait to report your incompetence to the generalissimo!" Frunhiem shouted, pounding his fist in his hand. "I hope he will allow us both to assist in impaling you!"

"How much gold do you think is left in the car, Sergeant?" Guzman asked while the Germans continued to rave.

"I don't know," the sergeant replied. "A million, perhaps two? It is still a lot of money."

Guzman looked back at his five mounted soldiers, all young peasant boys from the hill country. "More money than any of us will ever see in our lives?" he asked quietly.

"As I said, it is still a lot of money," the sergeant replied. Their eyes met and fixed knowingly on one another while Stienven and Frunhiem shouted at both of them.

Guzman reached down, unsnapped the flap on his holster, raised his big German pistol and shot Steinven squarely in the forehead. Before Frunhiem could respond with anything more than an openmouthed gasp, the young captain turned the pistol toward him, aimed and pulled the trigger again. The two Germans lay silent in death, a spray of blood splattered on the front of their white linen suits.

" 'Uncivilized monkey,' eh?" Guzman spit down at the two bodies. "Now look at you."

"I thought they would never shut up," Sergeant Valdez commented quietly.

"Me neither," Guzman said. Then he took a deep breath and said, "Send two men down for the wagon." Turning to the stunned men he called out in a jovial tone, "Good news, everybody! We have quit the army. Come let us draw our pay. We will all ride to Tejas!"

The young soldiers stared at one another; then as it dawned on them what Guzman had said, they shouted and laughed and gigged their horses forward, waving their hats in the air and spinning them away. . . .

In the distance, Sam and Hector heard the two gunshots, but they had only stopped for a second and looked back when they heard a weak, broken voice call out from a stand of white oak along a dry creek bed lying ahead of them.

"Listen," Sam said to Hector, turning toward the sound. "Did you hear that?"

The two sat listening intently until the voice called out again, "Memphis . . . is that you? Help me . . ."

The two hurried forward, spreading out, wary of a trap. But as they spotted Earl Caplan lying bloody alongside the creek, they slipped down from their saddles and hurried to him, their Colts drawn and cocked. When Caplan saw it wasn't

Memphis Beck coming to his aid, he cried out, "Get back, get away from me!"

Drawing closer, Hector slowed to a halt, crossing himself as he stared down at Caplan's decapitated right arm lying beside him. *"Santa Madre,"* he whispered, crossing himself. Caplan turned loose of his sliced-open stomach; Hector saw his intestines lying piled beneath the gaping wound as Caplan tried reaching his holstered Colt with his blood-slick left hand.

"Easy, Caplan," Sam said, recognizing him as he hurried down beside him as he untied and yanked his bandanna from around his neck. "It's Burrack. I'm not here to hurt you." As a precaution he slipped the Colt from Caplan's holster and pitched it away. Then he wrapped a quick tourniquet around the bleeding stub of Caplan's arm and tightened it down. The bleeding slowed, but didn't stop.

Kneeling beside the ranger, Hector took off his bandanna and handed it to him. "Keep watch for us, *Guardia,*" Sam told him. He wrapped Hector's bandanna around the stub and tightened it down also. On the ground not far from Caplan lay a straw sombrero and a bloody, discarded machete. Sam didn't have to ask who had wielded the machete. Instead he concentrated on stopping the blood.

"They took . . . my gold, Ranger," he said, his voice sounding weak and distant, "those tattooheaded . . . sonsabitches." In spite of his condition he managed an ironic chuckle and said, "Imagine . . . a thief like me . . . getting robbed."

A fresh, thin fountain of blood spurted up from amid his intestines. Sam hurriedly closed the gaping wound and held it shut with his gloved hand. Blood still seeped out around his fingers.

"Lie still, Caplan," Sam said.

"It won't matter . . . will it, Ranger?" Caplan asked with a weak but knowing look. "I'm never stepping up from here."

Sam let out a breath, knowing it was true. "Where's Suelo Soto?" he asked bluntly. "These Satan's Brothers are his people."

"I don't tell . . . nothing to the law, Ranger," Caplan said, his eyes glazing over.

"Listen to me, Caplan," Sam said, still holding his guts in for him. "Suelo Soto is likely going to have these demons kill every one of you. Is that what you want?"

"Nice try . . . Ranger," Caplan murmured.

"Listen to me," Sam insisted. "I'm not after any of you, not Beck, not any of your pards. Just Soto, do you understand me?"

"Just Soto, eh?" Caplan mumbled the words, then managed to get the strength to say, "I know that snake . . . was behind this."

"That's right, he was," Sam said. "I want to get to him before he kills anybody else. Beck could be next. You boys made a bad mistake this time. You didn't take in a thief like yourselves. You took in a bloodthirsty murderer. Help me fix it."

"Beck kept the woman . . . chased him off. I don't know where . . . he went," Caplan said, sounding weaker, more distant.

"Then where're Beck and the woman headed?"

Sam asked, deciding Soto wasn't about to stand
for Beck taking the woman away from him.

"Pier—Pierman's place . . . near the border,"
Caplan said, starting to gasp for his breath. "If
you're lying to me . . . I'll see you in . . ."

His words trailed as his last breath fell to a
whisper, then stopped. Sam turned loose of his
stomach and said quietly, "I'm not lying to you,
Earl Caplan. Soto's the devil I want."

Beside the ranger, Hector stood into a crouch
and walked along, studying three sets of hoofprints on the ground as they led off into the white
oaks. "Two of these demons at the hacienda, now
three more here," he said. "Suelo Soto has all of
the demons of Shadow Valley doing his bidding.
They will not stop until everybody is dead."

Sam stood up, his gloved hands covered with
Caplan's blood. "Or until they know Soto himself
is dead," he said with grim determination.

"Which way do we go now?" Hector asked.

"Back to the hacienda," Sam said. "Caplan said
Beck's gone there with the woman. If he has the
woman, Soto and his demons won't be far behind." Sam looked off in the direction of the hacienda and added, "Those bodies we dragged out
onto the porch ought to tip him off that Soto's
demons are prowling around."

Chapter 22

Before Sam and Hector had ridden five miles, looking to their left they saw another body, this one propped against a cottonwood only a few yards off the trail. From seventy yards away it appeared to be a man lying asleep; yet upon approaching cautiously, they saw that both arms and legs had been severed, and all that leaned against the tree was the bloody torso, its stomach slashed open from crotch to sternum.

"This is Bowen Flannery," Sam commented quietly, gazing at the blank, dead stare on Flannery's face. The man's fingers lay scattered about like trinkets spilled from a broken necklace.

Again Hector made the sign of the cross, but this time he sat in his saddle in silence and watched Sam walk over and look all around on the ground as if searching for clues. Sam shook his head after a moment and said as if speaking to the dead train robber, "There's little we can do for you, right now, Bowen Flannery. We need to push on if we're ever going to stop this man and his demons."

As Sam stepped back into his saddle and turned the stallion to the trail, Hector asked, "When you say demons, are you mocking me and my people's belief in such creatures?"

"No, I'm not, *Guardia*," Sam said in earnest. "I apologize if I've given you that idea. I surely didn't mean to."

"*Gracias*," said Hector. They rode in silence for a moment. Then Hector said, "So, you yourself believe in *demons*? You believe Suelo Soto is a *demon*?"

Gazing ahead, Sam replied flatly, "No, I don't. I surely didn't mean to give that idea either."

"Then what is it you believe?" Hector pressed, looking curiously at the ranger.

"I believe there is such a thing as evil," Sam said, "and I believe we're facing a powerful lot of it in Soto and his demons."

"You do not believe there is a force of Satan directing these demons? That Soto or any of them possess Satan's power?"

Sam turned and looked at him. "I believe that their *belief* in the force of Satan is as strong and evil as anything Satan could conjure up on his own."

"But you do not believe that Satan himself is real, or that he has power over man?"

"Real? I'm not the one to ask," Sam said. "But the more I acknowledge Satan's power, whether he's real or not, the more power I give up to him.

Suelo Soto's demons are only as powerful as I allow them to be over me."

Hector thought about it. "Then you have no fear in facing them?"

"No," Sam replied, "I had better not, unless I want them to win. When a man becomes too afraid of his enemy, he'll give up his fight without firing a shot. He starts to think it's useless to even try." He looked at Hector with a raised brow and asked, "What about you, *Guardia*, are you afraid of your enemies . . . afraid to even fight your demons?"

"You saw me kill one of the demons who stood over me while I sat sleeping," Hector said in defense. "You tell me if I am afraid."

Sam allowed himself a thin smile. "You're afraid of nothing, Hector. But you're still young enough to question those things you were raised to believe in."

"You do not question those things you were raised to believe in?" Hector asked.

"No," said Sam, "my job is to stop evil men, not question evil itself. The evil I see in some men would cause Satan to run for cover." He nudged his stallion forward; Hector did the same beside him.

They rode on.

By midafternoon, the two stopped in the shelter of the treed hillside overlooking the Pierman hacienda. Gazing down onto the front yard and checking all around for any sign of Soto or his Satan's Brothers, Sam said, "Seems peaceful enough

down there. But for all we know, Soto and Beck
could be lying in wait. As much as I want to believe Memphis Beck would have no hand in what
we've seen, he's still an outlaw . . . a tricky one
at that."

Looking at the big paint horse standing beside
Beck's at the hitch rail, Hector said almost with a
sigh, "There is my brother Ramon's horse. I am
taking it back with me, the way Ramon would
want me to do. . . ."

Inside the hacienda, Beck looked out the window with a pair of binoculars raised to his eyes,
a rifle leaning on the wall beside him. He scanned
the hillside and trail for any sign of Soto or the
men in their white peasant clothes, like the two
whose bodies he had dragged inside the hacienda
and into the bedroom earlier. "Two riders coming,
Clair," he said over his shoulder to Clarimonde,
who had gathered the dead men's straw hats and
stood feeding them into the hearth fire.

Beck took the binoculars down from his eyes
and continued watching the two figures as Clarimonde slipped in beside him. "It's Ranger Burrack," Beck said, recognizing the ranger's pearl
gray sombrero, then the man himself. "I don't
know who the other man is."

"Is this going to be trouble?" Clarimonde asked
quietly, staring out with him.

"Sam Burrack is always trouble," Beck said.
"But he's fair for a lawman. Anyway, he's got
nothing on us. We'll see what he wants and try
to get rid of him as quickly as we can."

As Sam and Hector neared the weathered and

crumbling hacienda, Beck called out from the open window, "That's close enough, Burrack. The next step gets you a bullet in the belly."

The ranger motioned for Hector to stop his horse beside him. Then he allowed his stallion one more step and brought him to a halt. "I'm hunting Suelo Soto," Sam called out.

"He's not here. What else?" Beck replied, the barrel of his rifle visible at the open window ledge.

"I didn't think he would be," Sam said. "But I believe he will be soon enough."

"Oh? Why's that?" Beck asked.

"Because he and his pards, in white clothes and straw sombreros, are tracking your men down, killing them one by one," Sam said. "We've found two of them dead so far."

Beck winced at the thought. But knowing the ranger wouldn't be lying to him about such a thing, he had to ask, "Who'd you find, Burrack?"

"We found Earl Caplan, not far from the train robbery," Sam said. "Then we found Bowen Flannery, four or five miles farther on. They'd both been robbed. Both of them were hacked to death with machetes."

Beck made no reply. After a silence, Sam asked, "Do you have the goatherd's daughter, Clarimonde, with you?"

"Yes, she's with me," said Beck.

"You've got to set her free," Sam said. "We're taking her back where she belongs."

"I'm not giving her up, Ranger," Beck said. "She doesn't want to leave me. You see what kind of murderer Soto is. What do you think he'll do to her if she's on her own right now?''

Sam couldn't argue with his reasoning, but he said anyway, ''If she wants to stay, I'll have to hear it from her. She'll have to make me believe it.''

''Tell him,'' Soto said to Clarimonde, standing beside him.

''I'm staying with Memphis,'' Clarimonde called out the window.

Sam and Hector looked at each other, both glad to hear her voice, after all their time trying to catch up to her. But then Sam called out, ''That's not good enough, Beck. Both of you step out on the porch and put some space between you. I want to believe she doesn't have a gun to her back.''

Beck shook his head. ''Always the rough, tough lawman, eh, Ranger?'' he said.

''Out on the porch, right now, Beck,'' Sam repeated, without acknowledging Beck's words. ''I want to see her and know she's all right.''

Slowly Clarimonde stepped out of the hacienda and to one side of the porch, Beck coming out cautiously beside her, the rifle raised in his hands. ''I'm keeping you covered, Burrack,'' Beck said, his thumb over the rifle hammer. ''Don't try anything.''

''Hector, if you hear his rifle cock,'' Sam said, ''don't wait for me. You drop him.''

''*Sí*, I understand,'' Hector replied, his hand on his holstered gun butt.

''Ma'am,'' the ranger said, touching the brim of his sombrero toward Clarimonde, ''we're both grateful to see you alive and well. Now, if you'll please move farther away from Memphis Beck, we'd be obliged."

Clarimonde did as she was told, but only after a nod from Beck. "I'm all right as you can see, Ranger," she said, "and I do appreciate you both searching for me." She looked back and forth between Hector and the ranger. "It wasn't Memphis Beck or any of his men who kidnapped me. It was Soto and Nate Ransdale, nobody else."

"We know that, ma'am," said Sam. "We followed the string of killing and bloodletting those two left behind them." He looked her up and down, making certain for himself that she wasn't being forced to say anything against her will. "I've got some good news for you. Your shepherd dog that Soto thought he killed was alive and mending when we left the old mission. I expect she'll be eager to see you real soon."

"Oh my, Bess is alive. . . ." Clarimonde raised her hands to her mouth; her eyes welled. She turned, teary-eyed and smiling, toward Beck, to whom she had told everything on their way to the hacienda.

"We're obliged, you both coming here," Beck said to the ranger. "As you can see, she's all right. I won't let nothing happen to her. You've got my word on that." He stared closely at Sam and said, "As long as Soto thinks she's alive, not only she, but her father and their animals are not safe. You know what Soto is. You know I'm right."

"Hector and I are taking him down, Beck," Sam said with determination.

"Best of luck, Ranger, but you and Hector haven't done it yet," Beck replied.

Sam stared at him, realizing that he had a plan of some sort in mind. Knowing Beck, whatever it was, it would be as good as any he and Hector could come up with. As long as Soto and any of his demons remained alive, Sam understood that Clarimonde's father and their way of life would be in danger. That was something he and Beck could both agree on.

Seeing the conversation about to wind down, Hector said to Beck as he pointed to the big paint horse, "That horse belonged to my brother. Suelo Soto killed him for it. I must take it back."

"Take it," said Beck.

Hector eased his horse over, lifted the paint's reins from the hitch rail and pulled the animal in beside him.

"Where's he headed, Beck?" Sam asked suddenly.

"Back to where he came from, Ranger," Beck said without hesitation, both of them knowing he was talking about Suelo Soto.

"You mean to Shadow Valley, where all the Satan's Brothers will protect him," Hector cut in, a concerned look coming upon his face.

"That's where I would look," Beck said as if concluding the conversation. His expression softened a bit and he said, "Thanks for telling me about Flannery and Caplan."

Sam only nodded at Beck. He touched his fingers to the brim of his sombrero and said to Clarimonde, "Ma'am," and turned his stallion back out of the yard toward the trail.

As the two lawmen rode away, Beck stared after them and said to Clarimonde, "Well, that's done. I know he means well as far as helping you goes. But he lives strictly by the book. He refuses to ever look the other way, or step short of the law for any reason. It's hard to trust a man like that."

Clarimonde also stared off behind the ranger and Hector, her eyes still misty. "I am so happy my Bess is alive. I must go to her. I want to hold her, to tell her how much I love her, and take her home to Papa, so he will see that we're both all right."

"All in time, Clair," said Beck. "But if you want your papa and your shepherds safe, this comes first, the way we agreed to do it."

"Yes, I know." Clarimonde sniffed and dabbed her sleeve to her eyes. "Do you think those two will ride all the way to Shadow Valley, tonight?"

"Yes, I believe they will," said Beck. "He knows that sooner or later Soto is going to be there. He wants him bad enough, he's willing to go there and wait it out. Meanwhile, we had better get ready, and do what we need to do here."

Fifty yards along the trail, Sam and Hector veered up onto the hillside. "Do you think Soto and his demons will be coming here tonight?" Hector asked, leading the big paint behind him.

"I'm counting on it," Sam said. "So is Memphis Beck, the way I read him. He's got something in mind for Soto when he gets here. He thinks it's something he can't trust us with. That's why he wanted to send us off to Shadow Valley. He wants us out of his way."

"But whatever happens tonight, we will be here waiting for Suelo Soto and his demons, eh?"

"Without a doubt, Hector," Sam said, "we're going to be here, whether Memphis Beck likes it or not."

Chapter 23

———

As darkness fell moonless and black around the hacienda and the surrounding hillsides, Clarimonde heard Beck walk away from the corral, leading his horses and the horse that had belonged to Dave Arken off toward a stand of woods. A moment later she heard him returning toward the hacienda, this time alone, having hitched the horses to a scrub juniper inside the tree line. "We can't risk finding them butchered in the corral," he said, stepping inside through the rear door.

"Did you see anything, hear anything?" Clarimonde asked, a bit anxiously.

"No," Beck replied. "But I wouldn't anyway, not unless Soto wanted me to." He reached out, took her by her shoulders and drew her to him firmly, but gently. "It's going to be all right. You'll see. I know how this man thinks—so do you. We both know how he is going to come at us. We'll be ready."

She allowed herself to relax for a moment in

Beck's arms, feeling safer than she had for a long time. "Perhaps we should have told the ranger—"

"Shhh," said Beck, cutting her off. "We can handle ourselves. Look at everything you've been through. The ranger might have been on his way, but he wasn't there. You did it on your own. You're the one who found your way out from under Suelo Soto. You freed yourself."

She thought about it, and decided not to question the matter any further. Instead she said, "Now that I know my shepherd, Bess, is alive, as soon as this is over, I want to go to her and take her home."

"We can do that as soon as it's safe for you," Beck said. "Did you give any thought to what we talked about?" On their ride to the hacienda he had invited her to travel with him and the gang. She hadn't responded and he didn't push the subject too hard right then.

"Yes," she said, "and I'm afraid that is not the life for me. I have lived wild and dangerously in the past. All I want now is to live simply, and to sleep well of a night. I am sorry if I disappoint you."

"Don't be sorry." Beck smiled. "I haven't given up on you yet. I still have some time. I plan on talking you into it."

"No," Clarimonde said amiably, "if I were interested you would not have to talk me into it." She gave him a tired smile.

"Seeing Paris, sunny Italy, South America? Instead of being Clair, your new name would be

'Lady Dynamite'? None of that excites you?" he asked.

"Lady Dynamite . . ." She shook head slowly. "There was a time, perhaps, when it would have excited me," she admitted. "But not anymore. Life had its way with me long ago. Now I want only to tend goats with my papa and spend time with my shepherds. Please don't try to dissuade me. It will only make me feel bad, turning you down."

"Ah," said Beck, seeing an opening and reaching in for it. "If it makes you feel bad turning it down, maybe you just need to think about it some more?"

Clarimonde looked at him closely and said, "I know that if you talked enough about it, I will give in. I know that if I think enough about it, perhaps I will change my mind. But try to understand that I do not want you to talk me into it. I do not want to talk myself into it. A terrible event has taken place in my life. Now that it is over, I don't want to let it change anything. I want my life to go on as it was."

"But shouldn't you be able to take something good out of it?" Beck asked.

"I want nothing from it," she said, "except to wake up and have it gone, like someone awakens from a bad dream."

Beck sighed and relaxed his arms around her. "All right, I give up," he said. "But we've still got a deal on you mixing explosives for me?" As he spoke, he turned an oil lamp down low and carried it to the bedroom.

"A deal is a deal." She smiled, following him. "I will be back with Papa and the herd as soon as it is safe. When you need me, you will know where to find me."

"All right then," said Beck. "Now for the rest of the deal." He set the dimly glowing lamp on a nightstand, and said as he turned it even dimmer, "It's bedtime, Clair. Are you ready to ride?"

"Yes, I'm ready. Are you?" Clarimonde smiled. She loosened her clothes, stepped out of them and let them fall in a heap on the floor beside the bed. Beck looked at her standing naked before him in the dim glow of the light.

"Oh, yes," said Beck, as he unbuttoned his shirt and took it off. He tossed the shirt onto a chair beside the nightstand. He took off his hat and his gun belt and hung them both on a chair back. Then he slipped his Colt from its holster and held it to his naked chest. "After you," he said in a gentlemanly manner.

From across a short stretch of flatlands to the west of the hacienda, Suelo Soto had seen the lamplight go low. He smiled thinly to himself watching the dim glow travel from window to window through the hacienda, like a ghost. Behind him Satan's Brothers waited with the horses, keeping the animals as silent as themselves.

But Soto was in no hurry. He gave Beck and the woman all the time they needed—plenty of time to sate themselves with one another, he told himself. He could wait. While he waited, he sat deftly cutting cord for the two canvas-wrapped balls of clay he had tied together. Down between the two balls he had stuck three vials of pure nitroglycerin. *A gift from hell, all for you, Memphis Beck and Clarimonde . . .*

When a half hour had passed, just as the brothers behind him had begun giving one another questioning looks, their eyes adjusting some to the darkness but still unable to see clearly, Soto rose into a crouch, a black cigar smoldering in his mouth, and moved away toward the dimly lit window of the hacienda.

Once beneath the half-opened window, he pulled himself up enough to look into the dim light. He saw where Clarimonde and Beck had shed their clothes. He saw the empty holster, knowing that Beck would be the kind of man to sleep with his gun beneath his pillow. But tonight his gun wouldn't help him, Soto thought, easing down the deadly balls of explosives by their cord until they rested on the floor.

I hope the whore was worth it, Memphis Beck . . . , he said to himself, looking at the exposed arm lying draped sidelong out from under the sheet. Instead of puffing the cigar to stoke it, he jammed the cord down into the blackened tip and twisted it back and forth until it found the buried fire and began to sizzle to life.

Easing back to the ground beneath the window, he waited only a second with his gun drawn, making sure the burning fuse cord didn't awaken the sleeping lovers. Then he slipped away into the darkness as silently as he'd arrived. . . .

Lower down on the hillside where the two lawmen had set up watch from the cover of the trees,

Sam had noted the faint, reddish glow of fire from
the cigar move down the hillside toward the hacienda. Instantly he'd recognized it and realized
what was going on. "That's him. That's Suelo
Soto," he'd said to Hector, sitting eight feet away.
"He's making his move."

Hector had seen the cigar at the same time. He
rose quickly, followed Sam to the horses and
jumped into the saddle. Leaving the big paint
horse hitched to a tree, the two lawmen raced
across the stretch of flatlands toward the house.
But halfway across, the air around them came
alive with whistling bullets slicing past their
heads. To their right along a hill line, heavy rifle
fire flashed like angry fireflies. Rather than sacri-
fice his stallion, Sam reined up quickly, grabbed
his rifle from its boot and leaped from his saddle.
Giving the stallion a slap on the rump he shouted,
"Go, Black Pot!" Then he dived to the ground.

"There must be an army—!" Hector shouted,
his words ending abruptly amid a volley of fire.

"*Guardia?*" Sam called out. He could not see
Hector, but he'd heard his horse neigh pitifully as
it took a tumble and a slide along the stony
ground. Then the neighing fell to a moan.

"I'm hit," Hector said in a strained voice.

The ranger crawled hurriedly to him, following
his voice more than the dim, grainy image lying
sprawled in the darkness. "Easy, *Guardia*," Sam
said, hovering over him, a bullet slicing the air,
dangerously close. "How bad?" As he asked, his
fingers felt the warm blood on Hector's chest. He
heard the young man struggle for breath.

"Don't . . . worry about me. . . . Get to the hacienda in time," Hector said in a rasping voice.

"I'm not leaving you, *Guardia*," the ranger said above the whistling bullets.

"Leave me," said Hector. "These demons . . . see in the dark."

But the ranger ignored him, knowing the riflemen could see no better in the dark than they could. Crouched, he dragged Hector along by his bloody shirtfront, realizing that the rifles had been firing blindly at the sound of the horses' hooves. Now that the stallion had run away and Hector's horse lay dying, the shots had started spreading out wildly.

"*Por favor* . . . leave me," Hector pleaded in a waning voice. "I am . . . bleeding so bad. . . ."

"No," the ranger said stubbornly, crouching lower as a volley of fire seemed to find them in the dark. As soon as the volley relented, Sam stared toward the dim glow of light in the bedroom window of the hacienda. What about Beck, he wondered. Hadn't he heard the shooting?

But as he dragged Hector forward again, any questions he had about Beck no longer mattered. Two hundred feet away, the hacienda turned as bright as day. "Oh no," Sam managed to say. For a moment the whole adobe structure seemed to rise up and hang suspended in the air. Then it flew apart in thousands, hundreds of thousands, millions of fiery pieces, before the ranger could even drop to the ground out of the blast.

At the distant hill line where Satan's Brothers had been firing into the darkness, Soto hurried in

among them and jumped into his saddle. While
the blast still stood high in the air, rolling in a
whirlwind of fire, he looked out across the flatlands. A grin of satisfaction came to his face; fire
reflected with a glitter in his dark eyes. He saw
the ranger stagger back up onto his feet after
being knocked to the ground. "Ha! Not a bad
night's work, eh, *mi hermanos*?" He spoke in Spanish to his brothers in Satan. They looked surprised,
knowing his hatred for his native tongue.

A few feet from where the ranger fell, Hector
lay sprawled, his mouth agape, his horse lying
dead a few yards behind him. Turning his horse
toward a trail leading down out of sight, Soto
said, gesturing toward two of the brothers on foot,
"You two, run down there and finish them off."

The two Satan's Brothers handed their rifles up
to some of their mounted comrades and, bare-
footed, looped away across the flatland. "Let's
ride," said Soto, jerking his horse's reins toward
the trail, leading the men away while fire boiled
high in the night. . . .

On the far side of the hill, Memphis Beck
stopped his horse beside Clarimonde and said,
"Well, that's that. I kept my part of the deal. I
killed you off." He smiled. "I even died with
you . . . something I've been meaning to do lately,
to give myself a new start."

"You did it," Clarimonde said, looking back
with him toward the fire as it lit up the night.

"We did it," Beck corrected her.

"All right, *we* did it." She smiled. "We fooled
him, those two bodies in the bed. He would never

have wasted precious explosives if he hadn't believed it was you and me lying there."

"My thoughts exactly," said Beck. "With everything else wrong with him, Soto is also a jealous man." He looked Clarimonde up and down, recalling how she'd looked earlier, standing naked before him in the soft light. "Not that I blame him in that regard."

She wore one of Pierman's shirts and a rolled up pair of trousers they'd found in a clothes trunk in the bedroom. Beck wore a shirt from his saddlebags. He wore his Colt in a shoulder harness he'd found in the hacienda, having given up his holster to the explosion.

Clarimonde said, in a delicate way as if to slow down anything he might have in mind, "Let's be friends for a while first, Memphis. Can we?"

"Yes, I understand," Memphis said quietly. "The fact is—" He stopped short, and jerked around in his saddle at the sound of the ranger's stallion limping along the trail behind them. His gun came out of his shoulder harness, cocked and pointed. But seeing the empty saddle, he looked confused and said, "What is this?"

"On no, look, Memphis!" Clarimonde said, pointing down onto the flatlands where Sam had tried once more to struggle to his feet, only to fall again. They both looked across the flatlands in the flickering firelight at the two figures lopping barefoot toward the ranger from a hundred yards away, machetes in hand.

"That blasted ranger," said Beck, "he had to stick his nose in. I had everything under control!"

He saw Hector, lying motionless, the dead horse nearby. "Damn it," he said, "I ought to let them eat him alive."

Clarimonde only stared. Black Pot, the stallion, limped up to Beck as if seeking his help. Blood ran from a bullet graze across his withers. Scratches from flying debris had bloodied his shoulders. He staggered; a cut ran deep along his foreleg.

Beck looked back down toward the ranger, who, a knee rocking back and forth and his hands clutching the ground, lay on the ground, trying to get a grip and push himself up. "The poor bastard." Beck winced. "We never liked one another, but I hate seeing this." After short consideration, he looked at Clarimonde and said, "Get off the trail and keep the stallion with you. I'll put him down when I get back." He shook his head. "I must be nuts. If I get killed trying to save a lawman's life—especially this damn ranger—swear you'll never tell a living soul."

"I swear. Now go," she said.

Chapter 24

The ranger lay helpless, feeling the world swirl around him in a flickering glow of firelight. The blast had left him unable to hear; the impact of it had stunned him so badly he could hardly string a thought together, let alone put it into action. His face burned, blasted by grains of sand and chips of stone. His hands stung; his sombrero had been swept from his head; his gun belt lay twisted around on his waist, the tie-down keeping the tip of it in place at his thigh. His Colt had been slung from the holster and lay on the ground ten feet away. His rifle had been yanked from his hands and hurled away by the hot blast.

"Hec-Hector . . . Black Pot," he said with much effort, his eyes squeezed shut. His voice sounded distant and detached from him. A dull ringing persisted inside his head.

"*Pote Negro?*" a sinister voice said above him, repeating the stallion's name in Spanish.

Hearing him say the stallion's name, Sam opened his eyes and struggled to keep them open.

"Sí . . . Pote Negro," he replied weakly, "Where is he . . . ?"

"Pote Negro? Pote Negro?" another voice said, the rounded point of a machete poking him in his stomach, not stabbing him, yet leaving a shallow cut each time. He managed to open his eyes and keep them open, seeing the faces of the two men standing above him, their machetes in hand.

"You're not . . . demons," he rasped, feeling himself slip away again, struggling not to let it happen. Beneath him down in the ground, he felt a rumble of running hooves. Didn't they feel it? No, not up there where they were, he told himself.

"Demons? Yes, we are demons," one answered in Spanish, "as you will see."

Sam felt the rumble of hooves come closer; he saw the two men raise their machetes over their heads. But that was all right, he told himself in his addled state. All he had to do was get onto his feet. These men weren't demons. There was nothing supernatural here. These were ordinary murderers, lowlifes, the kind of men he was used to dealing with every day. Relieved, he felt his eyes close once again.

Standing above the ranger, the Satan's Brother on his right was the first to hear and see the large image of man and horse bearing down upon them from out of the darkness. He shouted out in warning, but his warning came too late. Across from him, the other brother had started to bring his machete down, to lop off the ranger's head with one swift, dreadful stroke. But suddenly he was gone, picked up by the speeding horse and launched twelve feet into the air. His machete fell to the ground with a metal twang.

Turning away from the ranger to the sound of Beck's horse coming to a jolting halt, the brother crouched, his machete poised, his hands spread in a fighting stance. Firelight from the burning hacienda flickered in his eyes. Stepping closer, Beck stooped and picked up the discarded machete, not wanting a gunshot to draw Soto's attention and bring him and the others back.

He glanced down at the unconscious ranger, then stood over him like a protecting hawk. "Turn and run," he warned the Satan's Brother, a grim look on his face. But he knew that wasn't going to happen; and if it did, what then? Everything he and Clarimonde had just set up would have been in vain. If this man lived, Soto would know everything and be upon the woman like the rabid animal he was.

The brother's only reply was something dark, sinister-sounding, like some evil, ancient curse in a language Beck did not recognize. Then he stalked toward Beck. "That's what I thought," Beck said, sidestepping away from the ranger, raising the machete and moving it back and forth slowly, drawing the man's attention to it.

Wearing a strange, tight grin, the Satan's Brother moved in closer and made a testing jab with the rounded tip of the machete. Beck jumped back a foot. Growing bolder, the man made two more plunges, then a quick slash with the blade. Each move sent Beck farther away, leading the man away from the downed ranger.

Seeing his opponent was afraid, the brother grew more aggressive. He lunged harder, slashing the machete back and forth in a bolder move. Then with a war cry he raced forward, only to be stopped in his tracks by Beck's hard boot heel landing in a vicious kick to his chin. The man staggered in place, stunned but not going down. Beck stepped in before he could regain his senses. With a hard swipe of the blade he opened the brother's throat and stepped back quickly.

The Satan's Brother stood for a moment longer, dropping his machete and clasping both hands to his bleeding throat. Then he sank to his knees for another moment before pitching face forward into the dirt.

Beck tossed the machete aside and walked to where the ranger lay trying to bat his eyes and bring himself to consciousness. "Take it easy, Burrack," he said. "It's me, Memphis Beck. I've come to help you."

"Help me?" Sam rasped. "I thought you . . ." His words trailed.

"Yeah, I know, you thought the woman and I were blown up," said Beck. "That was a plan I put together to throw Soto off Clair's trail. I figured it was a good time to let everybody think I was dead too. But you've ruined that for me." As he spoke he looked the ranger over and helped him sit up on the ground. "Don't move," he said. "I'll get my canteen."

Seeing his horse in the shadowy firelight, Beck hurried over to it, took down his canteen and started back to the ranger. But before he'd gone

ten feet, he heard a terrible shriek and saw the
other Satan's Brother charging toward him, having
picked up the discarded machete while Beck had
walked to his horse.

Beck let go of the canteen and made a grab for
his Colt in the shoulder harness. But he saw it
was too late. He had no time to draw his gun, or
deliver his reliable roundhouse kick. The man was
already upon him. He saw the machete go back
for a hard swing. But the machete stopped as if
frozen in place when a gunshot exploded and the
brother stiffened, a gaping hole spewing blood
from his chest.

Looking past the fallen Satan's Brother, Beck
saw Hector up on his knees, his bloody belly covered with dirt from crawling to retrieve his lost
pistol. The young Mexican lawman tried to say
something—Beck couldn't make it out—then he
fell forward onto the ground.

Gunshot . . . ! Would Soto hear it? If he heard
it, would he be coming back? Beck looked off
quickly to where Soto and his men had disappeared only a few minutes before. He couldn't
take any chances. He hurried to the ranger, canteen in hand, and said, "We've got to get out of
here."

"Hector's alive?" Sam asked, his mind seeming
to be more clear.

"Yes, he is," said Beck. "I've got to get him and
get you both out of here."

"That's good to hear," said Sam, referring to
Hector being alive. He struggled up onto his feet
with Beck's help. "Go help Hector. . . . I'll be all

right." He looked all around for the stallion, and called out his name.

"He's not here, Ranger," Beck said, on his way to help Hector. "Clair has him up on the hillside."

"Is he all right?" the ranger asked.

"No, he's not," said Beck. "He's bullet-grazed and he took some of the blast."

"Oh no," Sam said, hanging his head.

While Beck stooped down beside Hector, Sam walked over and picked up the reins to Beck's horse and led it back.

From the shelter of the wooded hillside, Clarimonde kept watch on the flatlands in the firelight's glow while she helped Beck attend to the young Mexican's wound. Nearby, the ranger watched them work as he held the battered and wounded stallion's head against his chest and patted the animal's muzzle. He sighed in relief when Beck turned to him and said, "I believe he's got a chance if we can keep the bleeding stopped."

"Thank God," Sam whispered. He turned loose the stallion and walked over to look down at Hector. "If you can hear me, *Guardia*, I want you to know, I haven't forgotten my promise to you. I said I'd get Soto for you whether you're with me or not."

Beck cut in, saying, "Ranger, you're crazy. You can't go after Suelo Soto, not now, not alone. The shape you're in, he and his demon men will cut you to pieces."

"Don't shoot my stallion, Beck," Sam said, not

responding to Beck's words. "I looked him over.
He's going to be all right."

"I won't shoot him, Burrack," Beck replied.

"Give me your word," Sam said strongly.

"My word?" Beck said, bemused. "You mean
you'd take *my word*—the word of a train robber
like me? Ranger, what low level have you stooped
to?"

"I'm obliged to you for saving my life, Beck—
Hector's too," the ranger replied. "But I've got no
time for jokes and nonsense. I'm going after Soto,
and I want your word that you won't put down
my stallion."

Jokes and nonsense . . . Beck gave him a harsh
stare. But he nodded and said solemnly, "You've
got my word, Burrack. I won't put him down. I'll
keep him with me and give him time to mend.
Hector too, until he's able to ride."

"Obliged," Sam repeated.

"I have a question," Beck said, watching the
ranger raise his Colt, check it and drop it back
down into his holster.

Sam just looked at him, his face scratched and
cut and burned from the blast, his clothes ragged
and scorched.

"How are you going after Soto? Are you going
to walk?" Beck asked, sounding exasperated by
the ranger's determination.

"I've got the paint horse," Sam replied. "Hector
left it hitched in the woods."

Beck shook his head. "Go on then, if you're that
big of a fool. As soon as I can build us a travois,

we're pulling out of here. The stallion can walk with his leg bandaged and his bullet graze cleaned. When you come for him, he'll be in Hole-in-the-wall with me and all of my pals. If you don't come for him, I'll just figure he's mine. How does that suit you?''

Sam heard the challenge in Beck's voice. But he didn't have the energy to answer it. Instead, he picked up a lariat from his saddle, fashioned a hackamore around the stallion's head for a lead rope, and picked up the bridle he'd taken from Black Pot's battered head. "Obliged," he repeated again. Throwing the bridle and saddle up over his shoulder, he turned and limped away.

"I mean it, Burrack, damn it!" Beck called out, hoping it would stop the ranger. "I'll keep this stallion if you don't come get him. You've got *my word* on that too!" He saw Sam fade into the darkness along the hillside. "This doesn't make us friends, you know! I don't owe you anything. . . . You don't owe me anything. Nothing's changed between us!"

Beck and Clarimonde stared after the ranger for a moment. "You're wasting your time trying to stop that one," Clarimonde said. "He does not stop until he has done what he set out to do."

"Yes, I know how he is. . . ." Beck, staring into the darkness, let out a long breath. "Sometimes he reminds me of myself. The hardheaded fool."

Chapter 25

———

Suelo Soto had heard the gunshot, but he wasn't going back to see who had fired it. Now that he knew Memphis Beck and the woman were both dead, he had no interest in the Pierman spread or the members of the gang who would be gathering there over the next few days. His only interest in the gang was how many he and his men could kill and rob on their way back to Shadow Valley. He and his men circled high around the hillsides throughout the night, with no regard for the two missing brothers they left behind on foot to finish off the two lawmen. He knew they would return in time.

At daylight he led his men higher up into the hill country, taking a shorter route to the far end of their dark valley lair. As they climbed the trail, he left two of the brothers behind to keep watch over the lower trails and make sure no *federales* picked up their tracks and followed them.

No sooner had Soto and the rest of the men ridden out of sight than the two Satan's Brothers found themselves an overhanging ledge that afforded them a view of the land, much like that of a soaring eagle. For more than two hours they sat in silence, their horses hidden on a grown-over hillside behind them.

But then, as they were about to pull up and ride closer to Soto and the men and take a new position, they spotted two riders move into sight on a thin trail fifty yards below. One of the brothers nudged the other and gestured toward the bulging saddlebags behind the two riders' saddles. They looked at one another and smiled. Then they moved forward and down over the edge like rock lizards closing in on prey.

On the lower trail, the two riders stopped quickly, Max Short throwing his arm out and saying, "Whoa, Hunt, is that who I think it is?"

Hunt Broadwell gazed down with him, the two seeing the ranger step down from his saddle and limp forward, leading the paint horse to the edge of a narrow stream. "Damn right it is." Broadwell grinned. "It's that ranger, Sam Burrack, the one who gave Memphis Beck such a hard time in Little Aces."

"What's wrong with him?" Short asked.

"I don't know," said Broadwell. "He looks like he's been dragged through a dry creek bottom."

As they stared, Sam kneeled down stiffly, sank his canteen and let it fill while he and the horse watered themselves. "Think he knows about the train robbery?" Short asked, backing his horse out of sight, Broadwell doing the same beside him.

"So what if he does?" said Short. "That's Mexico's problem. It's no concern of his."

"Burrack's known to stick his nose in where it doesn't belong," said Broadwell, drawing his rifle from its boot and stepping down from his saddle. He hitched his horse to a tree.

"What are you doing?" Short whispered. He stared at Broadwell, even as he stepped down and hitched his horse at the same spot.

"What does it look like I'm doing?" said Broadwell, levering around into his rifle chamber. He nodded toward his bulging saddlebags. "This is the biggest cache of gold that's ever come my way. I'm not taking a chance some flea-bit ranger is going to take it away."

"What about Beck?" said Short. "He don't hold with killing."

"So? We're not on a job. This is me protecting what's mine." Broadwell grinned and stepped over to a rock at the edge of the trail. "Besides, I never held much with that old Hole-in-the-wall belief about not killing. Do you?"

"Now that you mention it, no, I never did," said Short. "I never said anything because I don't ride with them, except now and then."

"Well, if Beck had any sense, he'd thank me for this," said Broadwell. "All the same, don't you tell him about it."

"I won't say anything," said Short. "Make sure you don't miss. I don't want to spend the day trying to outrun him, especially with these heavy saddlebags."

"Don't talk stupid," said Broadwell, kneeling down, propping his left elbow on top of the rock and leaning into the rifle stock to take aim. "Even a greenhorn could make a shot like this." He eyed down the sights and slipped his finger across the trigger. "Good-bye, Ranger. You're dead."

Behind him Short made a muffled sound as a hand came from behind and wrapped across his mouth. The blade of a machete sliced along the side of his neck, sinking deep into his throat.

"Keep quiet while I make my shot," Broadwell said over his shoulder. He settled onto the rifle stock, aimed the sights dead center of the ranger's back and began to squeeze the trigger. On his right, he heard the sound of metal slice through the air in a full circle swing, lopping off his head just as his rifle shot exploded.

At the stream, Sam rolled sideways, rose up into a crouch, and raced away into the cover of brush. Bits of chipped rock and dirt stung the paint's forelegs and sent the animal bolting across the streambed, out of sight. On the steep hillside Sam heard Hunt Broadwell's head rolling, bumping, bouncing and tumbling, down through brush and rock. But he had no idea what it was until it bounced out onto the trail and came to a halt in front of him.

Atop the higher trail, the Satan's Brother looked down and back and forth only for a second, out of curiosity. Wiping his blade on Broadwell's back, he stepped away from the bloody rock, turned and shoved the other brother away from the bulging saddlebags. Taking the reins to both horses, the two swung up into the saddles and rode back up to where their other horses stood waiting.

From the brush the ranger ventured a look up in the direction of the rifle shot. His Colt was out, cocked and ready. But after waiting so long that the paint horse came walking back warily toward the steam, Sam eased forward with caution. Taking the paint horse's reins, he looked down at Broadwell's head, then up along the edge of the higher trail, long enough to decide what had just happened. Rolling the head off the trail with the toe of his boot, he stepped up into the saddle and rode away.

When the trail he rode switched back and climbed upward, he found both bodies where the Satan's Brothers had left them. Broadwell lay headless, sprawled across the bloody rock, his arms spread and his rifle lying between them. Short lay in a bloody heap on the ground. Sam looked all around and saw where their killers had ridden off on their horses. Without realizing it, the Satan's Brothers had saved his life.

"See?" he said to the paint horse, as if talking to Hector. "Even demons make mistakes." He tapped his heels to the paint's sides and rode on.

No sooner had Soto and his men arrived in the dark end of Shadow Valley than he began making enough explosives to bring the valley walls down on anyone foolish enough to come looking for him. There had been no one on his trail, but he realized the region was crawling with *federales* who were searching everywhere for the shipment of gold.

Let them come, he told himself, looking at the empty buckboard wagon that the brothers had taken when it was loaded with gold, after killing Captain Guzman and his soldiers. "Even the Mexican army is no match for Satan's Brothers, eh, my brothers?" he said to the men gathered around him. "When I am finished placing these loads, we will ride out and take more gold for ourselves."

The entire community of brothers had stood watching him load bundle after bundle of freshly rolled dynamite sticks and glass vials of extra nitroglycerin into a large canvas pack and swing it carefully up onto his shoulders. Before he turned to climb the crude, chiseled steps up the rock wall of the valley, one of the brothers stepped forward, and spoke to him in Spanish.

"We have watched you make and place your explosives throughout the length of Shadow Valley for three days," the brother said. "When will you be finished?"

"We have many enemies," said Soto. "If we are pushed here into the dark end of the valley, we must have an ambush prepared for them."

"But when will it be enough?" the brother asked.

"When I say it is enough," Soto said with a snap, giving him a dark glare. "When is anything ever enough? With us there is always a need for more of everything. More gold, more explosives, more blood." He picked up a coil of fuse cord and slipped it over his shoulder. "This is the world we create. This is what the ancient ones bequeathed to us. This is what Satan has sworn us to."

The brother stood back and watched him step up onto the jagged rocky wall and begin climbing the steep, narrow steps toward the top. Every ten yards he stopped long enough to reach back over his shoulder, pull out a bundle of dynamite and stick it tightly into a crevice before continuing on.

At the top of the wall he still had three bundles of dynamite and the vials of pure nitroglycerin when he climbed over the top edge and stood up, brushing dirt from his chest. The sound of a horse caused him to stop brushing and look in disbelief at the big paint horse standing twenty yards away, staring calmly at him.

Looking quickly all around, Soto started to slip the pack from his back, but he stopped when he heard a gun hammer cock and saw the ranger step out from behind a large, embedded boulder. Keeping his hands on his pack straps, Soto gave a slow, menacing grin and said, "I should have chopped you apart myself, Ranger."

"It's too late for 'should haves,' Soto," Sam said, making no mention of arrest.

Soto shook his head and said, "I go to all this trouble setting up an ambush in Shadow Valley, and you ride all the way around the valley instead of through it. Why did you do that, Ranger? It makes no sense that you would go to all that trouble."

"I try never to do what the devil predicts," Sam said flatly.

"I think it's because you are that afraid of me, and of my kind?"

"Of you and your kind, no," said Sam. "You and your boys are nothing new . . . just one more handful of fanatic idiots who're feeling bold, thinking you've got backing from hell."

"Oh, but we do have, Ranger!" Soto said, his eyes a dark, fervent glow. "Satan's Brothers are ancient, and we are indeed brothers of the devil himself, as you will find out as soon as I signal for the men below to ride up and kill you." His grin returned. "You won't get away. This time I will eat your heart. I swear it to the devil and to hell!" He backed to the edge and signaled down to the men on the dark, narrow valley floor.

"The devil and hell . . ." Sam shook his head. "Soto, you're a fraud. You've never known the devil or hell, either one"—his Colt leveled in his hand—"until now."

Hearing the shot from the valley floor, the brothers looked up as they scrambled to mount the horses and follow Soto's command. They stopped suddenly, seeing Soto in the air above them, the impact of the shot picking him up and hurling him backward off the rocky edge.

Knowing what came next, the ranger turned and raced farther away from the edge. Below him he heard the demons scream loudly in unison, some strange chorus from the bowels of hell. But their scream stopped suddenly. Grabbing the paint's reins and bracing himself, Sam heard and felt the first in a string of terrible blasts as Soto's body struck the side of the valley wall on its way down.

Ducking low, Sam rubbed a gloved hand along

the paint's side, settling the frightened animal as the explosions raced violently along the length of Shadow Valley. For a full minute after the last blast, he stood listening, feeling the cavernous ground beneath him rumble and settle and adjust itself back into place.

"Easy, boy, it's over," Sam whispered to the paint, feeling grit and tiny pieces of debris shower down around him. He stepped up into the saddle, turned the paint and rode almost a hundred yards before escaping the worst of the billowing dust and smoke. When he stopped the paint, he turned it and stared in awe, witnessing for a moment what terrible force man could create for the destruction of his own.

"We don't need the devil," he said to the paint, rubbing its neck as he contemplated man's resource and the lack of reluctance on the part of men like Suelo Soto to use it. But he didn't think about it long. He needed to get back across the border. The *federales* would be stopping and questioning anybody riding these badlands until they found out what happened to the gold. He didn't have time for it. He had a long ride ahead of him, all the way to Hole-in-the-wall, Wyoming. *A dangerous place for a lawman*, he reminded himself. But that's where Beck told him his stallion would be. He gave a thin, wry smile, turning the paint away from Shadow Valley, back toward the high trails. Yep, if his stallion was there . . . that's where he was headed.

Turn the page for a preview
of Ralph Cotton's next book,

RIDE TO HELL'S GATE

Coming from Signet in September 2008

Matamoros, Mexico

Lawrence Shaw, aka Fast Larry, aka the Fastest Gun Alive, aka the Mad Gunman, aka Chever Reed, had been too drunk for too long to be standing in a dirt street about to do battle. *Yet here I am*, he reminded himself through a whiskey haze. He held his right hand poised at the butt of the big Colt holstered at his hip. He stood with his feet spread shoulder-width apart, not so much in preparation for a gunfight, but rather to settle the unsteady world beneath him and keep himself from falling.

"I know who you are," Titus Boland called out from thirty feet away, stone sober, advancing slowly toward Shaw as he spoke.

So do I . . . , Shaw answered to himself, not sure what he meant, or if he could have formed an intelligent reply even if he'd wanted to. Instead he only nodded; he dared not attempt a step forward, not until the world stopped spinning and wobbling before his bloodshot eyes.

"You're sure as hell not Chever Reed, the attorney from Brownsville, the man you've tricked everybody here into thinking you are. You're Lawrence Shaw, the murdering coward from Somo Santos, Texas," Boland called out. "I aim to take from you what you took from my poor brother Ned in Eagle Pass—*your life!*"

All right, now on with it . . . Shaw nodded again; he didn't care. He stared at Boland, feeling his bleary eyes began to focus. He wasn't the least bit concerned with Titus Boland's angry threats, even though he knew Boland meant every word he'd said and had every intention of killing him, right here, right now, drunk or sober. *It makes no difference to Boland,* Shaw thought, *or to me either.* He took a deep, drunken breath.

Lawrence Shaw had long forgotten how many men had shouted pretty much the same kind of threats at him from countless dirt streets, from hastily abandoned saloon bars, from overturned card tables, from hotels, restaurants, houses of ill-repute . . . Death threats all sounded the same; they had for a long time.

"Let's get it done," Shaw managed to say flatly without his thick tongue betraying him. He almost attempted a step forward now that this senses seemed to be returning. But unsure, he stopped himself at the last second and remained standing perfectly still.

"I've been killing you in my sleep for over three years, *Fast Larry!*" Boland bellowed. "Today I'm bringing everybody's chickens home to roost."

A few feet behind him, to his left, one of Boland's gunman pals, Albert McClinton, looked sidelong at Vincent Tomes and whispered, "What the hell is he talking about, 'chickens roosting'?"

"I don't know. Hush up," Tomes replied nervously without taking his eyes off Shaw. "This Shaw fellow is faster than a rattlesnake. We do not want to be caught unawares by him."

"Yeah, but *chickens roosting*?" Albert persisted, still in a whisper. "I don't see what chickens roosting has got to do with any—"

"It's just a figure of speech, damn it!" Tomes growled. "Now spread out, so's one shot don't kill us both! I wish I'd never got talked into this."

"That goes double for me," McClinton murmured.

Okay, there's three of them. . . . Shaw grinned to himself. *Good . . .* Maybe these three were the ones who would do it. Maybe this would be the day the undertaker closed the lid over his face and lowered him into the ground forever. *Mexico, eh . . . ?* So this was where it would happen. He cut a glance across the wide street, seeing colorful banners and streamers fluttering on the breeze in front of the American Consulate building a block away.

Mexico will do, he told himself. He'd always liked Mexico. Rosa was from Mexico, not far from here. That was good enough for him. *Ah, Rosa. Dear, precious Rosa,* he said silently to his deceased wife, half closing his eyes. For a numb, drunken moment he felt a deep joy sweep over him. Was she here? Could she see him? He hoped so; *God,* he hoped so. *I'm coming to you at last, Rosa,* he spoke silently to her, even as the three gunmen settled into position.

"Here it is, Shaw!" Boland shouted, his fingers opening and closing restlessly. "Anything you want to say before I send you straight to hell?"

Shaw slowly shook his head, a dreamy smile on his lips as he thought of Rosa, seeing her loving face, her dark eyes. He could feel her warm arms around him. "Get it done," he said, his hand poised and relaxed near his holster, as if he might or might not decide to draw it when the time came.

"My god, look at him!" Tomes whispered to McClinton in a shaken voice. "He's as calm and cold-blooded as any man I've seen! He has no doubt what's about to happen here."

"Because he knows for damn sure that he's going to kill us all," McClinton replied, his voice turning strained and shaky.

"Go for your gun, Shaw!" Boland raged, seeing Shaw's indifferent attitude, "else I'll kill you, anyway. It makes me no never-mind if you fight back or not!"

Still wearing his drunken, reposeful smile, Shaw slapped his hand to his gun butt.

Instantly Boland made the same move, his Colt coming up cocked and firing as Shaw's hand seemed to stick to his holstered gun. McClinton and Tomes stood stunned, not believing their eyes as they saw Boland's bullet punch Shaw in his right shoulder. They looked even more stunned as they watched Shaw pitch forward, unfazed by the gunshot wound, and pass out cold, facedown in the dirt.

"Watch it, Boland!" Tomes warned, sidestepping away with his gun drawn and ready to fire. "It's just a ploy!"

"*A ploy?*" Titus Boland cut Tomes a disgusted look as he advanced toward Shaw, who lay limp in the street. "This is no *ploy*. He's hit. I nailed him fair and square." He stopped a few feet away from Shaw and aimed the gun at the back of his head. "This one here is for my poor deceased brother."

But before Boland could pull the trigger, he and the other two froze at the sound of a shotgun cocking behind them. "Drop your guns, *hombres*," a voice said with urgent determination.

Without turning or dropping his gun, Boland said over his shoulder, "Oh? And just who is making this request?"

"It is no request. It is an order," the voice said. "I am Gerardo Luna, constable of Matamoros. But it will not matter to you who I am if you do not do as I say."

"Gerardo Luna? The one all the local vaqueros and rounders call Moon?" Recognizing the name, Boland lowered his gun and let his aim move away from Shaw's head.

"*Señor* Moon to you," said the Mexican lawman, stepping forward, in between Tomes and McClinton, nudging first one, then the other with his shotgun barrel. Their guns fell to the dirt.

"With all respect, *Señor* Moon," Boland said,

holding out, stalling, his gun still in hand, "but you're meddling in a fair fight. He drew first."

"His gun is still holstered," said Luna with an accent. "He is drunk. He passed out and fell. I saw it on my way here. Lucky for you I was not in range or *mi pequeño ángel* here would have shot you into the sky. Now you drop *it*, or I drop you."

Boland sighed. He uncocked his Colt and slowly let it fall to the dirt. He relaxed a little and looked at the shotgun in Luna's hands. "Your little angel, eh?"

"*Sí*, my little angel," Luna repeated. He gestured down at the ornate eight-gauge shotgun with its brass-trimmed fluted barrel and its tall hammers drawn back.

"Well, ain't that just sweet as can be," Boland said stiffly. "Maybe we'll meet someday while your little angel ain't handy, and we'll reflect back on this thing from a whole other outlook. You just might find that I'm a man you do not want to anger."

Almost before the words left his mouth, Tomes and McClinton winced at the sound of the shotgun butt snapping up into his chin. Blood and broken teeth spilled from his lips as he fell to the ground beside Shaw.

"Whoa!" Tomes said instinctively, "You had no cause to bust the man up that way."

"Oh, you think not?" Luna took a step toward him.

Tomes and McClinton both backed away. Tomes raised a hand in a show of peace and said quickly, "Although I can certainly understand how you might have thought it was justified. . . . Titus has a way of getting testy if he goes unchecked."

"Which, in all honesty, he is prone to do from time to time," McClinton joined in, also raising his hands chest-high in submission.

"I see," said Luna, the short shotgun still clenched in his fists. "I am happy that you both agree with my decision." He jerked a nod toward the knocked-out gunman and said, "Now get him up and out of here. It looks bad, *hombres* lying in the middle of my street."